# THE MEETING OF AIR AND WATER

## SHARON LaCOUR

CLAUDIA DRIVE BOOKS

# PRAISE FOR
# THE MEETING OF AIR AND WATER

In Sharon LaCour's debut novel, *The Meeting of Air and Water*, we are taken deep into the mystery and harsh reality of two women's struggles for life, for art, for freedom. From the fishing camp of Cocodrie, Louisiana in the 1920s to the allure and danger of New Orleans in the 1980s, we travel with Dolores and Elaine as they make their way through worlds that do not offer a safe place for them to flourish. LaCour does not allow her heroines to escape the pain of their lives, and because of that, we are able to see the love that prevails. LaCour's writing is that rare combination: lush and lyrical, stark and honest. This is a wonderful book!

—Patrick Cabello Hansel, author of *The Devouring Land,*
*Quitting Time* and *Breathing in Minneapolis*

Sharon LaCour's lifetime teaching and playing piano surfaces in this multi-generational tale in the ease and confidence with which she moves between lush, hard-scrabble Cajun country life of the early 20th century and New Orleans nearing the *fin de siècle*. The story includes the awakening through the naive photography of the protagonist's grandmother, as well as her struggles with unidentified mental illness, all within the context of a true love story. Her grandfather remains a character in both the early and late scenes, a hardy man whose many losses have not broken him. The granddaughter's own struggles bear unexpected similarities to her forebear's life, especially in her work as a photographer. LaCour has created characters and scenes in prose that is flawlessly engaging and always economical. In these vivid characters' lives, she deftly reveals the grace that guides the lives of decent people through storms of every kind. Beyond the compelling narrative, LaCour manages to imbue the story with such a palpable atmospheric density that weeks after finishing the read, one can still feel the location as if it were a personal memory.

—Ralph Adamo, poet and editor, *Xavier Review*

LaCour has penned a novel grounded in down-to-earth realism. While playful imagination informs her writing, she nonetheless knows her factual subject like an insider, because *she is an insider*, having grown up around the Cajun people she has chosen to write about, and is herself of Louisiana French descent. LaCour's plain-spoken dialogue and frank descriptions avoid a common pitfall of those writing about 'earthy' people — namely, self-conscious cutesiness. Instead, LaCour depicts lives neither caricatured nor idealized, but weaves a tale that come across as natural, unaffected, and most of all believable.

— Shane K. Bernard, author and historian

For Marjorie Peyton LaCour
(1922-2022)

# TABLE OF CONTENTS


Praise for *The Meeting of Air and Water* ............... iii

1. Cocodrie, Louisiana, 1917 ............... 1

2. Little Woods, New Orleans, 1988 ............... 6

3. Dulac School Ferry ............... 14

4. Charlotte ............... 20

5. Photographer, 1923 ............... 31

6. The Tight Spot ............... 43

7. A Storm from the Gulf ............... 56

8. The Meeting of Air and Water ............... 62

9. Intangible ............... 70

10. St. Roch and the Dog ............... 78

11. Brownie Girl ............... 83

12. Cocodrie, 1988 ............... 87

13. Death Mask ............... 94

14. Audrey ............... 98

15. Moonshine ............... 104

16. Sam ............... 108

17. Bal de Noce ............... 115

18. Arnie ............... 122

19. Angelus ............... 129

20. Tarpon in Lake Pontchartrain … 133

21. Bitter Hope … 140

22. Bellocq … 144

23. French Quarter … 150

24. Rally … 154

25. Sara … 163

26. Like a Little Child … 170

27. Francis … 176

28. Windows are like Photographs … 179

29. Darkroom Tragedy … 184

30. Elevated … 188

31. Crainte … 196

32. Walking on Broken Glass … 198

33. The Little Doll … 205

34. Like Satchmo … 208

35. Confession … 214

36. Revelations … 219

37. The River … 225

38. The Photographer, 1988 … 227

39. Adventures of the Pintail … 233

40. A Way of Seeing … 238

Notes … 241

Glossary of French Terms (in order of use) … 243

Acknowledgments … 245

About the Author … 247

# 1.

## COCODRIE, LOUISIANA, 1917

DOLORES SAT IN A CORNER of the parlor holding the doll the healer made for her the day her maman died. The doll was stuffed with the gray moss that made the trees look like they had long, curly hair. Her papa kept the room dark. He covered the windows with black, thin cloth from Marie's sewing because you don't want the sun coming in on all the sad people, that wouldn't be right, but the windows stood open, and the cloth was thin to let her maman's spirit out so it could leave when it was ready.

The box in the middle of the parlor was covered with the same black cloth. Candles burned around it, two at each end. The light from the candles made strange shadows on the walls, shadows of the people in the room, their heads nodding or their fingers moving when they talked.

The thin shape in the box wasn't really her maman at all. Before she went away, her maman said, "Didi, t'inquiète pas. Je suis ici pour toujours. It will not be me inside the wooden box. I will be out in the woods with the feux follets. I'll be dancing and carrying on out there. And I'll be with my God for sure."

But Dolores went out every night looking for those lights in the woods and never once did she see one. Her arms were covered with welts from mosquitoes. Those feux follets were a strange thing. They lead you out into the forest and make you get lost. If you stick a knife in a tree, they will leave you alone. They're the lonely souls of the unbaptized babies, Maman said. Dolores thought they needed somebody to play with, that's why they trick you into the woods.

Every time the front door opened the sun lit up all the pine trees and the cypress trees against the bright blue sky, and more than once Dolores thought of running as far away as she could from that room, but she knew her sister Marie would become crazy folle with her if she ran off on their maman's veillée.

This time when the door opened it was the healer coming inside. She headed right over to Dolores. She smelled like bayou water and the bay leaves Marie picked for soup. Her hair was as long as the moss on the trees, and her skirts covered her feet. Dolores pulled away when she felt her hand on her head.

Marie said, "Didi, you let the traiteuse rest by you. She was good to Maman."

The traiteuse stroked Dolores' head. "Pauv' p'tit bébé, pauv' p'tit bébé."

The traiteuse would come visit and pray over her maman, sometimes sing, or rub her with smelly oils. Papa said the traiteuse healed people. She told Dolores that her maman had gone to heaven, but Dolores knew it was another way of saying she was dead, just gone, like that, not here anymore. Other things died around her before, like snakes boys kill on the edge of the bayou. She hated those boys for killing the snakes, but she didn't know the snakes, not like she knew her little cat. He got sick like her maman and went away, too, just like that, gone. It felt different when you knew the one who died.

More and more people came, and they brought all kinds of food. The smells filled the house like Sunday dinner—plates of fish, oyster stew, even roasted chicken and rabbit, and sweet things like bread pudding and sweet potato pie. Papa had made a little altar out of wood for people to leave things; even though Maman couldn't use them now, people left them anyway. Everybody had to put something there. He put her worn-out prayer book. Marie put her rosary and a kerchief Maman wore. The aunts and cousins put seashells and stones, other carvings and a little grass doll. All Dolores had to put was the cross her maman made for her one day in the woods out of sticks and moss. She put her drawings, too, the ones she used to make while she sat on the floor in Maman's dark room keeping her company.

Finally, Papa said it was time to go and everybody started to leave the house. The box went out first with uncles and cousins carrying it. The traiteuse took Dolores' hand and led her outside where everybody lined up to make a parade to the church. They put the box up on a carriage. Even Lita, the horse, had black over her back. Dolores thought her maman would like the part with the horse. Father Martin and Papa walked on the sides of the carriage. The sunlight from the morning was gone now, and the sky had a layer of clouds, not the big fluffy ones, but smooth like a blanket. Maman's sister, Adèle, kept leaving the parade. She shut the gate of a chicken yard, then the door of a shed. The houses on the path to church looked like a storm was coming. Everybody's shutters were closed even though it was warm and nice outside.

"Why is she closing things?" Dolores asked the traiteuse.

"They don't want Adine's spirit wandering into their houses by mistake."

Another shutter closed as they passed. The woman inside made a sign of the cross.

Inside the church Dolores squeezed between Papa and Marie. Marie's new baby cried most of the time. Jesus looked peaceful hanging above the box, even though he was on a cross like that. She always wondered why he could look so peaceful when it must hurt to be on a cross. Father Martin shook the thing that the smoke comes out of, and the church filled up with smoke and a spicy smell. Dolores' legs swayed under the pew, the words went on and on, she didn't understand any of them or what they had to do with why they were there.

One thing she had decided before the day started was that she would not watch the box put into the ground. As soon as Mass ended, and Dolores got to the doorway, she bolted down the church steps straight past Father Martin who called out her name more than one time. She pretended not to hear him.

She ran to the bayou and slowed down when she saw Earl on a pine stump, shaving wavy layers from a chunk of wood and letting them drop into the water. Nobody was coming after her, but they might later. There was a light drizzle that cooled her down after all that running. She sat apart from Earl and tossed little sticks into the bayou that floated past his shavings. She wondered if they'd end up out in the Gulf of Mexico.

"My maman died, and they're over there burying her." A line of turtles jumped off a log one at a time when she started tossing close to them.

"I know that. Why you're not over there, then?" He stopped carving for a minute, then started up again. "With everybody else?"

Dolores scooped up some rotten leaves from the shore. They let off a dark musty smell. She made little piles of them in the dirt. Three crows on top of the mountain of oyster shells started their loud cawing.

"My maman died too," said Earl. "It's hard to lose your maman."

"Are you some kind of my cousin?"

"Yeah, some way. I don't know how exactly."

She pointed to his carving. "Can you show me how to do that?"

"I don't think it's safe for a little girl. Too sharp." He leaned away from her.

"It's easy to talk to you," she said.

"I'm sorry about your maman."

Cicadas buzzed above her head, but they were quieter now that fall was coming. It made her feel funny when they were so loud sometimes in the summer, like her head was full of them. "You ever see the feux follets?" said Dolores. "I wish I could see them. They light things up at night in the woods. They try to trick you to play with them."

A baby alligator lifted its head, and the mud made a sucking sound. It crawled into the water a few feet away from them.

Earl held out his carving and turned his head to the side. "That's just a story, that's not a real thing in the woods. You don't need to believe that."

Dolores could see it was a heron he was carving. "How old are you?"

"Just turned eleven, last week. You?"

Marie's voice came from behind them. "Didi, c'est toi? Didi! Viens!"

Dolores stood up and brushed the dirt and leaves off her dress. "Almost eight. Good-bye, Earl. My sister is calling me."

"Good-bye, some kind of a cousin."

Dolores said, "I believe in the feux follets. One day I'm going to see them. I'll wait out all night if I have to."

Marie pulled her close. "Didi, ça va, p'tite? C'est tout fini. It's all finished. You come eat now." Marie cried a little bit and kissed the top of her head.

# 2.

## LITTLE WOODS, NEW ORLEANS, 1988

Elaine Landry opened her eyes, discouraged again to be back home even after three weeks of waking up every day in her pink high-school bedroom. The familiar lake smell and cries of the gulls consoled her, but the gulls reminded her of the noisy garbage trucks in Minneapolis that used to interrupt her sleep. She woke up some days thinking she was back there with her ex, Ethan, snoring next to her.

Her grandpa hadn't changed anything in the bedroom in fifteen years since she was in high school, and everything was as worn out as she felt. Stiff curtains dulled the sunlight, a torn, faded Joni Mitchell poster hung on the wall, and all her dusty diaries and sketch pads were piled on the bookshelf. She had left home right after college and followed the Mississippi River to its source, hoping that getting married and out of New Orleans would relieve her restlessness. Now she was back where she started, feeling more lost than before.

Her hair was starting to fade in the sun, and brown highlights had shown up. She took out a hairband and fought with the thick mess to braid it. Her arms and legs were already dark from all her daydreaming on the dock and the running she'd started to counteract her new smoking habit.

"Laney," Pappy called outside her door. "Elaine! It's your mother on the phone."

God, her mother again. "Not now."

"What?" he called louder. "Your mother!" His hearing was worse than the last time she was home for Christmas six months ago.

Elaine yelled back, "Tell her I'll call her later." She got up and went to the window. A great white egret lifted one of its legs from the mucky sand, and the breeze ruffled its feathers. She traced its curved neck and long back with her finger on the window screen, remembering how she used to sit for hours at this window, drawing. The memory of it brought a sensation of longing which baffled her.

Pappy's wheelchair squeaked outside the door. "You gonna get yourself up, young lady? It's almost 9 o'clock."

"I'm coming." She squeezed her eyes shut against the memory of the night before, groping in the back seat of Peter Melancon's car, the sticky vinyl scratching her thighs. It must be a divorce relapse, this stupid sex thing with her college boyfriend. He was married with three kids in grade school, and even worse, she had been friends with his wife, too, although they'd lost touch over the years. It was crazy to be hanging out in a parked car on a scary looking block off Esplanade Avenue. In New Orleans, things could change from block to block, and it was hard to tell what was safe and what wasn't. She should have been terrified, but the gin and tonics had made her careless.

She rubbed her face and reached for the pack of Winstons crumpled on her little-girl desk. It lay next to the splayed contents of her grown-up-girl purse: lighter, tampon, condom, lipstick. The contrast was laughable. Resting her elbows on the windowsill, she watched the smoke swirl over the water towards the brown pelicans resting on the ruined camp next door. Snatches of music and voices carried over the water from the convenience store across the street that Pappy had grown to despise as a sign of the neighborhood's decline.

*Hey man, where you been? You been gone a week or more.*

*I've been at my sister's in Mississippi. She's real sick.*

*That's right? Sorry to hear that.*
*She's got the stomach cancer real bad.*

The egret spread its wings and took off. The smell of brackish lake water came in with the wind, renewing that nostalgic longing.

She stubbed out the cigarette and went to the bookshelf to investigate some of her sketchpads. A brass frame with a black-and-white photograph of her grandmother, Dolores, sat on her desk. It was the only photo of her that Elaine had ever seen. Behind Dolores was a simple white cottage with an open front porch. The branch of the live oak tree she was sitting on had grown out from the massive trunk for over ten feet and hung inches from the ground. Wavy, dark hair fell around her face, and her eyes seemed sad and serious, but also had a curious, searching intensity, like she was trying to figure something out.

Elaine found it strange that this woman had given birth to her mother. The girl in the photo showed a depth that Elaine couldn't imagine in Charlotte.

Elaine put on a pair of shorts and a T-shirt that had been lying on the floor and went down the short hall to the living room. She blinked against the bright morning sun streaming through the screens and windows in the large main area of the camp. She stretched and did a few forward bends to try and shake the fog out of her brain.

The dark gloss of the lake shone through the cracks in the floorboards. Pappy had said they were for ventilation, but she thought that the camp was falling apart. She remembered Ethan being baffled by her early descriptions of where Pappy lived until she explained that the house was built on stilts in the lake over a hundred feet out from the shore. In Minnesota the camps are on the shore and the view is of the lake, not the other way around.

She went to the front windows and balanced on one foot in a tree pose. A narrow walkway led from their porch over shallow water towards the shore 150 feet away. She remembered when her grandpa had the zigzagged ramps installed on both the lake and street sides of the levee next to the straight wooden steps. It took a long time to build, and he couldn't resist sitting on the walkway watching over the workers, telling them how to do everything.

She switched to a different yoga pose and followed the line of the levee. It looked like there were even fewer camps than the last time she was home; maybe there'd been a storm that she'd missed. Some of the walkways started at the levee and went out into the lake, then stopped at a collection of debris and pilings.

Pappy coughed behind her.

She said, "It's so sad. It won't be long before there aren't any camps left out in this lake. You'll probably be the last one, and you'll blow away with it in the next hurricane."

"Phooey. Here's your coffee. Don't expect this kind of service every morning." Her grandfather passed the cup to her with trembling hands.

"Pappy, when did I first move in here? Do you remember?" She lifted one leg after another in a dancer's pose.

"I think you and your mother started having big trouble when you were about twelve, why?"

"No reason." She was used to her grandpa being without legs, she didn't know him any other way. Sometimes she could imagine him as a young man, and he would look like Henry Fonda, long and lanky, with a sweet smile and disposition. He'd always been thin, but he managed to keep his strong shoulders from relying so much on his arms and from carpentry. "Hey, you know that picture of Dolores? Is that the only photo you have of her? She looks kind of troubled."

Pappy headed into the kitchen. "Your coffee's getting cold. Your grandmother was troubled on and off. Always needed something more than everybody else. You need to call your mother, so she stops bothering me."

Elaine followed him and opened the fridge. "What happened to the half and half I bought?" She leaned against the refrigerator door. "What do you mean she needed more?"

"Don't hang on that door like that. You threw the carton away yesterday. Why don't you use the Pet milk? You used to like it. It's not good enough for you now?"

"It's funny you still use evaporated milk. I mean, why? It has a weird taste in coffee. Anyway, the war is over you know, you have refrigeration." The canned milk swirled into her coffee, and the happy looking cow on the label was upended in the process.

She went to the sink for a spoon, and there was Sam walking a woman to the end of his deck and kissing her. Elaine's coffee spilled when she jerked back from the window. Seeing Sam again was always going to be tricky, but she hadn't expected jealousy. It had been at least six years since they broke up.

Pappy sat at the stove stirring a steaming pot of grits. "I happen to like the taste of evaporated milk. It doesn't go bad either. Sam uses it in his coffee, too."

"You expecting company? That's a lot of grits you're making."

His hand was trembling, and the spoon shook. She felt a mix of concern and fear for him. A speck of spit dripped from the corner of his mouth. He seemed a lot older since his heart attack a few months before. "How old is Dolores in that photograph in my room?"

"We can fry the leftover grits up for dinner." He added a long stream of salt and black pepper. "Why are you watching me so close?"

"Because Mama's going to ask me all kinds of questions about how you're doing." She took her coffee and sat at the oak table in the living room. She traced the lines from the Exacto knife where she'd matted her photos in high school. "It feels like you're watching me all the time, too. What did you mean when you said Dolores needed something more than everybody else?"

"Making sure you're doing okay, that's all." The spoon clanked against the pot.

He blew on a spoonful of grits. "Elaine, you're going to have to see your mother. It's been two weeks since she was here looking for you. You off today?"

"Yeah. It's Sunday, right?" Already after nine. Weekdays, in St. Paul, she would have been up and out the door by seven, briefcase in hand, in her suit and heels, off to meetings and campaigns, using her drawings to sell overpriced stuff that nobody needed. God, she was glad to be out of that stuffy atmosphere, even if she was making a lot more money than she was as a waitress.

"Sunday. All day. You look kind of green around the gills. Late night?" Pappy joined her at the table. "Here comes Sam."

Sam had already reached the bottom of the levee steps and started down the walkway.

"Wait a minute. I can't see Sam now." She ran over to the wall mirror and raised her arms. "Look at me. And I smell terrible."

"You look fine. Now he was a good man for you. I don't know why you ever broke that off. He's a man with character. Not like that one you married. I never liked that one. A suit and a haircut and he smelled like perfume. Your mother liked him, though. Don't look so shocked—I know what I'm talking about."

She stared at him, trying to make sense of his tirade. The door opened. Sam leaned in, and the screen bounced off his back.

"How're you doing, Elaine?"

Elaine felt something inside her do a little flip. It was the way he looked at her; it had weight, like a current pushing up against you. Either she felt warmed by it, or the opposite. She wasn't sure which it was.

The screen door bumped shut. Sam continued to hesitate in front of it.

Pappy said, "Hey boy. You're letting in flies. Come on in here."

"Hey, Earl. I see you got your girl back. He's been talking about you coming for months."

"How are you, Sam?" Elaine said. It was always awkward talking to someone who'd been a lover, but her guilt over the breakup made it worse. Standing there in her dirty T-shirt looking at him, she felt another twinge of longing. At that moment she couldn't remember why she had chosen somebody like Ethan over this man who was gorgeous and loved her like crazy.

"I'm good. You?" He looked away from her towards Pappy. His discomfort made him seem vulnerable—endearing, but sad, too.

"You two look like you never met each other before. Elaine, you been away too long. People in the South hug each other. I hope you didn't turn into a Yankee. Get him some coffee, will you?" Pappy moved his chair over to make room at the table. "Sit down, Sam. You made yourself scarce the past couple of weeks."

"Just giving y'all some time to catch up." Sam pulled out a chair and leaned back in it, his long brown legs stretched out to the side.

"I wouldn't still be here if it weren't for Sam. He's a lifesaver," said Pappy.

"Oh, I don't know about that. You do pretty well for the most part."

She put a cup of coffee on the table in front of him and sat at the other end. The edges of his shirt were frayed, and his shaggy, dark hair looked like he cut it himself. He had three days' beard going, and he smelled like the lake and the sun. Elaine cringed at the contrast with Peter in his fine blue suit and tie and manicured hair and nails. Even in college he'd been better groomed than anybody else.

"Y'all hear anything about two, three this morning?" Sam asked.

"No, not me. Why?" Pappy waved his long, bony fingers at a fly.

"Shooting across the street at the store."

"Two or three?" Elaine tried to remember what time she'd come in.

"Dammit Elaine." Pappy pounded the arm of his chair with a fist. "You see, that's why I don't want you coming in at all hours. It's been a while since anything happened over there. I thought that element had moved on."

Elaine went to the store often since she'd started smoking. She'd even gotten to know a couple of the kids who worked there. She didn't remember seeing anything the night before. "I don't know how to avoid it. I have to work late sometimes."

"Well, that's no good," said Pappy. "But what can anybody do? These people want to kill each other. That's part of their culture. Laney, put those biscuits in to go with the grits. You need to eat something. There's plenty of grits, we can fry some bacon too. Sam, you hungry?"

"No, no, don't go to any trouble for me. I'll get some more coffee though." He started to get up, but Elaine stopped him.

"I'll get it," she said. "Pappy, I need to go see Mama, remember? Have to get a shower." She went into the kitchen with Sam's cup.

"But you didn't eat anything. Well, I'm gonna eat even if y'all won't." Pappy followed her into the kitchen.

She brought the pot in and filled Sam's cup. "I was so sorry to hear about your dad. That must have been hard."

"It was hard, thanks. I got your card."

"He had such a great laugh, and he loved everybody."

"Yeah, generous to a fault."

Pappy came out of the kitchen with his plate of breakfast and set it on the table.

Sam stood up and gulped some coffee. "Well, I have to get going."

Elaine grabbed a towel from the laundry hamper near the bathroom. "I'll see you around."

"Before I go, Elaine, I wanted to tell you, I have some wood pieces showing at a coffee shop off Esplanade. Café Lola. I can give you the tour. If you're interested. You can let me know. Number's the same."

Sam opened the door, and Elaine ducked into the bathroom. The pipes started squealing as the water started up.

Pappy said, "I've got to do something about those pipes." He lowered his voice. "She's restless as a bobcat lately. It's a big adjustment, divorce, and everything. Give her some time. She'll come around."

Sam started to say something, and Pappy interrupted him. "Don't even try, boy, I see the way you look at her. Mark my words, give her some time, then, well, we'll just see."

# 3.

## DULAC SCHOOL FERRY

"ÇA S'APPELLE THE EDUCATION ACT, Papa. Didi doit aller à l'école. Now it's a law. All the children in town will have to go to school."

Dolores was listening hard. Her oldest brother, Louis, held a newspaper in his hands.

Papa said, "They can tell me how I raise my own children? How do I know they going to teach them the right things? You doing fine, you didn't go to school."

"I had to learn by myself to help you with the business, to read and do the figures. It would have been a big help to have some schooling. And she can learn English. Everybody speaks French here, but we're in America, she needs to learn to speak it and read it."

"I never heard of such a thing. The government telling me about my own kids."

Dolores said a prayer that Papa would win the argument. She didn't want to go to school.

Papa went on. "Our people never needed schooling. We managed good until now teaching our own school. How to live and work out here on the bayou. My parents, they didn't trust nobody with something that important, not the government, not the church, nobody."

Marie sat down at the table next to Papa. She wiped her hands on her apron then held them up to him. "Look at my hands, Papa. See how they're all red and puffy. This is my life, work, work, work. I'm not complaining about me, but maybe Didi could have a different one if she wanted. Maybe she could be a teacher someday. We, all of us, we let Maman keep that child too close because we knew she was dying, and we did anything she asked us. But Didi has been shut up too long with an old woman. She needs something different."

Louis said, "She's right. Marie is right. Didi was a good companion for Maman, but it made her so she's not used to other children. It will be good for her."

Dolores stood next to Papa. "But I don't need something different. I can cook and clean. I can help Marie with the babies. I won't give her any trouble. Please, Papa. I don't want to be around all those people."

The day turned into evening and then into night. Marie went back to the stove. Louis went outside like always to close up the chickens. The last calls of the cardinals and crows made an echoing sound.

Papa finally said, "You have been alone here for too long, and for that I am sorry." He folded his massive, strong hands together on the table. Shaggy bits of white hair fell over his ears, and more hair came out of them. "You are the baby of the family. You spent too much time in this dark house with a sick old woman. It was not good for you. Now she's gone, I see that. Time for something new. You go to school."

<hr>

On the first day of school, Dolores stood next to the warm stove drinking her coffee and hot milk. Marie had made the white school dress she needed out of a new piece of coarse cotton. The ironed fabric scratched her neck and back. She blew on her coffee and watched the steam from it rise up and disappear into the cold room. The only sound came from Marie's baby's gurgling and the fire crackling in the iron stove. The room smelled of coffee and wood smoke, of porridge and the sweet potatoes Marie baked for Dolores' lunch. Papa and Louis and Marie's husband, Antoine, had left before sunrise to take the shrimp boat out for the day.

Marie sat at the kitchen table nursing the baby. Her other two children, a three-year-old and a two-year-old, sat on the floor at her feet with their fingers in bowls of rice porridge.

Marie said, "You'll see, it will be some fun. I wish I had gone to school. And all you do since Maman died is mope around the house. You're too quiet. You need to see other kids your age. Learn how to talk to them. And you need to learn some English. You can't speak only French for the rest of your life."

Dolores looked away to stare at the wall of the kitchen where she used sticky dough to hang the pictures she cut out of newspapers and magazines. There was a bridge over a wide river and a giant statue of the Blessed Mother on a mountaintop. She wondered how they took pictures like that. She reached over and traced the back of a horse with a long mane. Underneath it hung a drawing she made of the same picture.

"And while you're gone, I want to open up this house up a little. Give it a good cleaning. Maybe take some of those pictures of yours off the wall."

Dolores jerked her head towards Marie.

"Some of it is peeling off, it's been on so long. I'll only take those down. Don't worry. I won't throw anything away. I'll put all the pictures and drawings on your bed." Marie dropped a cloth bundle in front of Dolores. "Now hurry up and get on, the boat is waiting. That's your lunch, and don't give none of that away."

Dolores put her cup down and picked up the bundle. She started crying. Other than going to Mass with her mother and to the occasional Saturday fais-do-do party, she had not left her home, and never Cocodrie. Dulac was a different town that she had only heard about.

Marie put the baby in its basket on the table. She wiped Dolores' face with a rag. "Hey, chérie, none of that. Now, go, you hear. And take your jacket, it's cool today."

The morning was cool and foggy. Dolores pulled on the short black wool coat that had been her mother's and ran to the dock where a dozen or more children sat close together on a long wooden ferryboat. She had to decide whether to sit on the benches outside around the edge, or to go inside under the awning.

The boat man stood with a tall pole and waved at her to come. She stepped onto the dock and a blue heron lifted off from the shore next to her. She ducked her head as the bird flew over, and the man called to her to hurry. Earl leaned over the railing and waved.

Dolores climbed in and squeezed herself between Earl and another boy. The boy stuck his elbow in Earl's side and said, "She's your girlfriend, that little baby." Earl's ears turned red.

Dolores always felt better when she was around Earl, ever since she talked to him that day they buried her maman. She had trouble talking to most people, but not Earl.

The mud sucked at the pole and water lapped around the boat. In the middle of the bayou, the man put the pole down. A loud motor started up, and Dolores grabbed Earl's arm. Earl patted her arm and pointed to a flock of poules d'eau that flew up in the air. They looked like somebody tossed black ash against the white sky.

At the schoolhouse all the children were together in one big room. Dolores had never seen so many children in one place before, even on Saturdays at the fais-do-do. She followed Earl and tried to sit near him, but the teacher stopped her.

"What's your name?" The teacher asked Dolores.

Earl stood right by her. She understood what the teacher said, but she felt like she couldn't move or say anything. "She don't have much English yet. Her name is Dolores."

"She doesn't have much English. Doesn't not don't." The teacher took Dolores by the shoulders and led her to a seat in the front of the room. She said something, but Dolores didn't understand any of it.

She craned her neck every few minutes to find Earl in the back of the room. The teacher's voice went on for a long time. Dolores tried to watch the other kids and do what they did. They wrote numbers and letters with chalk on pieces of slate.

Outside at lunch, Dolores found Earl and asked him a lot of questions. Earl told her to be quiet. "Didi, tu dois parler anglais. You have to speak English."

"No French spoken in this school. I've told you four times already today."

Earl took Dolores by the shoulders and put himself between her and the woman. They talked to each other, and Dolores understood that the teacher was unhappy with her for speaking French.

Dolores shrank against Earl's long legs and watched their mouths back and forth, understanding a little bit. The teacher's voice rose higher and higher and got angry. Her clothes seemed strange to Dolores, not anything like the dresses and wood shoes they wore at home. She said this to Earl.

Earl wiped his forehead with the back of his hand. He shifted his weight from foot to foot. He seemed upset.

The teacher gripped Dolores' arm and pointed to the door of the school. "You, too, Earl." Dolores shook her head and pulled against the teacher.

Earl followed them into the schoolroom. He asked the teacher something and said please, but she fussed at him. She opened a cupboard and took out a basket filled with yellow corn. She dropped a handful of the kernels onto the floor and pointed at it. "Down," she said. When Dolores did not respond, she tapped the back of Dolores' legs until her knees bent and dropped onto the hard corn. It felt like the time she slipped on the oyster shell mountain and cut her knee.

"You, too, Earl. Down."

Earl knelt next to her and reached for her hand. "Don't cry, Didi, it's okay."

Dolores wiped her eyes and runny nose with the sleeve of her blouse.

Over the months Dolores had to kneel many times in the corn because she forgot to speak English. She had to write the lines, *I will not speak French in school,* until her hand hurt. One time a different teacher even hit her hand with a ruler. Every time it happened, Earl would walk by her table and wink or make faces so she would laugh.

After a while, Dolores stopped talking and didn't get in trouble as much, but she never learned to pay close attention to her lessons, or to make friends. The girls made fun of her and called her names behind her back. She always sat with Earl on the boat transfers to and from school and ate lunch near him. The kids laughed and said she and Earl were going to get married one day.

# 4.

## CHARLOTTE

CHARLOTTE STOPPED AT THE STOP sign a block from her house and waited for a few cars to pass. The a/c in her Chevette had lost some of its umph over the years so she turned it up as high as it would go. The charming houses she had walked or driven past for over thirty years appeared shabby and worn in the glare of the sun. In 1950, right after they married, she and her husband were thrilled with the idea of moving into a new suburban neighborhood walking distance to the lake. They had looked up the name of the area to find out that Gentilly meant gently or nobly, as in people who behave like the gentry or nobility. They laughed, as if they were anything close to gentry, a carpenter, and a librarian. When Jack died suddenly just four years later, she clung to the house as her consolation. That and her little job at the library which went full time when Elaine started school. It was sad that the neighborhood was deteriorating.

She put her car in drive then paused again while the Schweigerts, an old couple who lived on the corner, crossed the street. They didn't respond to her wave; they were too intent on watching their steps on the rough asphalt.

She pulled into her driveway and opened the back car door to retrieve the groceries. Her toe caught for the hundredth time on a crack in the concrete where the roots of the crepe myrtle trees had pushed the pavement up. The cracks were filled with dandelions and creeping charlie. Charlotte sighed and wondered how much it would cost to put in a new driveway. From what she could tell driving around, the whole city was crumbling and being taken over by weeds and vines. She laughed, it was like that book, *Love in the Ruins* that she read years ago where the main character suffers hives through the entire book from drinking gin fizzes while New Orleans evolves into a jungle around him.

Charlotte heaved the bags out of the car and reached for her keys. A blue jay landed in a myrtle tree by the sidewalk and squawked like it was angry at her. Then she noticed Elaine's car parked under in the shade of a Japanese magnolia. She must have remembered where Charlotte kept the spare key.

"Elaine?" Charlotte pushed the door open with her hip and went straight to the kitchen and set the groceries on the table. When she went back to shut the front door, the smell of stale cigarettes hit her. It was dim in the parlor where the drapes were closed to keep out the heat. Her eyes took a minute to adjust to the filtered light. Elaine was rolled up in a ball on the sofa asleep with one hand under her face and her knees pulled up to her chest. Her lips were parted, and wisps of hair pressed against her damp forehead. She looked much the same as she had at four years old.

Charlotte went to the hall closet for a sheet and covered Elaine's bare legs with it. The smoke smell mixed in with the sour odor of Elaine's worn clothing. Her breath came and went in a slow peaceful rhythm. Let her sleep; she looks like she needs it.

She washed the lettuce and laid it out on paper towels to dry, took out the remoulade she'd put together the day before and stirred it with a wooden spoon. The shrimp were peeled, trimmed, and ready to go. Mixing the sauce and the shrimp too early made everything wet and soggy. The French bread was covered in a basket with a cloth napkin. A pitcher of iced tea sat in the fridge, along with a defrosted container of gumbo to heat in the microwave.

Charlotte sat at the table with a glass of tea, tired from all her efforts to make lunch for the daughter she hadn't seen since Christmas who came over in dirty clothes and fell asleep on the couch. Things seem to have a way of not turning out the way you expect them to, the way you hope they will. Like losing her husband that way, a lightning strike of an aneurism. Now Elaine's divorce. Charlotte had had high hopes for the marriage and for Elaine's big job in Minneapolis. It all seemed so perfect. Ethan had been such a smart dresser, and so clever and gracious. His family was well-to-do, and he had landed a job at a fancy law firm. Even if he was from up North, that didn't necessarily mean anything bad. She was grateful that they hadn't been together long enough for kids. Divorce was so hard on children. She hoped Elaine would be okay and not fall back into that depression she'd suffered in high school. It wasn't something Charlotte would ever ask her about.

She got up and took the shrimp and remoulade out of the fridge as Elaine started grumbling in her sleep, a familiar sound that usually meant she was waking up.

The cold, pink shrimp were a good size, firm. Charlotte bit in, good flavor. They would be good for stuffed mirlitons, too. She stirred the remoulade again and shook the shrimp into the bowl with the sauce, gently tossing them until they were coated. She put the container of gumbo in the microwave and went back to the parlor to check on Elaine.

Elaine was slouched in the corner of the sofa holding her head in her hands. "Geez, sorry. I must have fallen asleep."

"I know you're smoking. I can smell it. Do you want to take a shower?"

Elaine looked down at her cargo shorts and old UNO T-shirt. "I took one this morning. I just didn't have any clean clothes to put on."

"Did you bring your laundry? You can bring it here if you want. How late do you have to work at that bar?" Charlotte rolled up the sleeves of her sweater. If Elaine hadn't been there she would have taken off her khaki slacks and put on a housedress. "Whew! It's warm today."

Elaine arched her back in a stretch with her arms above her head. "It's a restaurant, not a bar. Sometimes midnight. This room looks different. You changed something. Why is it so dark?"

"I hate to think of you hanging out in a bar. Your hair is so long! I have a really good hairdresser if you want me to give you her name."

Elaine rubbed her eyes. "Wasn't there a low chair over by that window? Seems like I remember sitting on it, looking out."

"Oh, that thing was so beat up. You used to sit there a lot when you were a little thing. Reading and playing." Charlotte leaned in the doorway. "Seems like just last week."

"I used to draw a lot in that window." Elaine stood up and went to a round Duncan Phyfe table by the window. She picked up a ceramic figure of a Victorian woman sitting in a straight-backed chair. "I wonder where all those drawing pads are now. And all that computer paper. Remember that? You'd bring it home from work." She peeked out the drapes. "Man, those oleander bushes next door have gotten huge."

"I kept a few of your things, but you can't expect me to keep everything. I threw some of it away. You had reams of that stuff." Charlotte went into the kitchen and poured the gumbo into bowls. "You were such a solitary little thing. I had to make you go find kids to play with. Are you hungry?" She called her from the kitchen.

"I'm starving. It smells really good. Hey, what's this stuff under the piano? This is Dolores, isn't it? You're giving this away?"

Charlotte rushed into the parlor. She'd forgotten all about the photograph, and really did not want Elaine to start investigating Dolores. Pappy had called to warn her that she'd been asking questions. "That's just some old junk I'm going to bring to the church garage sale." She took the picture out of Elaine's hands and put it back in the box. "I'm getting rid of clutter. It is Dolores with your grandpa's cousin, Violet, in Cocodrie, a long time ago." The lid of the flimsy box flopped open. Charlotte tried to stuff the things down and force the lid closed. "Now come on and eat." She could tell she was getting winded from the exertion, but also from her exasperation of having the box exposed like this for Elaine to find.

"You can't give this away. It's like only one of two pictures I've ever seen of her. Unless there are more I don't know about." Elaine came into the kitchen with the picture.

Charlotte scrubbed her hands at the sink. Sweat poured from her scalp and dripped onto her forehead. "I am so hot all of a sudden. I wish these hot flashes would stop. I'm sixty-five years old." She raised the back of a soapy hand and gestured towards the house next door. "Just look how ridiculous that is; at her age Pearl is still smoking. She's at least 90." That wisteria vine had to go; it was crushing the fence. Pearl looked like a wraith, she was so thin in her threadbare housecoat and fuzzy pink slippers. She seemed so vulnerable sometimes; Charlotte reminded herself to go visit her soon.

Charlotte tried not to sound agitated. "Her geraniums are choking on weeds and vines. Smoking. With emphysema. People are stupid. My cousin walked around for months with an oxygen machine trailing behind him and cigarettes hanging out of his mouth before he finally died. Then that man we knew across the lake, remember him? He reminded me of Pappy. He lost half his face to lip cancer. Did I tell you Lydia's son got killed a few weeks ago? He stopped to help someone on the highway. They always say don't stop. You want to be good hearted and help people, but a car came by and hit him while he was changing the tire. It's terrible."

"Jesus, Mom, slow down. Why are you scrubbing your hands like that, you look like you're about to perform surgery."

Charlotte turned off the water and dried her hands. She went to the table and scooped the remoulade onto plates and added the shrimp on top. "Get the iced tea out, will you?" She wiped her hands on a tea towel and went to get the gumbo from the counter. There was the photo again, turning up like a bad penny. "You got this out again? It's dirty, I told you to leave it in the box."

Elaine poured iced tea and sat down. "You really don't like that picture, do you? The one I have, she seems depressed or something. How well do you remember her? I know you were little when she died."

Charlotte took a bite of shrimp. Her usual tactic in these situations was to avoid the subject. "Mmmm, these are such good shrimp. I have to ask Bernie where he got them. They remind me of the shrimp we had when I was young. You know Bernie and I have been doing more together. I'm finally getting out and about a bit in my old age."

"Cool. How is Bernie? His son doing okay?"

"Yes, he's in remission. It is a miracle, really." Charlotte could hear herself chattering like she did when she was nervous. She went on about Bernie's son's trip to Medjugorje, happy to get Elaine off the subject of Dolores. "You know he believes that's what did it. He went there and one of the children touched him."

"Do you believe that stuff? I heard that one of the kids asked her if his soccer team would win the Cup. These are some of the best shrimp I've had in a while."

"That's ridiculous. Of course, I believe. I mean we're supposed to believe it. It hasn't been debunked by the Church. Well, not yet anyway."

"Oh, well then, it must be real."

"Elaine that's sacrilegious."

"Well, I'm glad his son is better anyway, and that you're doing more stuff, getting out. That's great."

"What about you?" Charlotte got up to get spoons for the gumbo.

"What about me, what?"

"Well, how are you? Have you applied to graduate schools yet? Are you dating anyone? I hope not, it's really too soon for that. Have you talked to Ethan? Poor thing."

"Poor thing?"

"Well, I feel bad for him, too, he must be so unhappy. Anyway, what about graduate school?"

"I don't want to go to business school, I told you that. I don't know what I want to do. But not that."

"You have to pull yourself together. You've had a setback. Your marriage didn't work out. It's not the first time that's happened to anyone. You have to pick up the pieces, get yourself a good job. Although I don't know if New Orleans is the best place for you. Marketing and advertising aren't exactly booming here. If you go back and get your master's, you could get a job at a college or something. I mean you had a good job up north; you must be good at it."

"I hated it. I hated everything about it. It's nothing but sick manipulation. And I hate offices, copy machines, and fluorescent lights. I hate business. I really don't want to talk about this." Elaine went to the pantry and brought back a bottle of red wine and two juice glasses. "Here we go."

Charlotte waved her off. "It's too early in the day for wine."

"Come on, you only live once. This is New Orleans." She twisted off the cap of the Zinfandel and poured out two glasses.

"Well, okay, just one finger, not two. Why don't you use real wine glasses?"

"These are fine."

"Elaine, that's too much!" Charlotte took a couple of sips of wine, then leaned back and took a longer drink. "It's just too bad that you and Ethan couldn't work things out. You had such a beautiful house. And he picked it out and had it ready for you."

"You make it sound like it was all my fault, like I lost a good man. Like I wasn't good enough."

"I did not say you weren't good enough. It takes two in these things, I know."

"You don't know what it was like with him. He looks good, I know. The dream man, the dream house, the dream job. You didn't really know Ethan. You weren't around him enough to…"

"Okay, well, you haven't really told me very much. But you can't be a waitress forever."

"Why not? There's a couple of women at the Pontchartrain in their sixties who've been doing it for decades." Elaine dipped a piece of French bread into her gumbo.

"Oh, no, I can't believe the girl I raised would consider being a waitress for the rest of her life." She finished off the glass of wine.

"Well, you never know." Elaine brought the photo of Dolores to the table and refilled their juice glasses. "Did you know Violet? She was Pappy's sister, right?"

Charlotte felt the wine giving her that fuzzy-headed feeling. It was a bad idea to drink it in the heat of the day. She felt her face flush. "Why are you so interested in all of this? I remember Violet because she was a crazy one. They always said Violet had spells, but they were just trying to cover things up. She was a floozy. She had lovers, several lovers over the years. Her husband, his name was Paul, he started drinking more when all that started. That's what killed him."

"Why do you think she had lovers? Didn't she love Paul?"

Charlotte's voice got louder. She knew the wine was a bad idea. "It's not about love. It's never about love. It's about dealing with life or not dealing with it. She was not capable of dealing with it. He was crazy about her though." Charlotte picked up her glasses and put them on the end of her nose and held the photo close to her face. Memories came to her, vague ones, more of a mood, really, of people around a fire and a woman dancing. "She was exotic. Like a gypsy, tall with black hair like you and dark eyes. She used to remind me of one of those enormous butterflies, the bright blue ones, fluttering in a net. She had all this gaudy jewelry around her neck and wrists and one time she let me try some of it on."

"Maybe she needed lovers. Or something."

"Oh, come on." Charlotte pulled her glasses off and tossed them on the table. "She didn't need anything. That's no excuse. I don't care how unhappy you are, you just take care of your husband and your children like everybody else. What did all those men do for her anyway? They got what they wanted and made her think she was happy for a while, that's all."

"Not everybody is made to have babies and a house. Maybe she was forced into a life that she wasn't cut out for."

"That's no reason to run around and leave your children. No reason at all. You do what you have to do, no matter what. Thank God you didn't have any." Charlotte went to the sink and wet her hands under the faucet. She rubbed the back of her neck with the cool water. A monarch butterfly fluttered in the wisteria vine, and a cat pounced, crushing the butterfly under its paws. "That damned cat." She beat the window with her fist.

She wiped her hands with a towel and dropped back down into the chair. "Not to say you won't have children. I mean you have plenty of time, Honey." Charlotte took a sip of wine as Elaine studied the photo. There was a definite sadness about Elaine, a distraction, a lack of energy. She could see it in her eyes and the way she leaned back in her chair. It reminded her of how she was in high school when she got depressed.

"Pappy said that I remind him of Dolores. Do you have any other pictures of her?"

"You don't look like her. You look like Pappy and your father. Why all this interest in your grandmother all of a sudden? How's Pappy doing with his medications? You know, old people get confused. They forget. And watch that gas stove. He really should have electric."

"Can I have this picture?"

A loud clap of thunder shook the house.

"Sounds like it's going to storm. You should get going. I need to lie down. That wine got to me. I'll keep the picture for you. I won't get rid of it, okay?" She felt outside herself, disconnected and even anxious, which wasn't normal for her.

"You promise you won't give it away?"

"I promise." Charlotte opened the door to encourage Elaine to leave. "I want to look at it some more. I'm coming over in a couple of days with red beans. I'll see you then."

It seemed selfish to feel so relieved to have Elaine gone, but all the questions about her mother unnerved her. She leaned back against the door and realized that she was still holding the photo. Her mother appeared to be a young teen, and Violet in her twenties. Violet had a mischievous smile, but Dolores, with her serious, deep eyes seemed to be searching for something in the camera. She closed the picture inside a kitchen drawer and went into the dim refuge of her bedroom for a nap.

———◆———

Elaine found herself out on the concrete steps not quite sure how she got there. Her mother seemed eager to see her go. Maybe she was just tired, or maybe it was the wine.

To the right of the porch between the houses, the smell was dank and marshy, but as she went out into the front yard, the pungent smell of the huge white oleanders on the fence took over. The woody stems weighed down the fence and hung over onto the sidewalk where the neighbor, Pearl, was leaning on the papery trunk of a crepe myrtle. She smoked a cigarette and gazed at the sky where ominous-looking black clouds pushed in from the lake.

"Hey, Miss Pearl, how are you doing?" Elaine rested her hands on the Cyclone fence.

"Who's that? That you Elaine? Look at you. Come over here. Lemme see you." Pearl put her hands up to Elaine's face. Her eyes were clouded with cataracts, and her gaze seemed to focus elsewhere. "You visiting your mama?"

"Yes, ma'am."

Pearl put her hands on Elaine's cheeks, and her breath touched Elaine's neck. "You remember when I used to watch you sometimes? You were so serious, with your colored pencils and your paper. You used to stick your little tongue out on the side when you were drawing. What are you doing now?"

"You mean for work? I'm a waitress right now. I used to…"

"Not for work. I mean for you. I'm talking about what you do for you here." She pointed to her chest. "For the inside you. The God in you. That part."

Elaine wondered if Pearl had started to have some dementia.

"Because when you find it, you will know it for what it is. Your heart will tell you but you gotta follow your heart. You see?"

"I think so."

Pearl patted Elaine's cheeks then raised her hands and face to the sky. Elaine wondered how much she could see.

"You see them clouds. They're coming in. I remember when there wasn't nothing out here. Open spaces, cypress trees. We used to take the little train, the Smoky Mary they called it, to the lake. From downtown. City girls, put on our cute dresses and ride through this swamp to go to the amusement park at the lake. Have a sno-ball, hope to meet some nice boys." She giggled, and it sounded like she was all of ten years old instead of almost ten times that.

The air got cooler suddenly as the pressure dropped, and the sky darkened. Pearl put her cigarette out in a clay flowerpot filled with damp butts. "This might be from that tropical storm out in the Gulf." Pearl leaned on her worn cane. "You better get where you're going. It's gonna be here in a minute from over that lake." She tapped her chest. "Your heart, Laney."

# 5.

## PHOTOGRAPHER, 1923

OLORES DUG HER TOES INTO the warm mud at the edge of the bayou and touched her arms where the willow fronds tickled them. Her maman would be surprised at how tall she grew in the past five years, tall like her papa. Children called her épouvantail, scarecrow in English, the way her brown legs stuck out of her cotton dresses.

Morning sun leaked through the trees making leaf shadows that jumped around the surface of the water. Dolores loved the patterns of light and shadow. In the shallows by her feet, her three little cousins were teasing a yellow and green baby water snake. She turned her head to the side trying not to look at the poor thing. Finally, she couldn't stand it anymore and picked up a stiff splinter of wood to lift the snake. It skittered off on the surface of the water.

"Fofolle, Didi folle! Why did you do that?" One of them splashed her with water and they all ran off laughing.

Dolores was waiting with Papa and her uncle for a stranger who was traveling along the coast in a houseboat. She heard them talking the day before about the man, saying that he had a camera and was taking pictures of the French people along the bayous and prairies of Louisiana. They sounded suspicious.

"Say he's got four or five of them things. I don't know why he'd be coming here. I don't want no pictures of me, no," said one man.

Papa said, "He says Cadiens are fearless to live in a place like this with storms and alligators and mosquitoes. Says we're poets, too, us."

"Poets? What the hell he mean by that?"

"Something about laughing in the face of death," said Papa. "Strange talk, hein?"

"They say he's not Cadien either. I don't know what he is, maybe came from France. I don't like it one bit."

Dolores wrapped her fingers around strands of her hair and held them to her mouth. When the breeze stopped, the water turned still as brown-green glass, then the breeze came again, and the sun broke into tiny sparks. Mosquito hawks bounced off the dark water, and the sun glowed through their lace-etched wings. Dolores wondered if a camera could stop a mosquito hawk right at the minute when the sun sparkled on it.

When she heard about the camera a couple of weeks before, she couldn't think of much else except this man coming to town. The last week of school the library was giving away old magazines and one of them had some pictures in it by a famous photographer. Earl read it for her. Next year would be her last year of school, but she still wasn't picking up reading, not like Earl. He kept on reading books even though he'd been done with school now for a couple of years.

"Steichen, that's the fella's name," Earl read from the magazine, 'did the series of the Flatiron Building in New York at different times of day. The most famous is one at dusk where the streetlights glow. Shadowed figures walk the sidewalk, and the building is lit by the lingering sunset'."

"It's like the camera stops time," she said. "It stops those people right there at that minute. And it won't be the same again."

"I guess so," said Earl. "I never thought of it that way."

"You can pick how you want it to be when it stops." She stuffed the magazine into her bag. When she got home she stuck the pictures on the wall of her bedroom where Marie had hung all her other ones.

Now the day was here that the photographer would be coming to Cocodrie. Dolores wondered if he was famous like that man in the magazine. In the water by the fishing shack a screened holding trap held a bunch of fish, mostly buffalohead and catfish. Every few minutes she would squat and toy with the latch. She ended up moving to another spot on the shore away from the trap, frustrated at not being able to free the fish. The trapped fish made her feel trapped, too.

The little cousins who had tortured the snake were playing under the covered gallery of the fishing supply shack. Papa and Uncle Red sat on a wood bench. She could smell the lye and the bait tanks from the gallery. She couldn't see past the line of stilt houses in the water where the bayou curved. The hanging clothes on their porches made it hard to see into the distance. At least most of the trawlers and oyster barques were out for the day, so when the man's boat got close, they'd see him.

They heard him before that happened. Papa stood up and Uncle Red followed.

"That must be him," said Red. "My cousin in Dulac said his motor sounded sick."

A couple of women and more children came over to the marina dock near the shack to see what the sound was. Dolores kept her distance.

The motor grew louder and louder until a strange type of boat appeared. It looked like the houseboats Dolores saw some of the Biloxi Indians use when they came to town. It had a rough cabin that looked like it was dropped onto the deck at the last minute. The motor did sound sick, like Uncle Red said. Dolores went closer.

A tall man climbed out of the cabin onto the deck. He wore mid-calf rubber boots, a straw hat with a wide black band, white baggy pants and a faded button-down shirt. He had thick black eyebrows and a trim mustache.

Dolores felt a hand on her arm. Earl was standing next to her. "Are you going to ask him about the camera?"

Dolores shrugged her shoulders.

"It would be alright to ask him if you could see one." Earl stood a head or more taller than her, and his straw hat shaded his face. He was always leaning over to talk to her or maybe to make himself seem less tall. Uncle Red went around a pile of screened bait boxes to shake the man's hand. "I'm Red. Those were my cousins you were visiting up in Dulac. What you got running this thing, boy? It sounds like it needs a little help."

"It's an automobile engine, sir from a wrecked Model-T. It's got one speed and no reverse, but it keeps going for me. Name's Adrian Dozier."

"A model T, hein? Well, they will *all* have noisy engines soon enough, I think. Here, let me help you." Red helped him unload a canvas duffel bag, a metal ice chest and two sturdy cases covered in oilcloth. They piled everything onto the dock. Dolores wondered where the cameras were. Her cousins tried to get closer to him and started running up and down the dock.

Red said, "Leave the man alone. You'll see him tonight. We have a party planned for you. We don't get too many visitors here being at the end of the line. Not much left before the ocean once you get to Cocodrie. Right now, we thought you'd be hungry, so my wife Estelle fixed some lunch at the house. You can settle in. Just up this way a bit."

"That's nice of you. Thank you."

Earl and Dolores stepped up closer, and Earl nudged her forward. "Go on. It's a good time. Ask him."

Dozier leaned down to lift the duffel bag onto his shoulder. When he stood up again, he seemed surprised and took a step back from Dolores and Earl. Dolores looked down at the ground.

Earl spoke up. "She'd like to see one of your cameras."

"Of course, I'll get one out. Have you ever seen one? Red, can I have a minute to show her?"

Red nodded at Dozier and set down the cases he was carrying. "She's my godchild. This is her papa here. She's been eager to see a camera."

Dozier squatted and took out a small rectangular box from one of the cases. When he pressed a button, the thing opened up like a squeezebox and let out a sigh. The kids jumped back from it and squealed.

Dolores smiled and said to Earl, "Comme un accordéon."

Dozier nodded. "Yes. It has a bellows just like an accordion."

Dolores inched even closer to him, her face riveted on the camera, her fingers opening and closing at her sides. "Is it true you can stop time with it?"

Dozier tilted his head to one side. One of Dolores' cousins laughed at her, and the others copied him. The cicadas whined so loud above her head that she almost couldn't hear.

Red said, "It's not a time machine, Didi."

Dozier cleared his throat and held the camera like a baby in his hands. "In a way, yes, you can stop time with it." He talked like he was looking for the right words. "In fact, that's how I got this camera. I found myself a few years ago, with a bit of extra cash, so I bought a watch. I thought I needed something to help me keep track of time. But the next day I realized that wasn't at all what I really wanted to do, keep track of it. I saw this camera in a shop, and I knew I wanted to, well, as you say, to stop time. And here I am."

He stared down at the camera, then at Dolores, and seemed to have lost his train of thought. After a funny laugh he began to put the camera back in its box.

Dolores said, "I'd like to try it."

He pulled it back out again. "Of course, yes, you are welcome to try it."

"Estelle is waiting for us," said Red.

"Oh, of course. So sorry," said Dozier. He picked up his bags again but didn't move on.

Dolores squinted up into his face with her hand over her eyes to block the sun.

Dozier said, "I'll be here by the fishing shack later today if you'd like to try." He gestured towards Red and cleared his throat again. "I have to go now."

<hr>

That afternoon Dozier brought out his field camera and settled it into a tripod not far from where he'd come in. Three little boys stood around him watching his every move and posing in front of the camera. A sail-powered lugger with trawling nets approached the marina, and more boats followed, the water glistening on their big nets like sparks of fire. Dozier switched back and forth between his portrait camera, his new 35 mm Kodak, and a folding field camera.

Dolores finished her chores as fast as she could and ran back to the fishing shack. She followed close to the water and came out almost in front of Dozier from a cluster of willows on the shore. He was lighting a cigarette. He blinked and stepped back; his cigarette fell from his lips. "You surprised me. It seemed like you were coming out of the water." He leaned over to pick up his muddy cigarette and threw it in the bushes. "You're the girl from this morning. You're interested in cameras?"

Dolores held a hand up to shade her eyes and nodded. Two white ibis flew overhead with pink feet trailing behind them like tails on a kite.

Dozier followed the birds then turned to her. "Well, this one I have out already is pretty interesting. It's called a 'tropical camera'. It's teak, a special kind of wood, it holds up in hot places like Louisiana."

She reached over and touched the surface; it was smooth as glass. Then she felt embarrassed and pulled her hand away.

"It's alright. You can get closer. Here. Look through this opening. I'll get out of your way." He fixed the camera stand so it was right for her, then stepped back to where a carryall bag sat open on the ground. He pulled out a pack of cigarettes. "Go ahead and try it. You can't hurt anything."

She leaned over the top of the thing and tried to find the place to look through.

"You can tilt it," he said, "different angles to affect the focus. Focus is what makes it clear or blurred. Is it alright if I show you?"

She nodded. He pointed to the place where the opening was, and as she looked, he tilted it. The water in the bayou and oleander flowers got clear, then fuzzy, and clear again. He tilted it again, and she could see above the water that the sun was starting to melt into the wispy clouds, turning them pink, red and green. When he moved the camera the water would get fuzzy then clear.

"Does it always have to be on a stand, like so, or can you hold it, too?"

"My, you have good questions. How old are you?"

"Thirteen."

"Not everybody here is interested like you. Some fellows out on a shrimp boat got pretty upset with me this morning when I tried to take some pictures. They seemed angry about it."

"They're afraid of something new. Afraid to get their picture taken. I heard them talking to my papa." Dolores felt the heat climb up her neck like it did whenever she talked to somebody new.

"Ah, that's interesting. To answer your question, yes, in fact, here, I have a couple of other cameras in my bag. Let me show you."

"I wish I could hold it and look up at the clouds."

"Of course, yes. It's nice to hold one." He rummaged in his bag. "Here's one you can hold. But you can't really look at clouds with this one. This was my first camera a few years ago. It's called a Brownie, and it's easy to use. It doesn't have any film in it right now so you can't take any pictures. When you look through this you are going to see things upside down. You can hold it up this way or put it on its side. Hold it close to your body," he demonstrated, "about at your waist and look down into it."

He put the Brownie into her hands, and she was so nervous to break it that she held it like it was one of Marie's babies. "You don't have to be so careful," he said, "it's a very sturdy camera. Try not to drop it, that's all. Look through right here." He pointed to a square window on the top of the box. "That's called the viewfinder."

It was like seeing things through little windows, little bits at a time. A crow flew into the window and startled her, then she moved it around, putting the crow in different spots and putting other things around it. The bird took off, and she wondered if the camera could stop the wings when they move through the air.

Dozier said, "May I take your picture?" He put his eye to his camera, pointing it at Dolores.

She nodded and stared into the pointer imagining what she might look like in his window.

His camera clicked a few times then he laughed and cleared his throat. "For some reason it feels like you are taking my picture instead of the other way around." He was a funny man, thought Dolores, and went back to looking through the window. "May I walk around with it?"

"Yes, yes of course. Take your time. I'll get it back from you later."

She walked up and down the shore pointing the camera at everything. The sky lit up bright orange as it sank into the bayou. The green water frogs started to chirp in the mud near the water, and the cicadas got louder which usually meant it was time for her to go home. She brought the camera back to Dozier and held it out to him.

He took the camera from her. "What did you think?"

A flock of mallards flew down towards the bayou making a lot of noise. "I think it makes me feel quiet," she said. "It slows things down."

He nodded his head a few times slow like he was thinking hard. It made her feel impatient, and he could probably tell because she started to shift from one foot to the other.

Finally, he said, "How about this? I'll put some film in it for you and you can take your own pictures while I'm here. Then I'll take the film and have it processed and have the photos sent back to you. Would you like that?"

His face was lit up by the leftover sun. "You mean put the pictures on paper?"

"Yes, on paper. You call it processing, well, and developing. I can send them back to you."

Dolores turned around when she heard someone walking up behind them. Next to the church across the road people were getting ready for the fais-do-do that night. The party was usually on Saturdays, but tonight was special because of Dozier. The smell from the hot pepper in the seafood boil reached all the way to the bayou.

Earl came up and stood next to Dolores. "Didi, Marie's looking for you to help with the food."

Dozier offered his hand to Earl. "I'm Adrian Dozier."

"I know," said Earl. He shook the man's hand.

"This is Earl," said Dolores.

"Earl, I was just showing Dolores how to use the camera. But it's getting late. I think there's going to be a dance. So, I'll show you first thing in the morning if you want to meet me here. Earl, you can join us, of course."

The next morning Dolores woke up before the sun. She let out the chickens, fed them and cleaned out their shed. Marie went to take care of the cows. Dolores had to watch the babies because the men were gone in the boat. She paced around the kitchen with a baby on her hip afraid that Dozier would be gone by the time she made it. Marie didn't even have the chance to find out where she was going because Dolores was out the door as soon as Marie walked inside.

Dozier was taking pictures by the water when Dolores got there all out of breath.

He said, "Ah, Dolores. Hold on one minute. I'd like to get some of these boats while they are getting ready to go out." Dolores watched how he looked with his eyes first then with the camera. After he finished, they walked back to the place where he left his bags.

"Dolores, you are very patient." He reached into one bag and took out the same box camera she had held the day before. "Here's the Brownie. I'll load it for you, it only takes a minute." He talked as he worked putting the film in. "It takes only ten pictures, so choose carefully. There are only three things to set. All you have to do is adjust it for how much light you want to come in." He snapped it shut. "You open this hole bigger or smaller to let different amounts of light in." He pointed to a lever on the side of the box. "If something is in the shade you want to open it here." He pulled the lever up all the way and the opening enlarged. "If it's sunny, close it more, like this."

He gave the Brownie to her and pointed. "Okay, you see this little red window? It says 'one'. After you take your first picture, wind this little knob until it says two. Then it's ready for your next photo. This metal piece on the side slides down to take your picture."

She moved the lever up and down and watched as the hole opened and closed.

"Keep it steady when you shoot. I'm going to set the opening for you now to medium. You can't be too close or too far from something. Keep it about this distance." He paced back and forth a few feet in front of her. "That way it will be clear. If you're too far away from something it will be fuzzy. Just keep it steady. I'll be here a few days so I can show you how to change the film. It's easy."

For the next few days Dolores spent all her free time with the Brownie. Dozier showed her how to change the film, and she used up three rolls. Whenever she could get away from home, she watched him take pictures around town. Little by little the town stopped being so afraid, and more people wanted him to take their picture.

Five days later, Dolores went down to the dock with Papa and some of the rest of the town to say goodbye to Dozier. The air smelled clean and grassy from a fresh rain. Dozier had made friends in Cocodrie; some of the people that did not trust him at first had changed and let him take photos of anything he wanted. Dolores had watched him take pictures of men working on their boats, of young boys collecting moss from the trees, women hanging clothes and working in the fields, pictures of dancing at the party, and of babies and kids. He told them he was going to make a book out of the pictures, and they would be able to see it.

People brought him presents: dried shrimp and oysters, oranges and plums, holy cards for protection, a bandana, and Earl gave him a wood carving of a heron.

Dolores set the Brownie on top of his ice chest along with the used film from that week. "Thank you," she said like Papa told her to, his hand on her shoulder.

Dozier squatted by the shore, tucking the gifts into his canvas bag. He adjusted his straw hat and took one last photo of the group. Then he picked up the Brownie and handed it back to her. "I want you to have it."

Dolores reached for the Brownie then stopped and looked at Papa. She didn't think he'd let her have it.

Papa squinted at Dozier and rubbed the stubble on his chin. "Non, Monsieur, we cannot take that."

"She'll be good with a camera, sir," said Dozier. "It is not an expensive apparatus; I've had it for years. Many people own them in the city to take family photos and the like. I can develop the film for her."

"What do you think, Didi?"

Dolores nodded.

Dozier handed her two more rolls of film. "It's time to pass this thing along, anyway."He placed her used film in his bag. "I'll send these back to you as soon as I can print them."

"Thank you, Monsieur. Very much."

Her father shook Dozier's hand. "We'll take good care of it."

The old engine sputtered a few times before starting. Dolores wandered along the edge of the bayou as Dozier's boat pulled away from shore. When she gazed back towards the sound of his boat, he was looking in her direction. He lifted his hand, and she waved back at him, then turned away as the motor faded in the distance.

# 6.

# THE TIGHT SPOT

Earl Rizan rested his elbows on the windowsill and lifted a pair of heavy binoculars to his face. The binoculars were old and clumsy, and the lenses ruined by humidity. He looked out over Lake Pontchartrain and the lazy clouds that drifted like the big whaling ships he'd read about. He was happy to catch a pair of brown pelicans flying over; he remembered that not long ago they were endangered because of that DDT stuff. He found Elaine dangling her feet over the water near the end of the dock. He'd been waiting all morning for her to wake up, then missed her when he went to the toilet. Now she might be out there for an hour daydreaming.

Earl had lived near Lake Pontchartrain or in this camp on stilts out in the lake a hundred feet from shore for most of his eighty years. He had lost his legs and a wife and raised two children while fishing and crabbing it. Water was one thing you could count on in this city: canals, bayous, lakes, rivers, and street floods after a summer rain. Ghosts were the other thing; not like white sheets flying in the wind, but glimpses of memories from the past and other pasts that nobody took ownership of. These glimpses had started to bother him more since Elaine was home, mostly because she reminded him of his dead wife, Dolores. It almost seemed like Dolores was trying to tell him something.

Elaine reached up and did something to her hair. Earl pulled the binoculars away from his face and shook his head. "There she goes again." Dolores used to do the same thing; it was like she was trying to sweep cobwebs off her head.

He wiped sweat off his forehead with a handkerchief. When he looked up again, she was headed back. *Finally, I can ask her.*

He had started to wonder lately, after his heart attack, if he might want to spend some of whatever time he had left with a woman. He'd had lady friends since Dolores died, more than one that lasted a few years, but he'd had Charlotte to raise, and after Elaine moved in with him, he didn't seem to have the energy for it anymore. Too much time without a woman made him forget certain things. He was forgetting how to behave like a gentleman, was letting himself go, dressing poorly and not washing up as much. But he figured it would be a miracle at his age, in his damaged condition, to find anyone who would be even a little bit interested in spending time with him.

Even so, he was willing to give it a try. He hurried over to the door to open it for Elaine. She almost didn't notice him, had her hand out for the doorknob, so fixated she was on a gull feather she was holding. "Good morning, princess. Do you want coffee? I just made some."

She guided the screen door shut with her bottom. Wisps of her dark, fuzzy hair fell out of her baseball cap and stuck to the sweat on her forehead, which was starting to turn red from all the sitting she did out there on the dock.

She said, "What's wrong? Do you need something?" She leaned down and kissed his cheek, the same as she'd done since she was tiny, except she used to have to reach up to do it. Now she towered over him, and seemed to be scrutinizing him all the time, looking into his eyes, then acting as though she was about to take his temperature and blood pressure any minute.

He rolled away from her, and she went into the kitchen.

He said, "Why do you always think I need something? You're acting like you did with that wounded robin I helped you with when you were ten." One thing about her was that she could be easily distracted. This time from fussing over him.

"Robin?" She poured herself some coffee from the white enamel pot. "I don't remember that." She stood at the window stirring her coffee. The lake was quiet. No sounds came from Sam's camp. "Oh yeah. Now I remember." Her voice went from distracted to sad and forlorn. "I was kind of obsessed with it. And then I fed it too many worms and it died. The day I was going to let it go." She picked at a few breadcrumbs on the cutting board and chewed them. "I guess Sam's out with a fishing tour."

He rubbed his head with his hand. It was not an easy thing to ask her, and she seemed to be deliberately making it more difficult for him. Why had he brought up that damn robin? "Look, I want to ask you a favor." He hit the arm of his chair with the side of his fist, a habit he had picked up years ago when he first lost his legs. It was a way of getting someone's attention and it seemed to work well with most people. But Elaine had been more exasperating than most lately.

"God, it's hot already." Elaine brought her coffee into the living room and dropped onto the sofa that faced the back of the camp.

Gulls had settled on all the posts of the dock, one on each post, like lookouts. Earl's fishing boat called to him from the end of the dock. The lake was calm, just a smattering of white caps, a great day for fishing.

Elaine said, "I've been thinking. Since your heart attack, you know, it's crazy for you to be out here in the middle of the lake in that wheelchair."

"Oh Jesus, not again. You sound like your damn mother." Earl sighed and rested his forehead in his hands. "Believe me I will be the first one to admit when it's time for me to get out of here. I guess you and your mother went on about me the other day. Plotting against me."

"No, not really. By the way, I didn't marry Ethan because my mother wanted me to marry him."

"No, of course you didn't," he sighed. "That what she says? You married him to get away from here. And from your mother."

Elaine fumbled with the fringe of a worn-out throw pillow. "Yeah, I guess I did. It didn't really solve much, did it? Running away?"

"Never does. At least not in my experience."

"We talked about Grandma a lot too. She has this picture she was going to throw away with Grandma and Violet. How old was Mama anyway when Grandma died?"

"I don't know. That was a long time ago. I guess she wasn't even in school yet." He took a couple of deep breaths. Now she was asking her mother questions about Dolores which he knew would upset Charlotte. He softened his tone and changed the subject. "Laney," he used his little-girl name for her. "I want to ask you to do something for me."

"Oh yeah. You said that before. I'm sorry. Sure. What do you need?" She turned the ceiling fan on high and sat back down. "You need me to get something for you?"

"Well, yeah, I guess you could say that. You know, I've been alone for a long time. It's nice you're here, but you need to get your life together and I, well, I'd like to meet somebody. Somebody my own age, a woman, to talk to. Don't give me that face, it's not about sex. Just some company, maybe keep you and your mother out of my hair." He rubbed his forehead again with the back of his hand.

"A woman, like somebody to date? Do people do that at your age?"

He turned his chair to get to the kitchen and the back wheel caught on the edge of the sofa. "Goddammit, this damn thing!" He slammed his fist on the arm. The chair was so much a part of him that he usually didn't notice it anymore, except in certain agitated moods. He'd had the same one for more years than he could remember and would not hear of getting a new one, even though the arms were black from the sweat and oil of his skin. "Sometimes I hate this thing!"

She set her coffee down and jumped up to help him.

"I don't need your help. I've been in this chair for forty years." He backed up and went around the sofa towards the kitchen.

"What do you need, let me get it." She tried to follow him.

"Sit down, I'm just getting a beer." He took the magnetic church key off the fridge and opened the cold Dixie with it.

The big wall clock had a Norman Rockwell painting of a boy and an old man fishing off a pier. Elaine had always loved the picture. She said, "It's only ten thirty."

"I know what time it is." He brought the beer back into the living room and took the tobacco pouch out of its place in the front pocket of his shirt. He held the pouch in one hand, poured in the tobacco then grabbed the string with his teeth to pull the pouch closed. He rolled the cigarette, licked the paper, lit it with a match and inhaled. "I want you to go down to see Ida and ask her to find somebody nice. She knows a lot of people from church."

"Wait a minute. You want me to go down there and ask Ida to find a woman for you to hang out with. Why me? Can't you call her or something?" She went back into the kitchen and poured more coffee. "Seems like a weird thing to ask me to do."

She stood at the kitchen sink staring out of the window, almost as though she had left the conversation and went off somewhere else in her head. Why was he asking her to do this? He wasn't sure, except for one thing, he wanted her to know he was thinking about it. He wanted her to be a part of it for some reason.

He said, "You're right. You're right. I could call her. I don't like to do things over the phone. But I see that it's a strange mission for a granddaughter."

She turned around, and he was struck by how tired she looked.

He said, "Listen, I still have a life, I want you to understand that. I might need some help, I'll need help until I die. But I want you to get on with your life, not be obsessed with an old man."

She stared at him with those pools of brown, another reminder of Dolores. Her eyebrows lifted, and she puckered her mouth and took a deep breath. "Okay," the word slid out with a sigh. "I'll go."

"Get yourself a po-boy. Take your time, but I'd like you to go today. I know you'll put it off, and it'll be weeks before you get down there."

---

Elaine pulled on a clean T-shirt and loose cotton pants and grabbed her cigarettes. She tied her shoes next to the back window and watched Pappy cast into the green-brown lake at the end of the dock. Choppy waves broke the surface of the water. Elaine was tempted to forget her mission and lie down on the levee to watch the huge clouds like she did when she was a kid. But she'd been wanting to go down there anyway to visit Ida, whom she'd known forever.

She put on a plain baseball cap to cover her dirty hair and pulled the front door shut. Sam's place was still quiet. She noticed her slight droop of disappointment every time she went out, and Sam wasn't around. She wondered what it meant. If her feelings for him were going to start nagging at her again, she had to be sure to watch herself carefully. She didn't want to stir him up, especially in the state of disrepair she was in.

The walkway groaned and swayed, always making her a bit nervous even though Pappy scooted up and down it in his wheelchair without a thought. The motion of the water three feet below made her dizzy. She climbed up and down the levee stairs and crossed over to the sidewalk.

The Tight Spot was a two-block walk past clapboard houses that now served as business enterprises mostly around food: J and S Seafood, Lakeview Restaurant, Binder's Bakery—she could sometimes smell the French bread from the house—and a new Vietnamese place, Dong Phuong. She passed a cramped hardware store and a couple of homes that were set back from the street.

Elaine loved the overgrown yards and slowed down in the shade in front of them. They were filled with oversized azaleas and oleander bushes, jasmine vines, and palmettos. The air that came out of them carried a fetid smell, like overripe fruit, and brought her nostalgia to the surface, like so many other things did here.

The neon sign above the door to the Tight Spot was a relic of another age. She had always enjoyed it with its two martini glasses, green olives, and a curvy white line like cigarette smoke rising behind them. Elaine pushed open the heavy wood door, entered the dark coolness of the bar, and slid onto a stool, breathing in the familiar scent of Ida's place as her eyes grew accustomed to the dimness.

There were a few people sitting in booths, no one she knew, an old couple and a table of oil workers, two guys at the slot machine. Ida's voice came from the kitchen, and the door swung open. Ida came out wiping her hands on her grimy apron. "Hey, baby, look at you! You finally came to see me. Sam told me you were in town." Ida lunged over the bar and grabbed Elaine in a bear hug.

Seeing old friends and relatives after a divorce was what it must be like after getting out of prison. Nobody wants to ask the obvious questions, so they don't know what to say. A lot of times they act like nothing happened. That was one reason Elaine had avoided coming down for the past month.

Ida went on. "How's that old bastard treating you?"

She smelled like smoke and fried food, same as always. Pappy used to bring her here, to Charlotte's dismay, buy her pickles and let her use the slot machine. She wanted to bury her head in Ida's arms and have a good cry.

"He's treating me fine. You doing okay, Ida? It's been a while."

"Same, same. A new ache and a new chin hair every morning, other than that it's all good." Ida's thick, pink arms rested on the bar, which she rubbed every few minutes with a rag. "What can I get you? You're looking thin. All you been through. I was sorry to hear. Me and the ol' man. We were sorry. How about shrimp? Ya want it dressed?"

Elaine nodded. "Sounds great. And a Dixie."

"Comin' up." Ida yelled the order to the kitchen and plopped a sweating bottle of Dixie in front of Elaine. The giant air conditioner above the front door had a loud hum and a rattle like some parts had fallen off and were rumbling around in it. Elaine took in the place, trying to remember if anything had changed in the past few years. The odor of stale beer and grease hung in the air, and the memorabilia hanging on the walls had taken on a dark sheen. There was an autographed poster of Archie Manning and a few other Saints photos. Lots of pictures of the Mardi Gras Indians. Dr. John at the jazz fest. The usual lighted beer signs included Dixie, and a new one, Abita. Elaine wanted to try it; she only ordered Dixie for nostalgia's sake; it tasted terrible.

The front door opened and the glare from the sun blinded Elaine.

Ida called out towards the door. "My lucky day. I got both y'all in at one time. Two of my favorite people." She pressed out her menthol cigarette. "Sam, you want an Abita?"

Sam crossed the room to the bar and stood next to Elaine. "Can I sit here? Or are you waiting for someone?"

She said, "No, no, have a seat." He smelled like fresh, woodsy air and mossy sweat. Elaine had loved the way he smelled, and it reminded her of how she had only tolerated Ethan's scent.

"Thanks." Sam nodded at the beer Ida put in front of him. "I'm surprised to see you here so early in the day."

Elaine pulled off her baseball cap and hoped her hair didn't smell too sweaty. She followed the outlines of the muscles in his arms down to his browned hands and stopped herself when she got to his jeans. His arm felt warm when it brushed against hers.

Ida said, "She don't need a reason to come visit her old friend. Do ya, Laney?" Ida filled two glasses with ice water and set them on the bar. "I hope the old man's not too cranky. Gonna run you off. I told him that before you came, you gonna run that girl off with your grouching and complaining."

Elaine said, "You see him much, Ida? Before he got sick?"

"Oh, this guy brings him down some." Ida was called back into the kitchen. "Sam, you gonna eat? The usual?"

"Sure, Ida, thanks. I don't bring him here too often." Sam pulled a pack of Marlboros from his front shirt pocket and offered one to Elaine. He lit them both with an old flip lighter that had initials engraved on the side. "I know he's not supposed to drink or smoke, or anything, I guess. But every now and then, you know, won't hurt, after a fishing trip."

Elaine took a long drag and determined again for the hundredth time to stop smoking as soon as she felt the heat hit her lungs. "That's his list of all the things he wants to do including the 'or anything'. He sent me over here today."

Sam shifted on the stool and took a long drink. "What do you mean? What else is he trying to do? Another building project?"

She laughed. "I wish it was that simple. He sent me here to ask Ida to find him a companion," she said. "A woman. I'm not clear on it."

"Really?" Sam's eyebrows lifted toward his hairline. "He's never mentioned that to me. Hunh. Interesting. A companion. Seems like a strange thing to ask you to do."

"That's what I said. He doesn't want her to help him with any-thing, just keep him company, talk. So me and Mama don't have to worry over him so much."

"But does he mean like someone to date?"

"That's also what I said. That seemed to irritate him."

Ida set a plate down in front of Elaine with a half loaf of French bread smeared with melted butter and piled high with fried shrimp.

"Jesus, I'll never eat all this." She started eating the shrimp off the bread with her fingers.

Sam said, "What's it like being back home?"

Elaine couldn't identify what was making her feel so nervous sitting next to Sam. She felt herself squirming on the barstool. She saw that look in his eyes, hiding behind the casual small talk. The same look she'd noticed the morning he came over. Like he wanted something from her. Or maybe it was hurt. Or maybe he felt as nervous as she did.

She said, "I saw a woman at your place the other day. Pappy didn't say you were seeing anyone."

Somebody put money in the juke box and a Fats Domino tune started, "Blue Monday."

He slumped a little and turned towards the guys at the slot machine who had started clapping and cheering. Then he sat up straight and drank from his beer. "She's nice. A nurse at Charity. Likes to fish."

Ida returned with an oyster po-boy for Sam. He pressed out his cigarette. "Ida, Elaine has a favor to ask you from Earl."

"Oh, yeah?" Her face was red with heat from the kitchen. She refilled their water glasses, then wiped the counter before resting both arms on the surface of the bar and leaning her bulk against it. "What do you wanna ask me? And why can't he come ask himself?"

"He sent me down here to ask you to find a companion for him. A woman just to keep him company and talk. Said you knew people from church? I guess he's just lonely."

"Well, that's something." She turned to her husband Walter, who was standing at the kitchen window. "Earl wants a woman, after all these years." She turned back and pointed to Elaine's plate. "Laney, you not eating anything, you're too thin."

Elaine bit another shrimp. "It seemed strange to me, but it makes sense that he'd want to meet people his age. Most of his friends moved away or died. Why shouldn't he want some company?"

Ida said, "Yeah, yeah, I know, it's just that he's, well he's never been too interested, maybe a couple of friends over the years. He just gave up on women a long time ago. Seems kinda late to start looking now."

Walter said, "Sounds to me like he's not looking for a wife, just some company. You gotta go makin' more outta nothing."

"Oh, shut up, old man," she waved him away. "Well, I do know a lady who visits people, older people. I mean she's old too, but in good health, laughs a lot. She has an accent, like Mississippi or Georgia, one of those places. I'll take care of it." She pushed herself up from the bar. "Y'all want another beer?"

Elaine said, "Not me, I'd like to get back."

Ida turned away, grabbed two brown long-necked bottles from a cooler behind the bar and set them on the counter. "Here, take 'em to go." She opened a brown paper bag and put the bottles inside.

Elaine said, "Ida, you knew my grandma, Dolores, didn't you?"

Ida set the bag down and started to wipe the bar around their plates. "Now you two stay as long as you like, I got work to do. I'll take care of the lady for Earl, her name's Audrey. Real nice, you'll like her. Tell him, okay? Elaine don't stay away too long. You either, Sam." She shuffled off with a steady if painful gait. Her stockings were pulled up to just above her swelling knees and held tight by garters. Her legs stuck out of misshapen slippers that used to be pink.

Sam set his po-boy down and spoke through a mouthful of oysters. "Who's Dolores? Your grandmother? I don't remember you talking about her before."

"She died young. I never knew her. And I'm curious about her— for one reason, because nobody wants to talk about her. She looks interesting in pictures." She snubbed out her cigarette and reached for a box to wrap up the rest of her shrimp. "I'll bring this to Pappy."

Sam said, "Wait, I'm almost done. I'll walk with you." He finished the po-boy in another bite and tossed some bills on the counter. "I'll get it. A welcome-home lunch."

He pushed his plate away and they both stood up at the same time, blocking each other's way around the stationary barstools. She felt his breath on her neck.

He said, "That girl. She doesn't mean anything to me."

"It doesn't matter to me. Why would you say that? You're not thinking of taking a chance on me again? You like risk?"

He smiled and lowered his eyes. "Maybe. Calculated. Ego driven."

She laughed, and he moved away to make room for her to pass. They went from the darkness of the bar into a mid-afternoon sun that hung below a layer of thin, ragged clouds. The lake opened at the top of the levee, blue green now with a skipping of white caps. Each time Elaine climbed to the top of the levee she felt like she was coming out of a cave into the world again.

Sam went with her to the end of her walkway. Pappy was sitting on the side porch towards the back of the house. He was fishing. "Looks like Earl got busy while you were gone on your errand. I'll leave you two. Call me if you need anything, okay?"

"Sure."

He touched her arm and turned to leave, then retraced his steps. "How about you? Are you seeing somebody?"

A dinghy sputtered near Sam's place where gulls were fighting over a scrap of something on the dock.

"Never mind," said Sam. "None of my business. I can meet you Wednesday afternoon at the café if you want to see my show."

"Wednesday? Okay, that will work." She wished she hadn't agreed. It seemed clear that he was wanting them to start over again.

The gray boards of the dock swayed as she walked the rest of the way around the side porch and sat down next to Pappy.

"I see you ran into Sam. Nice guy, like I said. He still really likes you, you know." Earl handed Elaine an extra fishing rod. "It's already got bait."

"Yep. Nice guy. He's got a girlfriend, Pappy."

"So?" he snorted.

"We talked to Ida." She let out some line and it dropped into the water under her feet.

"Oh, yeah? Good. Good." They fished until the mosquitoes started, then went inside and finished the po-boy with some leftover red beans. They watched old reruns of the Andy Griffith show.

When the news came on, Elaine felt herself starting to doze off. Lulled by the sound of the water and the dimming light, she remembered a lullaby that Pappy used to sing to her. "Dors bien, pauvre petite bébé ; dors bien. Les chattons viennent te voler. Dors bien, pauvre petite bébé." Sleep well, poor little baby, sleep well. Kittens come to take you away. Sleep well, poor little baby.

"I'm falling asleep, Pappy. Good night." She got up and she leaned in for a kiss.

"Sleep tight, babe." Without turning his eyes away from the screen, he scratched her forehead with his dry lips. "And thank you."

# 7.

## A STORM FROM THE GULF

ONE AFTERNOON DOLORES GOT HOME early from school because a storm was coming. It was the beginning of her last year of school, and she was happy for that. Early September is when the bad storms usually come, and Papa and the older people knew how to read the signs from the sky and animals and the water when their boats are out in the Gulf.

Her brother Louis was boarding up the windows of the house. "Didi, a storm is coming. You can help Marie in the house."

"Where's Papa?" she said.

"He's over at Aunt Titi's helping her with her windows."

Marie was busy gathering up bedding inside the house. "I'm glad they got you home early today. Change your clothes and come help me get ready. We have to fix up under the table for tonight and then make supper before it gets bad outside. I don't like cooking in the middle of a storm." Her two-year-old son, Raymond, had found a dead water bug and played with it under the table. "Raymond, leave that!" She kicked the bug away and picked him up. "How was school today, Didi?"

But Dolores had already gone through the house to the woods outside the back door. She liked the excitement of a storm. And it meant no school tomorrow. The air smelled bitter, like metal, and the sky swirled with yellow-green clouds. If clouds had feelings, these would be angry clouds. She held up her hands to make a square shape out of her fingers and squinted up at the sky through them. Except for the sounds of people boarding up windows and calling to each other over the wind, it was quiet in a strange way. No birds or crickets chirping, no squirrels and chipmunks scratching and scrambling. Dolores wandered away from the house and tilted her finger camera in different directions. She pointed at the sky, then at the gray fence, the brown cow with her new calf, and the baby red chickens. The tall pines had already started swaying in the wind. When she turned it toward a mass of azalea shrubs, the bushes vibrated, and Earl walked out.

"You scared me," she said. "I thought you were the loup garou."

"You and your stories. There is no loup garou. No wolf that steals little children. Those are all just make-believe. Fairy tales."

"How do you know? You ever see God? But you believe there is a God, don't you?"

Earl shook his head. "I see God every day. Every time I go out on a boat or look up at the clouds. Every time I look at you."

That stopped her in her tracks. "T'es fou, toi! There is a loup garou."

"I don't even know why I try to talk to you sometimes. You so stubborn."

She pointed her fingers at the clouds again. Louis came around to the side of the house. "Didi, you get inside now and help Marie. Hey, Earl, you need any help at your house?"

"No, I'm going home right now."

Louis went through the gate and started leading the cows into the barn. The chickens had already gone inside when the sky darkened. He spoke to Papa and their voices trailed off in the wind.

Earl said, "This storm is gonna be a bad one. I know you want to be walking around with that camera, but you need to be careful."

Dolores lowered her hands. "Papa won't let me out in it. I'll go out after." The wind tossed a good-sized branch across the path behind them. Leaves and dust swirled like the water going down the sink.

A cloud of dust blew into Earl's face. He wiped his eyes. "I can go with you. We can go check on the wood duck nest we found."

Marie called. "Didi, you should come in. It's starting to blow harder. Earl Rizan, you go home now before it gets bad." The wind picked up and the tall pines that looked to Dolores like skinny old women with big hats swayed back and forth like swamp grass.

Dolores helped Marie make a tent out of the heavy kitchen table. They piled blankets and pillows under it. Dolores remembered the last big storm three years earlier when they camped out under the table. Now that she had a camera all she could think about was taking pictures of it. She had been so careful with the film Mr. Dozier left with her, almost afraid to push the lever, and still had five pictures left before the rolls were done; then she could send them to him in New Orleans.

After dinner she and Marie and the children settled in under the table while the men stayed in the front room ready if they needed to deal with anything outside. The wind was loud in the trees and rain pounded the roof. Violent sounds came from outside, maybe trees falling, or debris being tossed around and crashing together. Dolores tried to stay awake with the grown-ups, but finally felt herself falling asleep, despite the noise.

By early morning, the storm had quieted, and Dolores sneaked by everybody out the front door with her camera. She knew Papa would want her to wait in case there were dangerous things lying around, but it was not even dawn, and everyone had such a long night, even Marie and the babies were still asleep.

A warm breeze lifted her hair as she stepped down from the porch into soft, wet grass. She wandered in the front yard through drifts of brown and green pine needles and fallen branches, some as tall as she was and full of leaves. The sturdy live oak that Papa said was over 300 years old had lost a few leaves but stayed strong like a guard over their home. Some of the yellow pines had snapped.

One tree had fallen over next to a garden in an open area. It lay on the ground with the crown at one end and the roots were all out of the ground pointing up at the sky. They were twice as tall as she was. It looked like a fairy tale monster with long gangly arms and legs and a deep crevice for swallowing things up.

She looked at it through her camera, but it was much too big for the Brownie, and it was still too dark anyway. She headed towards the bayou as the first birds began to wake up.

The path was covered with all kinds of things. Besides the tree branches and needles, there were things from households—a washbasin, a toy wagon, a metal pail, and a pair of overalls hanging from a high limb. On the dirt path that led to the bayou, a child's dress lay across the ditch like somebody had set it down gently after ironing. It was white cotton with lace, someone's church dress, but streaked with mud. The abandoned dress made her feel strange, afraid, and sad, but curious.

She noticed the world waking up around her, but it was all in the background while she looked at the dress. Birds started singing louder, and people came out of their houses, children splashed in puddles, women began to pick up in their yards and the men talked together as they looked at the damage to the dock and boats. The sun began to warm under the sleeves of Dolores' cotton shirt and to heat up her feet in her boots. She kept the dress in the viewfinder trying different angles and distances; she even tried laying down in the mud to get a certain view. It was like the dress put her in a trance.

Finally, there was enough light. She checked to make sure the stop opening was all the way open and framed the dress into the square holding the box firmly against her waist. She stopped breathing for the moment it took to press the lever on the side, like Dozier showed her.

With ten pictures per roll, she had to be real careful, so after four shots, she moved on to other strange sights. A bedsheet flapped like a ghost from an oak limb; an iron kettle was sunk into the mud next to a tractor tire and a ball of fishing twine. Two young pecan trees had fallen and lay with roots turned upward like the octopus that sometimes got caught in the nets.

The sky cleared and the light that came after was washed fresh, almost too bright, Dolores thought, preferring the dimness from the clouds or the yellow green of the storm sky.

She went to the dock and focused on some egrets in a dead cypress tree. Earl showed up in the viewfinder, and she lowered her camera. He lay sprawled on his back in the grass with his knees up and his straw hat pushed back on his head, a cigarette in his fingers. *He looks like a grown up.* Dolores sneaked up close to him, held her breath and clicked the lever as Earl raised his cigarette to his lips.

Without looking up he said, "Didi, is that you?"

"How did you know? I was real quiet."

"I don't know. I just did. I saw you wandering around over by the store, taking pictures. You must like me if you took my picture."

"Of course I like you," she said. "I've known you my whole life. But why are you laying here instead of working?"

"I'm taking a break. I know you like me, but that's not the kind of liking I mean though."

She dropped down next to him in the wet grass. Ducklings the size of handfuls hurried to keep up with their mother in the dull bayou current.

"What other kind of liking is there?" said Dolores.

Earl sat up and hugged his knees. He threw a pebble into the water, then another. "Di, you know how old I am?"

Dolores pointed her camera at the water where the ripples spread in circles. "I guess you must be 16." She set the camera down and drew shapes in the dirt with a stick. She drew the outlines of the mama duck with the ducklings behind her.

"That's right, sixteen. I'm a man now, soon it will be time for me to get married."

Dolores let her drawing stick drop into the dirt. She took her hands off her knees and sat up straight. "Married? You?"

"That's right. And you know what? I'd like to wait for you. I'd like you to marry me when it's time. What do you think of that?" He turned his face from the water to hers.

His eyes seemed to change from blue to green and then back again like the water in the Gulf close to the shore.

His smelled of cigarettes and coffee. She said, "Papa won't let me get married!"

"I said I wanted to wait. I'm good at waiting." He turned back to the water and started throwing pebbles again. "I gotta go before they find me doing nothing." He stood up.

Dolores stood up, too, brushed off her skirt and picked up the camera. "I don't think I'll have time for getting married Earl. I'm sorry."

"Dolores! Earl!" Father Martin called to them from the church steps. "Come, follow me!" He was walking fast through the church-yard, his cassock floating out behind him like a sail. "Venez, mes amis, venez!" He was calling to everyone he could find. A moment later the tinny church bell began to ring. When he had enough people gathered at the place where the Saturday parties were held, he stood on a box and called them all to pray.

"Merci, Almighty Father and the Blessed Virgin, Raphael and Michael, St. Anthony, and St. Jude, thank you for delivering us from this storm. We thank you for your blessings upon this poor community, we sit so close to the ocean and her great power, the storms we have had before this we lost so much. We thank you for sparing us this time and we vow to make ourselves worthy of your mercy from this day forward."

Father's eyes were focused on heaven and his hands raised high; the breeze played with the bottom hem of his cassock. Dolores held her breath and pressed the lever. It was her last picture in the roll.

# 8.

# THE MEETING OF AIR AND WATER

ELAINE GRIMACED AS SHE LEANED over the top of the stainless-steel counter and was singed by a blast of heat from the steam table. The plate of grillades and grits weighed heavily on her wrist as she yelled above the roar of the kitchen. "She didn't want grits with that." Her loud voice had never been very loud and was swallowed by the dinnertime chaos. "Can I get fries instead?" Sweat dripped down the side of her face into her limp uniform collar.

She felt her backside brushed by a waiter from the Caribbean Room, the fancy restaurant that shared a kitchen with the café, where prices were high and only men allowed to work. The waiter lifted four plates of trout amandine onto a large napkin-draped tray. "Can you move, hon?" the waiter asked without making eye contact while almost running her over her. She managed a glance at the cashier who rolled his eyes and stuck out his tongue at the waiter as he disappeared into the atmospheric darkness of the restaurant.

Elaine shifted to one side while a young kid came up behind her with a boiling drum of turtle soup. "Hot stuff, hot stuff!" he called out.

It was hot, frustrating work with little compensation, and Elaine was already tired of it after six weeks.

"Tiny," she tried again leaning in closer to the cook. "She wanted fries with it, not grits."

"Whatchyou mean she don't want grits? That's what comes with it. You want something else you gotta tell me, Honey." The cook, Tiny, who Elaine figured weighed in at about 300, liked to mess with all the waitresses from the café. But he always stuck up for them when the guys from the restaurant tried to belittle them. "What they doin' eating breakfast this time a day anyway? It's after 8! Maybe they lost track of the time." He started laughing, and his whole body shook. The sweat dripped down his puffy jowls and into the collar of his white starched apron to collect around the gold necklaces that hung between the folds of his neck. "Hon, you got to *tell* me these things, you know?" With a melodic slide on the "tell."

"Okay, okay." Elaine wiped her forehead with a linen napkin.

"Here you go, baby, here's her fries, grillades, and fries. You doin' alright today, baby? You lookin' tired with a capital T. I bet she's one of them nasty old white ladies, real old, too, huh?"

She laughed. "She is, actually."

Elaine hadn't come across this type of old lady in her neighborhood growing up in Gentilly—the rich uptown elderly widows, who moved into this fancy residence hotel, the Pontchartrain, and thought everybody who worked there was their servant. Especially in the café. They never ate in the dining room; that seemed to be for yet another monied group that Elaine had more experience with—politicians like Peter among them.

Elaine pushed the door open with her back, passing another waitress who was on her way in, and set the plate in front of a thin woman whose needle-fine wrinkles covered every inch of her face. She was wearing a rhinestone tiara and a mass of gaudy rings and bracelets. A cloud of cigarette smoke wafted into Elaine's face. She reached in her pocket for a clean ashtray, turned it upside down, and used it to cover the one already filled with lipstick-smeared butts, then picked them both up, returning the clean one to the table right side up. It was a trick one of the veteran waitresses had showed her one day when business was slow. It was a smooth move that they used in the Caribbean Room, and Elaine found it entertaining.

As she set the plate down on the table, a photo hanging on the wall of the booth caught her eye. Elaine was surprised she hadn't noticed it before since it was a place Pappy had taken her to many times when she was little. It never occurred to her until now that it might have some special significance for him, another thing she would have to ask him about. Even as a little girl the sculpture in the picture had fascinated her because, although it was made of brass, the fairy, as she called it then, seemed to be floating above a chalice-shaped fountain sitting in a shallow pool. Only the tip of one delicate foot was tethered to a sphere that separated her from the bowl of the chalice. It was magic how it hung there in mid-air. Pappy let her wade in the pool when it wasn't dry, which it usually was. He used to complain that the city was neglecting it. The card next to it said, "The Meeting of Air and Water. Artist unknown."

"Do you like that picture?" the woman asked. "Because I recall we ordered two Sazeracs a long time ago."

Elaine didn't realize how long she'd been staring at the picture. "I'm sorry," she said. "I'll get them right now."

The manager of the café, Alexander, appeared at the table out of nowhere. Elaine had noticed that he was gifted at defusing situations involving these types of women by charming them or distracting them from whatever complaint they were making. "Miss Angeline, Miss Thalia. How is everything?"

"Well, first she didn't bring my French-fried potatoes. Now we're missing our drinks. She's too busy staring at the walls." She gestured with a bony hand, and the thick tangle of bracelets jangled on her wrist.

"I will bring them myself, ladies, and they're on the house. And Miss Angeline, I have a special little treat for Toto, I know he's been poorly lately."

Angeline took Alexander's hand, and her eyes welled up with tears. Elaine thought the woman would start sobbing any second.

"Oh, thank you, dear. He is on the mend, but it has been very hard."

"I know, I know. They are like our children." He squeezed her arm as she turned to her friend and began describing the gastric issues plaguing her dog.

Alexander gestured for Elaine to follow him into the bar.

Elaine said, "I'm sorry, she's right, I did forget their drinks, and I was staring at that picture in their booth."

"No worries." He leaned against the bar and ordered the drinks. "I'll bring them. You can take your break now. You like that picture? I just put it up a couple of days ago."

"I love it. I used to visit that fountain a lot with my grandpa. I've seen quite a few photos of it, but this one is different, the way the clouds form the backdrop. And she's not centered in the middle of the plaza like in most of them."

Alexander set the drinks on a small tray. "Sounds like you've thought about this a lot. You're a fan of photography?"

"Especially black and white. Who's the photographer?"

"Good question. We found it and a few others at an estate sale uptown recently. No names on anything. I have a gallery in the Quarter." He reached into his jacket and handed her a card. "Come visit sometime."

Elaine held on to the card in her pocket and leaned against the bar after he left. The last time she had taken pictures was for her job. It was a shoot advertising a department store for an insert in the Sunday paper. There was very little if anything she liked about any of her assignments except maybe designing the ads, but she needed about a thimbleful of creativity to do the shoots. Nothing engaged her, with the exception of one shoot that included young children playing with different kinds of toys. The kids found interesting things to do with uninteresting toys, like turning plastic kitchen sets into forts and castles. She remembered feeling like the kids were the only genuine aspect of any of it, like everything else was fake, pure manipulation. That shoot marked the beginning of the end of that career for her.

When the piano player stopped playing and recorded music came on, Elaine realized she had been standing at the bar for a while.

Leroy, the tall, older guy who shucked oysters and helped tend bar walked over to her from his end. "You back with us again? You seemed like you were faraway there. It's Elaine, right?"

She nodded, feeling a little awkward. "Yeah. I got lost there for a minute."

"I could see that."

Leroy was one of the few interesting people who worked at the hotel. She knew from another waitress that he'd been shucking oysters for decades, but he didn't seem that old, maybe fifty. He had a full head of thick auburn hair, but his whiskers were graying, and he had the calm air of a wise soul. Elaine had liked Leroy from the minute she met him. He was respectful to the women who worked there, as far as she could tell, unlike a lot of men in the restaurant business, who were notorious for living for the notches on their headboards. She couldn't imagine him raising his voice or getting ruffled by much of anything.

"Do you think I could have a half dozen? Do you have time? I'm going on break now."

"Sure. Gimme a minute. You can go ahead and sit down."

He brought her the oysters at a small table for the staff in the back of the bar hidden by a curtain. "Thanks. I really appreciate it."

"You going out for a smoke soon? I'll join you."

"Soon as I finish these."

He went back to the bar, and Elaine stabbed the oysters, dipping them in cocktail sauce and following them with buttered crackers. From her spot she could watch people in the bar without being noticed, and she was thinking about her conversation with Alexander. It had nudged at something inside her that had been asleep. She noticed she was seeing in a different way, framing the faces she saw in the bar, and the hands that gestured in animated conversation. When the pianist started again, the music fed her imaginings. The bougainvillea and ivies in worn clay and ceramic pots of all shapes and sizes in the windows seemed to be hinting at stories. The whole city was like that, one hidden story after another, and suddenly Elaine felt herself seeing in stories.

She met Leroy in a dim patio outside the open door of the kitchen where the dumpsters were parked. The noise and smell of the kitchen drifted through the screen door: Tiny's laughter, the clanging of the pots and pans and the smell of heat and grease. Elaine thought if patrons stood out here for a minute they'd change their minds about eating in the restaurant.

They leaned against the bricks of the building, still warm from the day's sun. The area sat between the Pontchartrain and the brick wall of the bridal shop next door. In front of them a rusted metal fence circled the backyard of a rambling white Victorian house that was a good distance away from them. What little moonlight there was made the white stucco glow. Some of the red ceramic roof tiles had cracked and broken over the years, and black tarpaper showed under them. The lower porch was close to collapsing from a wild wisteria vine that had leapt over from the side fence. On the second floor a dark figure was standing in a tall window.

Leroy inhaled and said, "What brought you back home, Elaine? Folks say people from here just can't make it anywhere else. You heard that?"

Elaine shifted over a few inches to avoid a three-inch-long palmetto bug—a polite name for a giant cockroach—that was examining the garbage can. The roach approached Leroy's feet, and the man lifted one heel and crushed it against the pavement.

Elaine turned her eyes away from the roach smear and turned back to the house. The light in the window upstairs had gone out, and one on the bottom floor had replaced it.

"I'm not sure why I left in the first place, but I got a divorce and now I'm home taking care of my grandfather. He's in a wheelchair."

A figure appeared on the overgrown porch of the house, smoking, and leaned against the railing. Elaine couldn't tell if it was the same person from the upstairs window or not. She wished she'd had her camera.

"Hard for a man to be in a wheelchair. When did that happen? In the war?"

"No, he was around forty, I think, on a construction job. He pretty much raised me. He used to like to fish a lot, and he still does that with our neighbor. He still works with wood in his shop. But he's lived alone for a long time. I think he's getting kind of lonely."

"Once a man loses that physical power, it's hard for them to keep going. He must be quite a guy." Leroy bent to a squat. "Women, they're different."

"How so?" The cicadas whined loudly in the big oaks.

"The beauty queens, they have problems like that, but most women have relationships to fall back on. Being a mother, for one thing, for some that's all it takes. Being somebody's mother keeps them going. Not all of them, of course. I imagine somebody like you needs something more."

"Yeah? Like what?"

"Oh, I don't know, something artistic, maybe. You seem that way to me, I can't say why. Like you might be a musician maybe." He threw down his cigarette and stepped on it. "Are you?"

A weird cry came from the house, either animal or human, and the man who'd been smoking on the porch hurried inside. "Not a musician. But it's funny you should say that because it's what my grandpa says about my grandma. That she needed more."

Leroy slammed the screen door a couple of times to knock off the roaches and flies clinging to the outside of it. "You know what they say, open your ears to your ancestors to find your path."

He opened the screen door. "Who said that?"

He laughed. "I don't know, maybe it was me."

"I'll just be a minute." She inhaled the warm humidity and the scent of jasmine and wisteria coming from the overgrown yard. For a moment the sweetness overpowered the odors of the kitchen.

The figure came out again, and a quick flame appeared, followed by the glow of a cigarette. The way the house was lit up—its shadows and angles, its deterioration—reflected whatever drama was going on inside. Elaine imagined how she would photograph it. She took out her order pad and made a couple of quick sketches then opened the door to the steamy interior of the kitchen.

# 9.

## INTANGIBLE

DOLORES WENT TO THE POST office every day after the ferry dropped them off from school to check and see if her pictures from Mr. Dozier had come in. Mr. Hébert, who ran the store and the post office, would shake his head each day until one day in the middle of May. Dolores stopped on her way home to watch a pair of cardinals building their nest. The place they chose was at the top of a ladder that leaned against a shed outside the fishing shack. The birds took turns bringing leaves and moss to the nest and tucking them under the eaves of the shed on top of the ladder. It worried her because somebody would need the ladder, and the nest would be destroyed. She set her books down on the ground and tried to figure out what she could do about it.

Mr. Hébert stood on the steps of the store waving a brown envelope in the air. "Didi, viens ici! Come quick! Why you taking so long today? It's here, what you been waiting for."

She grabbed the envelope and sat on the steps. Mr. Hébert stood behind her looking over her shoulders. The whole town had watched while she toted her camera around taking pictures of everything. Sometimes they didn't realize that she might have been pointing it at them, but the number of times she took pictures was not that many since she only had so much film. But it was funny to let them pose anyway, and then they got curious about what they would look like in the pictures.

There was a shrimp boat, but it was too dark, and the top of the net was cut off. There was Marie cleaning fish, but only one of her hands showed. There was a good one, just like she remembered, with clouds behind a cypress. And then there was Earl and his carvings. And the dress, the little girl's dress laying in the mud after the storm, so forlorn and sad. Seeing that one was special like it was part of her on the paper.

She went through them for some time until Mr. Hébert grew tired of looking, then she turned the envelope upside down and piece of paper fell out. It was a note from Mr. Dozier. She could read most of it, but needed some help so she put everything back in the envelope and ran as fast as she could to find Earl who was a much better reader than she was.

Earl was busy helping his papa repair some nets.

"I got back my pictures." She had to slow down and wait for her breath to come back from running. "I want to show you. But I need you to read the letter."

"What letter?" Earl put down the net and the spool of string.

"Go on," said his papa. "Take a break." He took a pipe out of his pocket and lit it.

"Mr. Dozier sent back my pictures and wrote me a letter." Dolores sat next to him on the wood bench. "Here." She handed him the piece of thick writing paper that Dozier had written his letter on. It felt creamy, like a cow's belly.

Earl stumbled over some of the words, but he got most of them.

*Dolores:*

*What I see in your photographs is very touching—quite surprising for someone of your age just starting out. You capture a great deal of emotion in your subjects. There is a mood expressed in all of them, a sadness that is intangible but present, nevertheless. The images of the child's dress are especially beautiful and disturbing.*

*I am keeping copies for my files but have inscribed your name and the date on the back of each one. I am including several more rolls of film. Please use the film and return it to me, I am happy to process it for you. I am signing you up for membership in the Brownie Club. You will get magazines from them about taking photos. I'll enter one of your pictures in the magazine's contest. I hope that's alright with you.*

*Sincerely,*

*A. Dozier.*


"What's intangible?" said Dolores.

"I don't know," said Earl. "But he liked them. Can I see them now?"

She took out the pictures and lay them one by one on the bench between them. When she put down the picture of him, Earl stopped her hand. "I didn't know."

"You were busy working. Didn't even notice me at first. I put the camera down once you noticed."

"I can't believe I didn't notice you. I always notice you."

"You don't notice anything when you do that carving. Like you're in another world. But see here," she pointed to an area in the photo near his feet. "Look here. I didn't see that when I took it. Those reflections on the grass of the leaves and branches. That showed up all by itself. It's like I see one thing, and the camera sees more. And look how pretty those leaf shadows are."

"Yeah. I see what you mean."

"There's something like that in almost all of them."

Earl looked through the rest of them. "These are something. You're gonna be famous one day, you keep doing this."

She didn't know if she wanted to be famous, but she did like that Earl and Dozier liked her pictures. It made her curious that Mr.

Dozier saw emotion in them. She could not say how she felt when she took them, except that something drew her in.

Earl held the photo of himself up close to his eyes. "You were pointing that thing at me more than one time. I remember thinking you must like me at least a little. But if you get famous, maybe you won't want to marry me then, hein?"

She got quiet like she always did whenever he brought up that subject. It was the only time she ever felt that way around Earl. Around other people, she felt it all the time, that separateness, like there was a wall between her and the other person. She started putting the photos back into the envelope. "He sent more film so I'm going now."

Earl went on. "He say something about a contest? He's going to put one of your pictures in a Brownie contest. Maybe you'll win. I bet you will."

Dolores started walking back to her house. She didn't like when Earl talked that way about them getting married.

---

After the first package, Dozier sent Dolores film every month and as careful as she was sometimes the film ran out before the next package arrived at the post office with the postmark from New Orleans. Those times were hard. The camera started to feel like a part of her body, and now that she understood the way things worked from light to paper, when there was no film, the empty camera seemed like a weight around her neck. When there was no film in it, the way she saw things and talked to things changed. It was hard to think, hard to be in the world, it all seemed louder and brighter and like it pressed on her from the outside through her skin.

"It's a white feeling," she told Earl. "Empty. Everything is blank except for this pressing from outside. Everything closes in like that rat we saw at the store. Just his tail sticking out of that old copperhead."

One Sunday, she realized she was out of film. Papa and Marie and everybody were getting dressed for church, but Papa did not make her go since Maman died. He said she'd spent way too much time in church with her maman when she was little, and it would be bad for her. Dolores did not want to go, and still didn't understand why people went there. Or why Maman seemed to love God and Jesus so much. Marie tried to get Dolores to go because she thought it was a sin not to, that Dolores might go to hell, but she didn't believe that.

After they left, she went into her room and found Maman's prayer book under a pile of linens on a shelf. The book had sat there since the funeral when one of her aunts told Dolores to take good care of it for Maman. She rubbed the oily black cover of the book like she saw Maman rub it with fish oil. At church on Maman's lap, she would play with the silky ribbons and twirl them in her fingers. She took the book to the bayou and waited there while everybody in town went to Mass. The round, stained-glass window above the door of the church showed Jesus on the shore of a sea, holding bread and fish in his hands in a place that looked like Cocodrie.

The church doors closed, and Cocodrie was as quiet as it ever got because nobody was working or talking or running around. She could barely hear the music coming out of the church. All the water birds and bugs made noise, quiet noise, and the water would rustle now and then. She lay back, and the clouds, as big and still as mountains, hung almost close enough for her to touch. Sometimes when she closed her eyes, she imagined a night sky going out in all directions forever and ever until she felt like she was floating above the surface of the ground, and that her body was part of that forever sky.

The noise of people leaving church made her sit up. She waited until it was quiet and went up the steps to the open door of the church.

The moment she went inside the sun went behind the clouds, and the church grew dark. The candles burning on the altar were glowing. Father Martin was busy clearing things away on the altar. Dolores walked up the aisle towards him.

"Dolores, how are you? Where have you been? You don't come to church since your maman died. We miss seeing you." He pointed for her to sit down in a pew. "You must miss your maman very much."

He smiled and sat down in the pew in front of her.

"But what about the feux follets?" The question leapt out of her from somewhere. It was not what she thought about asking him. The prayer book was in her hands.

"Feux follets?"

"She said she'd be there with the little lights at night."

"She said that to you? That was the sickness talking, Dolores. She didn't know, none of us knows what will happen when we die. Anyway, that is just a story, that light. Maybe she meant that when you see those mouches à feux at night, or the swamp light, you are to think of her. Maybe they are meant to remind you that she is here," he pointed to his chest, "in your heart."

The sun came out again, and the glass windows lit up. Cool air flowed through the bottoms of the windows where they were propped open with wooden stakes. The room smelled of some spice and of the burning candles, and it gave her a nice feeling. The memory of Maman felt good.

She handed him the prayer book. "It's in French. I can't read it. She said she couldn't read. So why was it so important to her if she couldn't read the words?"

"Ah, I remember this book." He took it from her. "It was her grandmother's prayer book. She asked me to bless it for her. Just because she could not read the words doesn't mean that there was nothing for her in the book. It didn't really matter what the words said, she and God were having a visit together, and I think that the book helped her find a path to Him. We all have our ways." He shifted in the pew moving his hands down into his lap and facing the Crucifix behind the altar. "Do you pray, Dolores?"

"I don't know. I talk to Maman sometimes."

"Ah, well your maman is in heaven so she can intercede for you, that's good. You can visit her that way. But everyone has their own way to visit God, and this book was one way that she had to be with him. Your mother began to retreat to the next world long before God took her away from this earth. As I say, in her heart she left before her body did, and we cannot judge her for it."

Dolores wrinkled her brow at the idea that her mother had left the world before her body. "She left before her body?"

"I mean that the way she spent all her time alone with you at home, away from the world, not really speaking to anyone. She had entered a different place. I'm sure it was strange for a young child like you to be with her so much at that time. I think her spirit was gone."

"Like the night sky." It was the feeling Dolores had when she imagined the sky going on forever. "It goes on forever."

The wood pews of the old church creaked, and a light patter of rain fell on the windows and roof. "Yes, like the sky. 'For as the heavens reach beyond earth and sky, we live in mercy, as in an endless sea'."

Father used the pew to help him stand up and groaned as though it took a lot of work for him to do it. "Your way to God will be different from your mother. Perhaps it will be through your camera. There are many different paths, but they all lead to the same place. The place of quiet and stillness, here." He pointed to his chest. "For you also. That place inside you, that is God. And maybe the camera will help you find it."

"The camera can help me find God?"

"Faith is not about seeing more of something, but about seeing with more of yourself. I'm guessing you are learning how to see the world with that thing, and that you will learn to see it in a different way, with more than just here," he pointed to his head, "and more from here." He pointed to his heart. "Because it demands that you see all of something, at least if you are truly seeing with it, all of a person, or of a scene or an object, that you see it in all of its depth and meaning."

The white hairs stuck out of his ears, and he seemed to be growing tired as he spoke; his eyes seemed to open and close real slow.

"I think I see," she said even though she understood nothing of what he said about seeing. The only thing she did understand was that when she did take pictures, it seemed that her head did turn off and something else take over. Like Earl and his carving, she guessed it was the heart that did the seeing or the carving, whatever the heart was.

"I hope to see you at church sometime. But if not, I am always here for you. Now I must take my rest."

Dolores tucked the prayer book under her arm, happy to be out under the open sky again. She noticed at once the absence of her camera and felt the edge of the white feeling coming back. Instead of letting it take hold, she ran home and found the blank newsprint that Uncle Red had given to her and took it and her pencils to the bayou.

Earl waited there, at the pair of cypress stumps where they met evenings after supper or on Sundays after the big meal. He was focused on a carving. She took a seat on her stump and took out her pencil.

Earl raised his eyes from his hands and paused in his work. Dolores paid no attention but started a drawing of him. He smiled his crooked smile and went back to his carving.

# 10.

## ST. ROCH AND THE DOG

A s soon as Charlotte sat across from Father Joseph at the rectory she started wondering if it was a mistake for her to be there. She brought up the topic of Elaine and her questions about Dolores to him because he had known Charlotte and the whole family for so many years. But now all of it seemed a useless exercise. What had religion done to help her mother anyway? From Charlotte's memories and stories Pappy told her, it had only made things worse.

"Why does it bother you so much that Elaine wants to know these things?" Father Joe seemed a lot older up close than he did when he was up on the altar saying Mass. His white hair had grown a bit wild lately like he was letting his grooming slip.

"I'm not sure, but it worries me. All these questions. I mean does she have to know what happened? What good would that do? Just upset her. Make her wonder about things. All that pain." Her words were thick in her throat.

"I've known you since you were a young woman. Before you lost your husband. And of all the things you've been through, the death of your mother has been your most difficult wound." He went to a credenza near the windows and poured a fresh cup of coffee into a thick ceramic mug. He added cream and handed it to Charlotte.

The word *wound* struck Charlotte. It was such a strong word; she'd never thought of herself as being wounded. She'd never had patience for people who talked about their trauma or woundedness. They were enjoying acting like victims, using it as an excuse for not being able to function in the world. She took the mug and looked out at the barren school playground, now vacant in summertime. It felt lonely without any children, like a mausoleum of play equipment, and it gave her a queasy feeling.

"Well, yes, and I don't see the point in it. She's having a hard time in her life now with this divorce. Even before that she couldn't figure out what to do with herself; she was always unhappy." She sighed and sipped her coffee. "I know some of it was my fault. I kept her away from the things she liked, drawing, taking pictures. Just like Mama. Elaine was depressed when she was a teenager. Hurting herself. I was afraid. I didn't want to make her think there was mental illness in the family. I mean it was just Mama."

A garbage truck pulled into the parking lot and gripped a dumpster with its rusted hands. A few startled crows flew off.

"I understand how you were concerned, but it is part of her history. It might be important for her to know, like it is for people to know about heart disease or certain cancers." He spooned more sugar into his coffee, stirring. "Good could come of the connection. Your mother was ill, but as you said, gifted, a gifted artist. Perhaps Elaine has inherited that from her. And the final event of your mother's death was never established, so you could present it to Elaine any way that you want to."

Charlotte blew on her coffee. The priest's ears seemed overlarge and to have a significant crop of hair sticking out of them. "I'm not sure how to approach it. I'm so worried about her." She lowered her voice. "I think she's seeing a married man."

"Oh, dear. That's too bad. I'm sorry. That's never a good thing. I'd be happy to talk to her, I mean, if she'd be willing." He cleared his throat, and Charlotte detected a touch of judgment.

He coughed an old man's cough, deep and throaty. Charlotte had not remembered him being so old. Of course, it meant she was older too. She could not imagine Elaine listening to anything this man would say. "Oh, I don't think she would. But thank you anyway."

"Pray for her, Charlotte. That's what I tell everyone with children. They leave home, you cannot influence them much anymore, and it's very hard. All you can do is pray, and know that she has grace too, taking care of her, the same way you do."

The rectory parking lot was steaming from a light rain that evaporated almost as soon as it fell. Her car was so hot inside she had to wait before she could even touch the steering wheel. She used to leave the windows down in hot weather, but now she was afraid to leave them open with all the crime in the city. She finally headed towards Schwegmann's grocery with her windows down and the air conditioner blowing.

She passed the little park on the corner of St. Roch Avenue where she used to take Elaine when she was little. The play equipment was old and out of date with rusted metal poles and hard wooden swings. Two boys under school age climbed on a metal dome that had once been painted red and blue. The parents smoked cigarettes at a nearby picnic table, and a black and white spotted dog panted under a scrawny tree.

Charlotte pulled her car to the curb that edged the park. For once she was going to pay attention to that nostalgic tug that pulled at her at times. Something about the scene drew her in. The conversation with Father brought up memories from her own childhood.

She was seven or eight years old. They were in the kitchen, she and Mama and Papa. A collage of photographs hung behind the table, stuck on the wall with cellophane tape that was yellowed and brittle. Some of the pictures were torn. She hated that wall. It scared her because it was covered in faces. Some of the faces were old and wrinkled, others strange or deformed or mean looking. At the time, she didn't know they were photographs her mother had taken, but she knew they meant something to her. That if something happened to one of them, if Charlotte brushed up against one and it tore or started to come off, her mother would be angry.

It was early summer, but not too hot yet, and Papa had convinced Mama to go on a picnic. Mama rarely went out in those days, especially with the family, but this time she agreed to go, and Charlotte was excited. Mama stood by the kitchen table wrapping sandwiches in waxed paper. Papa put his arms around her from behind, and Charlotte heard him humming a song, like he was happy. He was swaying Mama from side to side.

Papa said, "You remember that song, Didi, from our wedding?"

"Yes, I remember." But Mama hadn't seemed happy to remember the song. She seemed upset by it and pushed his arms away to go wash her hands at the sink.

Charlotte's attention drew back into the park when the boys' father joined them on the battered jungle gym. He pretended to climb after them, moving slowly so they could get away easily. It was nice to see black families in the neighborhood, like it was a normal part of life. The mother smiled and relaxed with a Coke. That picture of life had never been part of Charlotte's experience, not as a child or as a mother since Elaine's father had died so young.

That day that Mama and Papa prepared for the picnic had wedged itself into her memory. She had tried to get her mother to the back window to see a cardinal and went to the sink and pulled on her skirt. But her Mama shooed her away. "Stop it. Get away. I don't want to see the bird."

Charlotte had run over to Earl and hid her face in his pants leg. "I'm sorry, Papa."

Earl said, "Do you have to talk to her like that? She's little."

Her mama told them to go on the picnic without her, went into her bedroom and stayed in there for what seemed like weeks. People came to take care of Charlotte and to cook meals. She would sit outside the door, drawing picture after picture, waiting for her mother to come out. After her mother died, she stopped drawing altogether and had no patience for anything like it. She would do anything to get Elaine interested in other activities, dance, and music, but Elaine always went back to her paints and pencils, and later a camera.

One of the boys on the jungle gym cried out and startled Charlotte out of her thoughts. She was embarrassed to discover tears on her cheeks and wiped them away quickly with her sleeve. The wooden placard next to the bench where she was sitting had faded, worn out lettering and a picture. *St. Roch Playground, 1955.* She recognized what was left of the painting as a rendition of the saint himself, St. Roch, shown as always, with a dog licking the sores on the saint's leg. When the nuns talked about the picture, they used to say the dog licked his wounds.

The image turned Charlotte's stomach even though she'd seen it dozens of times in other places. That word wounds again. Charlotte shuddered and went back to her car and headed home, too exhausted to do the groceries.

# 11.

## BROWNIE GIRL

*Dolores:*

*You are truly a Brownie Girl now! And much more! Have you gotten a magazine yet? You can submit more of your photographs in contests. What do you think? Enclosed please find four more rolls of film. I will be sending you a bigger package soon. It will be an exciting surprise. Something that Mr. Hébert can help you with.*

*Your friend,*

*A Dozier*

"MR. HÉBERT, PAPA SAYS A box came for me. Where is it? Did you open it?" Dolores couldn't wait to see what Mr. Dozier had sent her. "Mr. Dozier said last time that it was something you would have to help me with."

"It did. Not a little box like you usually get. It's a bigger box. Same return address. It came parcel post, cost him a dollar to send it. What do you think it is?" Before she could say anything, he said, "I know what it is, because he told me himself. It's for setting up a darkroom. He wrote me a letter." He reached behind the counter and held the box up in his hands. "I've already talked to your papa about it. He knows you're going to be over here doing this."

He opened a door behind the counter that went to a smaller room. A small window let in some light, but he pulled a string, and an electric bulb went on like they had at her school. He put the box on a table near a metal sink. The bell rang when the front door opened. "I'll be back." He handed her a tool to open the box.

The box was filled with newspapers. She pulled out an old camera from under the layers of paper. Mr. Dozier had shown her one when he was in Cocodrie, it had a thing called a bellows that did the focus. It had the name Sanderson on it.

The door creaked open behind her. Mr. Hébert said, "What do you have there?"

"I don't understand why he sent this; I don't know how to use it."

"Wait, I almost forgot." Mr. Hébert left for a second and came back with another package. "This came today in the regular mail." He pulled up a stool to sit next to her, but the bell sounded again.

This box had a stack of paper with a lot of writing, some film wrapped in tissue and a letter envelope with her name on it. She only had a little trouble reading it without Earl.

*Dear Dolores:*

*I am sorry to be so late in getting this film to you. I wanted to put this information together for you first. Hopefully you have received my other package and opened it by the time you read this. You may remember the bellows portrait camera I showed to you on my first visit. I have a new one, so I am giving it to you. But not to use as a camera. In this envelope you will find instructions on how to make your own darkroom using the bellows camera as your enlarger. You may need some help making a frame to hold your negative and also finding a source of light that works. But my instructions will give you ideas and specifics on how to use everything after you put together the darkroom.*

*You can use baking pans as trays and salt water for your fixer. Plain water will stop the process, although maybe not as fast as you would like."*

She picked up the bellows camera and shifted it around. He went on in the letter,

*"I wish that I could come back to visit you and help you with this, but I am starting my studio in New Orleans, and I hate to leave when business is just beginning. I took the liberty of asking Floyd to help, as he is so handy. I will send you some directions and tips for developing in a few days, I'm putting it together now. Good luck, Dolores!*

*Sincerely,*

*Adrian Dozier*

When Floyd came back, he sat down and read through the instructions.

"How did you learn to read English so good?" Dolores asked him.

"In the war," he said. "I was a telegraph operator."

After a few minutes he said, "He says we need it to be dark. We can cover up the window and put a kerosene lamp on the floor. He said we'd need water too. We'll do it together. You know I've put to-gether a few things in my life."

Over the next few days, they went over the instructions and began to set things up.

"Let's see now. He says there's a hole here on the bottom." He lifted the bellows camera above his head next to the light bulb. "Ah, here it is, see here? We put the bulb here then connect the camera so you can move the light and use the bellows. That's how you get the picture clear."

It took over a week to get it to work right. Dolores brought the things from home for the chemicals, vinegar for the stopper and baking soda mixture for the wash and the pans to mix them in. Floyd hung a fishing line above the sink to dry the photos and covered the window with a burlap sack. It was all very strange and mysterious to Dolores. The room was so dark it seemed like church on a cloudy day, and whenever she walked into it, it gave her the same feeling as going into church or into the deep parts of the woods. There was something holy about it.

People in town had started to talk. Marie said that some were saying Dolores was a witch and doing magic. Kids tried to look in the window to see what they were doing. After she figured out how to process her own film into negatives, Dolores asked Earl to come watch her try to use the bellows enlarger to make a print.

Earl gave her a funny look when he walked into the darkroom and saw the strange machine they had made. "What in the world?"

She showed him how it all was supposed to work, and she put in the first negative. The image started to appear on the paper. Earl was surprised. "It is like magic."

The pictures she had taken of the cypress knees appeared. She had always been drawn to the knees because they look like little forest creatures with personalities, and they are all different from one another. Some are shorter and fatter, and other ones tall and thin, like people. Some have smooth bark and on others it's peeling off in strips. She had taken a whole roll of them and by changing the amount of light on the paper, she could change the mood of the picture. It reminded her of the game she used play when she was little, making figures out of sticks and rocks and moving them around outside, hiding them in different spots, or making scenes out of them.

"I'll never see you now that you have this. You'll be in here all the time that you're not with the camera."

Dolores couldn't hide her excitement and kissed Earl on the cheek, which seemed to surprise him even more than the photographs did.

# 12.

## COCODRIE, 1988

I T WAS A GRAY DAY with a steady drizzle. Blessedly cool for June. The windows were opened a few inches to the freshness of the air. They'd been traveling about an hour on highway 90 at a steady clip from New Orleans when Sam had to slow down to a crawl behind some farm tractors. Earl stuck his head out the window. "Thank you, Sam, for going all this way. It's been too long. You smell that cane? You can smell it growing." The cane fields opened out on both sides, rows and rows of the bright green grassy stuff. "That brings back memories. Chewing on the cane."

A flock of water birds lifted off a pond, and the sun glinted off shiny wings. Elaine said, "What are those? They look shiny black."

"Must be ibis," said Sam. "Glossy ibis. Or could just be one of those diving ducks. Were they bigger than ducks?"

"Definitely bigger," said Elaine. "I'll have to look those up."

Sam said, "You're welcome. I'm interested to see Cocodrie again. Went fishing there years ago." Sam sat at the wheel of Earl's old van with Elaine riding in the back seat. "The way I hear it, one more storm could put Cocodrie right into the Gulf along with the rest of the Delta. Best go now before that happens."

They got off the highway on a smaller road that ran along the bayou. "Bayou Terrebonne," Elaine read the sign.

"Look at that cypress." Earl pointed towards the swampy woods alongside the road that ran alongside Bayou Cocodrie.

"What about it?" said Elaine.

Earl said, "See how some of it is grayed out and losing leaves. It's dying. The saltwater's killing it. The damn shoreline recedes every year and that saltwater starts pouring into these swamps. Cypress don't like saltwater. It's all those damn canals they built for the ships to come in and out from the rigs."

Sam said, "And they logged the hell out of it in the day."

"It's a damn shame. I don't know the solution, except to build up the Delta again, but how're gonna do that?"

"Isle de Jean Charles," said Elaine.

"What?" said Earl.

"That highway sign, it goes to Isle de Jean Charles. I read about that place. It's sinking into the Gulf. They relocated the Biloxi tribe there in the 1800s, and now it's sinking, so they'll have to relocate them again. Their cemetery is underwater, so is the land bridge most of the time."

"Same problem as the cypress," said Earl.

"It's still beautiful," said Elaine. "Some of them are huge."

Earl was glad to see at least some of the cypresses were bright green and healthy and probably at least a hundred years old. Their animal shapes reflected shadows in the water. "We used to pretend they were animals. Or animal spirits."

Earl felt the presence of the bayou next to him like a companion as he had when he was growing up. He fell into a dream state where vague memories came and went, but they were more like passing sensations. Maybe the years go by, and memories turn into something else. They weren't gone, just changed.

"Looks like we're coming up to CoCo Marina," said Sam. "That's where I chartered the boat. The restaurant was great." He slowed the car down when they reached a series of docks and the rustic fishing camps and resorts lining the bayou.

Elaine said, "Does it look familiar, Pappy? When's the last time you were here?"

"No, not familiar. Even from the 60s when I visited. It's modern now. That building, I think that's where the fishing shack was, but that's a new building. Not new anymore."

Elaine said, "I was gonna say, it doesn't look new."

"From the 50s I'd say," said Sam. "That sign is new."

Elaine said, "Pappy, do you want to find your house first?"

"Not my house. I want to find your grandmother's house. Go down this street back from the bayou. These are all newer houses now. Closer together. We had more land around us. Wait, stop. This little street, Crab Street. Try that."

The street angled away from the bayou into a long stretch of green. "These little cottages, that's more like what we had."

"These oak trees are huge," said Elaine.

"Here, this is it. Stop here, Sam."

Seagulls cried above them, and the air had that same sea smell Earl remembered. The tree towered above the abandoned cottage that Dolores had lived in; its arms stretched out to twice the length they had been, or that's what it seemed like to him. "I had those branches etched in my mind from sitting on her porch for so many hours. We used to wonder what year the one big branch would end up touching the ground. Now two of them are touching." Vines covered the ruined porch and a big limb had fallen and collapsed the roof.

At the end of the block next to another oak, another white frame house had come to the same fate. "That was her brother's house there."

Elaine said, "This must be the tree in the picture I have. She is sitting right where that bigger limb touches the ground. Do you want to get out here, Pappy?"

"No, it's too hot. Let's sit here a minute." He took out his tobacco pouch and rolled a cigarette. The day reached the point of heated quiet with most of the birds hiding out in the shade; only the sound of the gulls and the cicadas broke the silence.

"The first time I remember talking to Dolores, her mama was being buried that day. I don't know how old we were, but she ran away from that church like a rabbit while they processed to the cemetery and found me by the water. She said something about her mama being buried." He tossed his match out the window. "And then she asked me if I believed in the feux follets."

"The what?" said Elaine.

"An old folktale, but she believed it. Believed there were little lights in the woods, and they were people. Story says unbaptized babies, or some say souls, but she thought her mama was a little light in the woods. Used to sit up all night waiting for them to show up."

"You mean fireflies?"

"It's just a folktale, but she believed all those tales. A lot of people did back then. She didn't talk about her mama much, but she had some ideas about those little lights. She thought she could feel the dead with her. Lights or no lights." He threw his cigarette down. "Let's go to the Marina now."

Earl thought he felt a chill and that maybe he regretted coming back there after so many years. Maybe it was better to let the past rest. "Let's go down by the water. Come on."

Sam said, "Okay, I'm going. Keep your drawers on."

They parked at the Marina, and Sam helped Earl into his chair. The dock was crooked but sturdy and took them to a small platform they used to clean fish. The bayou got wider in two directions and was dotted with small islands and dark green vegetation along the shore—cypress, water oaks, willows and cattails. That was all the same as it had been back in the day.

"Boats are still out. I did love going out on the shrimp boats. Stay for days, sometimes." Earl squinted at the one shrimp boat that was left behind for some reason; the sun was reflected in the wet of the net like the boat had been out and come back in. One leg of the bayou opened onto a flat marsh with open water in the distance.

A great weight began to settle on Earl's heart. "I met her once on one of these docks. Not this one. I can't figure out which one it was." He was trying to look in all directions at once, to get his bearings. "Everything is so different but still the same. I was working on a net and felt eyes on the back of my neck. She was pointing that thing at me."

"What thing?" Elaine had a stick and was trailing it in the water.

"The camera." Earl realized as soon as he said it that it would open the can of worms. He didn't intend to say anything about the camera, but he knew at the same time it wasn't quite an accident that it slipped out.

Elaine dropped her stick and looked up. "She had a camera? Where did she get a camera?"

"I never saw a camera before that year." Earl began to rub his head with his hand then turned the chair around and started back towards the car. He wished he was able to think about Dolores and their past together without so many feelings. Sadness all mixed up with guilt and maybe even some anger. "So many years ago. Maybe I should never have come back."

"Why?" said Elaine.

"Everything is so different. It's just not the same place. I should've known, it was so long ago. I don't know what I expected." He stooped and wiped his face with his handkerchief. "I should have left it in my memory the way it was then. All those years ago. Sometimes it's better to leave the past in the past," he wiped his face again. "Let's go have some lunch."

"Let me push," said Sam.

They ordered as much as they could handle and tasted everything. Fried oysters and shrimp, baked redfish stuffed with crabmeat, boiled crabs, fried catfish. It was all good, but Earl was having trouble enjoying it.

"How y'all doing? I'm Danny Benoit. This is my place."

"Benoit, yeah. I knew some Benoits." Earl shook his hand. "Long time ago. I grew up here."

"Yeah? A little different then. A few hurricanes later. Hey, would you mind talking to my grandmère? She'd love to see somebody from her time. Hold on a minute, will you?"

A woman around Earl's age came to the table in a wheelchair and started talking to Earl in French. It took him a few minutes, then after she started telling some stories, he remembered her family. Dolores had taken some pictures of them. The owner ended up bringing them coffee and bread pudding, and the conversation went on for some time.

---

Earl fell asleep as soon as they hit the road and started back through the big expanse of swamp. Elaine thought about Pappy's description of the animal shadows from the cypress trees. With the late afternoon sun, they made monsters on the road and over the water. The light was gold and orange, so the smooth trunks seemed to glow.

Elaine said, "Did you understand much of what they were saying?"

"Some. They talk like my grandparents."

"They kept saying something about a 'dark room'. They said 'dark room' in English. Could you understand what the dark room was all about?"

"Not a dark room, a *darkroom*. For photographs."

Elaine closed her eyes and dropped her head back. "Of course. A darkroom. What about a darkroom? First, I hear my grandma had a camera, now there was a darkroom somewhere."

"Unusual for her to have a camera, much less a darkroom. Maybe somebody else had the darkroom in town."

"I never heard about her having a camera, but I've never heard much at all about her. She's a mystery. I wonder if she took many pictures with it. That's so weird. I mean I'm a photographer, or I was a photographer."

Sam said, "You are a photographer. But I wouldn't expect to get any more information about her from him today. From the looks of him, you're going to have to wait until tomorrow."

———⬦———

After Elaine went to bed Earl lay in bed exhausted but unable to sleep. He got into the chair and pulled down a misshapen cardboard box from a low shelf in his closet. He set the box on the bed and poured himself a bourbon from a bottle he'd hidden in his bedside table for rare occasions. The photographs were like a history of their life together, but also a testament to how little he knew or understood Dolores. Many times, over the years, he considered destroying them. Charlotte didn't want them, she made that clear; they brought her nothing but pain. Of course, she could change her mind. But it was Elaine he was thinking about now. Elaine reminded him so much of Dolores, her gestures and voice. And Elaine was an artist, or used to be, like Dolores. Maybe she should know, and maybe that's why he let the word camera slip out. He needed to find a new way to look at all of it. Life was all about suffering and how you deal with it. Who was he to shelter Elaine from Dolores, from either the painful part or the beautiful parts? Some of her pictures were beautiful, there was no question, she had had talent. One can't exist without the other, the bad and the good.

The photos were jumbled together without any order and held together in bundles with crumbling rubber bands. It was a shame he hadn't taken better care of them. He opened one bundle, and Cocodrie came back to life, the way it was then. Moss hanging down over the wood tables full of people laughing and eating; him whittling on a stump, all legs and skinny, a cigarette hanging out of his mouth.

He rolled a cigarette and went out onto the back porch. The lake surrounded him, still and black, no movement. The lights of the causeway made a thin line on the water's surface like the stripe of a brush; the car lights flickered like diamonds.

# 13.

## DEATH MASK

BEGIN TO UNDERSTAND NOW WHAT Father Martin said about seeing with more of myself. When I take the pictures, I think I try to save something. Something that might be lost if I did not capture it in that moment. For some of the photographs this is what happens. I took a picture of Earl making one of his wooden things. He carves birds and boats out of wood that he finds. When he is in the middle of doing it, it is the same thing, I think, as when I am behind the camera. He forgets everything else. He didn't know for a long time that I stood there with my camera set on him. Time stops for him when he carves. The world stops moving around him. At that minute there is only him and his wood. And I think also what he wants his wood to say, and how he tells his hands to move so that the wood does what he wants. And this is not a thinking. I know because he says he does not think when he does it. He says that what happens with his hands comes from somewhere else. He calls it his stomach, but I think it's his heart.

I understand. When I hold the camera, everything stops around me. Not just the thing I want to capture. The world. That moment for me, it stops. The moment for whatever is in the picture stops too. Earl is stopped in that moment of his carving. The dress on the road with the mud smeared on it—yet the rest of it pure and white—lying there right after a big storm as though it floated down from heaven and rested in that spot. It is a moment that will not happen again. But also, the moment that I am there, with the dress, or Earl, or a tree limb, or an old man, my heart connects with it, and everything else disappears. And when I disappear, then instead of looking at something to make the picture, I let the thing show me what it is, like it has its own voice, and I am there to let that come out.

Then what happens comes from somewhere else, not from me, and what can show up on the paper can come from out of nowhere. Things I did not notice show up. Things in my mind not important. I think it's a mistake, like when I tried to take a picture of a heron on the shore. An ugly dead fish was right next to it. I didn't like it so I tried to move the camera so the fish would not be there, but I got the ugly whiskers in by the heron's feet. But the whiskers, they make it special, you know? When I took Earl's photograph, I tried to leave out the pile of oyster shells next to him, but the edges got in there anyway. Then other things I don't notice show up too and they seem important. Like a message. Where did they come from? How did I miss them? Were they truly there in the first place or does something happen that adds them to the film later? I don't understand it.

In the picture I took of Marie, she didn't know, she was standing outside with her skirts pulled up picking weeds out of the okra. But what I didn't see in that moment was the sunburst that comes down from heaven out of a dark cloud and onto her head. Like the light you see coming down from God to Jesus. I did not know that sunburst was there. But it makes the picture different. Makes it more special even, I think. I would never show the picture to her, she would be angry, especially with her skirts pulled up like that. But I like her that way. It is truly Marie, I think, just like the other one is truly Earl.

When I took the one of the two cows behind the house, I could see the fence and the tree and clouds and the house. I could see the pond in front of them. But when the picture got on the paper it shows the roof and chimney reflected in the pond. It makes the picture beautiful. In the one where Marie is goofing and holding a raw oyster high above her head to drop into her mouth, Papa, and Jean, they are laughing. I didn't see the cat under the table behind them, but there he is in the picture, crouched down, waiting for somebody to drop one.

In the old man at the foot of the oak tree next to the bayou, a little bird shows up in the moss above his head. Things like that are a surprise. Maybe God sends them. Maybe those things are Maman talking to me. Who knows? They say you can talk to Jesus. The priest says I can talk to Maman. Maybe she can talk to me in strange ways. Like in my pictures.

— ❖ —

Dolores leaned in close to the baby's mouth, so close that strands of her dark hair brushed the collar of her white dress, and her ear felt the coolness of the baby's lips. Marie had warned her that seeing a baby who died would be too hard, and she told her not to do it, but the mother had begged Dolores to take the pictures. In one of the old magazines Mr. Dozier sent her there was a story about photographs of dead children. People had been doing it for a long time. Dolores didn't really understand it, but the lady had persuaded her.

The last body she had seen had been her mother's, but she tried not to think of it, and forgot as soon as she started to take the pictures.

The baby lay in a coffin on a tattered quilt streaked by light coming in the window through the bushes. Shadows of leaves and limbs from the leaves and branches fell over the dress and quilt. A thin white curtain lifted and fell. A dove began to coo, and Dolores remembered something her maman said about the souls of baptized babies being taken away by doves to heaven.

The baby looked beautiful, with dark lashes and fair skin. The dress reminded Dolores of the one she had photographed after a storm. It covered the baby in folds of cotton and plain lace to her feet, which were bare, the tiny toes perfectly formed, like pearls, on perfect feet. The fingers and hands too were perfect, resting at the baby's sides.

The mother stood back a bit in the doorway; she rubbed her hands together and kept glancing out the front window. "Mon mari, he will come back soon. He would not like you being here."

Three young children came to the door and pulled on their maman's skirts.

A dog barked and the mother turned away quickly. "Restez là." She pressed the shoulders of the children together. "Stay."

Dolores moved to a corner of the room and looked through her lens at the baby then at the children, the window, and the wood dresser. The tallest child came close to the coffin and touched his fingertips to the lace of the baby's sleeve. The other children turned from Dolores and her camera to look at the baby. The sound of the shutter made them all look up at her, and she clicked again.

Dolores worked on the pictures for days in the darkroom to get them right. She was not surprised any longer when things showed up like little messages in her pictures that she didn't notice when she took them. On the white curtain the shadow of a sparrow appeared. It was resting inside the shadows of the branches and leaves that Dolores did remember noticing, but she had not seen the bird at the time. Maybe it was another message from her mother.

The mother of the baby told people about the photos and others started to ask Dolores to take photos of their children or of a young married couple, even a new calf. It was like Earl said, she was either taking pictures or in the darkroom. She couldn't remember a time in her life when she did not have a camera. It felt like she was a child when she got the camera two years before, and now she was a woman and would be getting married in a year.

# 14.

## AUDREY

TWO WEEKS AFTER ELAINE'S TRIP to the Tight Spot, Earl got a call from Ida that she was sending someone over to meet him. A woman. That's about all the information he could get out of Ida.

Ida said, "I'm not sending you over a commonplace hooker, Earl Rizan. And what the hell were you thinking asking Elaine to get you a woman? I mean, really, sending your own granddaughter? You just need some company and I've got just the person for you. I think you'll like her."

"What kind of a woman is she anyway? I mean is this supposed to be like a date or something, because it's been years and years since I did anything like that."

"Just be yourself, Earl, she will love you."

He'd been in the bathroom for over an hour now, primping, and he needed to comb whatever strands he had over to one side. He reached for his comb on the back of the toilet. Elaine must have put it there when she was cleaning up. It fell to the floor as he tried to grab it. "Dammit." He'd already dropped his razor and spilled his coffee earlier that morning.

The bathroom was too small for his chair. Every time he did anything in there it took three or four turns, backing up, getting things just right. Now he had to figure out how to get to the damn comb. The grabber was lost somewhere in the house.

He backed the chair up against the toilet and leaned over holding onto the edge of the sink. Finally, he got a grip on the edge of the comb, but sat up again, winded by the whole ordeal. He rubbed his forehead with the back of his hand. His strong, carpenter's hands. Now with most of the muscle gone, they looked like a stranger's hands, thin and bony, with patches of brown skin. Sometimes he'd dream them back the way they used to be until he'd wake up fully and get a good look at them. In a way it was worse than losing his legs. He gave up on the comb and used his fingers instead.

He went to the living room to make sure Elaine hadn't messed up anything before she left for work. He hardly ever thought about the accident anymore, although once in a while he had a dream that was so close to the real event he'd wake up in a sweat, scared and confused. In the dreams, the sky shone as vivid a blue as it had been that day. The same helplessness would come over him when he watched that beam drop off the end of the crane. In the dream, it stops in mid-air. That's when he wakes up. But of course, that didn't happen. Time stopped and everything about that moment burned into his mind, all those things are the same in the dream, the sounds of the men's blurred cries, the sky, the yellow leaves of the big pin oak.

Shit, why was he thinking about all this now? Must be the woman. The idea of being with a woman reminding him of all he'd lost that day. He hadn't had time to think when it happened, but the first thing that came to him was his boat sitting up tied to the dock, all alone, after he was dead, waiting for him, like a pet dog waits for his master in the evening. But he hadn't died; the beam severed his legs just above the knee, cleanly and solemnly, like an act of God, an altar ritual. If it had happened forty years later, they might have been able to put them back.

Of course, Elaine had left her coffee cup on the end table with the crumpled newspaper. The coffee had dripped and left a wet smear. He got a kitchen rag and wiped it, then leaned his nose over to his armpits. "Damn. All that sweating, now I have to clean myself up again." He headed for the bathroom, but footsteps on the deck sent him to the door instead.

She stood in the doorway with the sun behind her, so her face was in shadow. The vantage point he had grown so used to, looking up at people, now seemed a great disadvantage.

She said, "Hey, there. You must be Earl. I'm Audrey. From St. Agnes, they said you needed a little help around here, some company?"

"They did?" His tongue felt thick in his mouth and with it a paralyzing dryness.

"You were expecting me, weren't you?"

Fool, standing here with your mouth hanging open. "Yes, yes of course. I'm sorry. Come on in." Her look of confusion was replaced with a beautiful smile. She glanced around the room like women do, sizing things up for whatever they look for, neatness or the furniture. He hoped she didn't look too close. She was an attractive woman, no question about it, not that much younger than he. "You a friend of Ida's?"

"I sure am. We go to St. Agnes together. This is right cute."

*Raaht cute.* Was it Georgia or Mississippi? "Being out here on the water must be so nice (*naahce*) for you. We used to come out here when I was a girl to visit my aunt and uncle. This place has some memories for me, good ones too."

Earl couldn't think of a thing to say to her. He liked the look of her, the uncoiffed hair, her blue jeans, the tilt of her head. He'd been expecting polyester, maybe done-up hair with lots of spray in it, too much makeup. This woman was natural; that's what he liked.

"I'm sorry, Audrey. I find I'm a bit nervous. It's been quite a few years since I've entertained a woman in my home. Or anywhere else for that matter and I'm out of practice."

She smiled.

He hurried up and added, "I mean not to say that you're, that we're…oh hell, can I get you some coffee?"

He took his handkerchief out of his pocket and wiped sweat off his neck.

She laughed. "I would love some."

"Sit down. I'll bring it to the table." He went to the kitchen and turned the burner up to warm the coffee, retrieved the cream from the fridge. The deep breathing exercise he'd read about in the paper helped calm him a little. "Is evaporated milk okay? My granddaughter makes fun of it, but I still like it."

"It's just fine. That's what I use too. Ida said your granddaughter, she lives with you for the moment?"

He brought out the coffee on a tray that attached to his chair and laid it out on the table. At least now, pulled up to the table across from her, they were at the same level. "Yes, she got divorced and she's between things now, trying to find her way."

"That can be hard. But this place is neat as a pin." She drank some coffee and looked around again. "It's so lovely to be sitting right here in the lake with the water on all sides. I always did love that about it here."

They both gazed out the windows and were quiet for a minute. He liked that they could sit like that and not fill every second with words. It was relaxing, comfortable.

"I love it out here, too. Not many live out here anymore. Only a few camps left for the vacationers. I think there's only four of us left who live out here. Where did you grow up, Audrey? Not New Orleans. Lemme guess. Georgia?"

"Well, yes, you got it on the first try. A little town in the mountains. We was dirt poor."

"So were we, so were we. People had to work so hard. That's all they knew. Nobody realizes that anymore. How hard they had to work just to get food on the table. Now they got TVs in each room."

"It's the truth. We had no indoor plumbing. Had an outhouse out back for most of my growing up."

"That's what we had, too."

"But you grew up here in the city, Earl?"

"Here, have some more coffee." He refilled their cups. "No, no out in the country. A little Cajun fishing town called Cocodrie."

They covered more ground in one afternoon than Earl had with anyone in years and years. He couldn't remember the last time he had felt so heard by somebody. They had moved to the sofa then to the back porch and back to the table again for crackers and cheese. It baffled him that it was so easy.

"I should be getting home, Earl. It sure has been a lovely afternoon." She went to the sofa to retrieve her white handbag. She sat back down on the edge of a chair by the door, a gesture he appreciated. "Ida said you needed help around here, but it sure looks like you and your granddaughter do quite well on your own."

Her hazel eyes were so lively, the eyes of a young girl. They stopped him for a minute—that, and his loss for words to respond to her. She was right, he didn't need any help. Was that what she came for?

She interrupted his pause. "Because I don't know about you, but it sure is nice visiting, if you ever want to do that again. I mean only if you want to."

He let out a sigh of relief. "Well, yes, I think that would be very nice," he chuckled. "Very nice."

"I hope I didn't talk too much, sometimes I get a little carried away."

"No, no you didn't. It was, well, it was perfect. I hope you'll come back soon?"

She stood up and smoothed her pants legs with the palms of her hands. "I would love to come back any time."

"Tomorrow?" he asked. Then he could have kicked himself, if he'd had the legs to do it. The last thing he wanted was to scare her off.

"Tomorrow?"

He went to open the door for her. "Just any time, Audrey, any time you have a few minutes. I've enjoyed it."

"So have I. I wasn't expecting, well I just don't know what I was expecting, but seems like the time just flew by talking to you." She smiled and he noticed—not for the first time— her straight, even teeth.

"I know what you mean. I didn't know what to expect when Ida called me. I was so nervous. But this has been a very pleasant surprise."

He went outside and sat on the deck as she made her way down that endless walkway to the levee. She turned and waved before climbing over to the parking lot on the other side. He went inside and washed the coffee cups and plates, and he realized he'd been whistling the whole time.

# 15.

## MOONSHINE



A WATERY IMAGE APPEARED IN THE water bath. Floyd leaned over her shoulder. "Look at that. Every time I watch you do this I'm surprised by it." He chuckled.

Dolores transferred the wet paper to the fixer tray. The picture began to take form, and shapes more defined. The rough wood grain wall of a shed was marked by three metal tools hung on nails in a neat row. A rake, a hoe, and a sling blade. In contrast to their determined simplicity, the softness of a girl child leaned her body against the grainy surface next to the tools. The girl's gaze was curious and dreamy, and strands of her hair frayed in all directions. Dolores made a throaty sound and drew in her breath.

"Now, that's something." Floyd shook his head back and forth in wonder.

"I understand now something that Father Martin said to me about the camera."

"What did he say?"

"He said it was a different way of seeing. That it shows you how to see with your heart. You see into something more. I can't explain it, but he said it had something to do with God."

"Hmmm."

Floyd left her alone and came back an hour later. "Didi, it's a good thing I'm closing up, because you'd be in here all the night long."

Dolores stepped out into the dim quiet of dusk and pulled on her sweater. The windows of Red's house behind the store glowed yellow orange from the kerosene lamps inside. The smells of wood smoke and cooked pork mingled with the scent of dry leaves. She started down the path towards her house then hesitated and followed the path close to the water. A couple of houses stretched out into the bayou before the shore became more wooded and another smaller bayou went off to the east. The two bayous were divided by marsh grass and edged with dark stands of swamp oak and cypress. A few lingering seagulls broke the quiet.

A collapsed dock had been turned into a lean-to where a barge was tied up. A pair of wood ducks were settling down in some tall cattails next to it and a possum walked in front of Dolores on the path.

"Aieeee, toi!" A man yelled from the lean-to. "What you sneaking around for? Get over here!"

Dolores backed away in the direction she'd come. "You stay there," the voice said again, "You hear me? Julee, go see what's that out there."

A bulky man came out of the shadows from deep in the woods across the path from the bayou. He stood in her way when she tried to turn around and head back. The ground there was spongy and soft. She tried going around him, but he grabbed for her arm and ended up with his hand clutching the waistband of her skirt. When she pulled away, he laughed and called back to the others. "It's that fou girl from town. The one with the camera."

The man pulled her closer and touched her cheek. "Too bad you so crazy; you pretty, you."

He let go of her with a grunt, and she fell back onto the path. Earl came from behind him and wrestled him to the ground.

"Get your hands off her you son of a bitch." Earl's arms and legs flailed.

The man laughed and straddled Earl in a scissors hold.

"Julee, what's that going on?" A voice from the water called out.

The man held Earl down. "Maybe you two spying on us, hunh? You got a revenuer in your pocket, boy? Or maybe she does?" He laughed again and hopped up, calling to his friends. "Nothing, ain't nothing going on."

The other man climbed up to the path from the barge. "Earl Rizan what the hell you doing out here boy?"

Earl said, "I understand now, how you got that new boat, Julee, and a new roof for your maman's house, a new porch for yours." Earl helped Dolores up and moved so she was behind him and wiped off his lip where he'd taken an elbow in the scuffle.

Julee laughed again. "They's lots of people trying to make a few extra sous doing this. Now take this crazy girl and get the hell outta here." He reached a hand to help him up, but Earl rolled over and stood on his own.

Earl said, "Goddamn rumrunner." He put his arm around her. They started on the path towards town with only a half moon for light. "Didi, did he hurt you?"

She shook her head. "What is Julee doing out there? It smelled funny."

"It's a still. They make moonshine not just for themselves, but to sell. So, they get all kinds of people out here and trouble comes from it. I could kill him for touching you."

The first two houses at the edge of town came into view with dim light in their windows. Children's voices came from inside. Fireflies winked in the bushes around the house.

They came to the place where the paths to their houses diverged. Dolores said, "Earl what were you doing out there?"

"I was coming to meet you at Floyd's and saw you walk out on this path. I was worried. It was almost dark. I couldn't figure out where you were going." His hands hung at his sides, and his head drooped. "I'm sorry. Where were you going?"

She took a step closer to him and leaned her head against his chest. He stiffened and stared out into the night, then his body softened, and he embraced her with both arms.

"You saved me," she said. "I was going to a spot maman used to take me to."

"Are you still looking for those lights? If he had hurt you, Didi, I think I'd have to kill him. Please don't go walking by yourself at night. Promise me?" He held her shoulders and positioned her to look into her eyes.

She kissed him full on the mouth then trotted away towards home. Earl was left there like a statue standing on the edge of the dark woods.

# 16.

## SAM

ELAINE WAS LATE MEETING SAM at the café and that made her more nervous. They had to get to know each other all over again, even though parts of it were still comfortable. A lot had happened in the past six years, but she thought that the connection they had was still there, under all the subterfuge of the break-up, move, marriage and divorce.

The coffee shop was crowded. People formed lines out onto the sidewalk or sat in benches in the shade of the trees on Esplanade Avenue. She peered into the place through a mass of shoulders and sweaty necks to find Sam at a small table in the corner.

A wide doorway next to him led to a spacious area that she guessed was where his work was displayed. The front room was too cramped for much artwork, except a few small photographs. Sam was holding a newspaper, but not reading it. He shuffled his feet as if he was a bit uncomfortable there. That was like him, always more at ease outside, in a boat, or in the woods. They took many trips in his boat on the bayous, crabbing and shrimping, when they were together. He'd wanted to show her why he loved it so much, the moss and the hidden island chains and inlets, the birds, the clouds, even the alligators. How the alligators calmly waded back and forth from shore to the tiny islands, not bothering anything. It was relaxing to watch them.

Sam looked up towards the door. He waved and stood up. "You made it," he said when she got to the table.

"Sorry I'm late. I didn't think I'd ever get into the bathroom. Pappy was in there for hours sprucing. I think that woman's coming over." She leaned over to look in the back room. "Is your stuff in there?"

"Yeah. They're too big and bulky for this area. I sat here so I could see when you came in. Here, I already got the coffee." He handed her a to-go cup. "Extra dry cappuccino, lots of foam."

"Lots of foam. You remembered." She reached for the cup when a voice behind her said something, and she felt a tug. A little boy in a stroller was pulling on the fringe of her bag. She shifted towards Sam to let them by, and his breath brushed her cheek. It felt so familiar and natural. It made her want to touch his arm, but she held back.

She took the coffee from him and stepped through the doorway to the back. "Thanks. I'm gonna go look."

One wall of the back room was all glass with large doors that opened onto a patio with more tables. It was surrounded by sago palms and flowering vines, wisteria, and gardenia, lots more that she could not identify. The ceiling fans spread a scented humidity from the patio that drifted around the room. Booths lined the other walls, and above each one hung one of Sam's wood sculptures.

Elaine had to be discreet because patrons sat in all the booths, but she was able to maneuver around the room and at least get glimpses of Sam's pieces. She stopped in front of one that hung outside a booth, and she sensed Sam's presence next to her.

"Yeah, you can't really see them too well with all these people." He took a sip of his coffee and stared at the wall as though trying to avoid eye contact with her. "I didn't know it could get this crowded here. Should have guessed."

She turned to him. "Sam. This is amazing. So far along from where you were a few years ago. It's so impressive. It must have taken you months."

He laughed. "More like years. Thanks. Earl helped with some of it, some of the carpentry I needed advice on."

The abstract carving was detailed with copper accents and twisted copper wire. It had graceful curves, and the wood had been polished to a high sheen. "It's birdlike, this one. It's so watery, like flowing water, and like a wing. You're really doing it. What we said we'd do."

"We made a pact not to let the world get in our way."

"Yeah, then I let the world get in the way," she said. "Or myself, not the world, I let myself get in the way."

"I was thinking of you when I did this one." The colors of the cherry, walnut and cypress swirled around shiny copper wire inlays. Patterns radiated from a circle of wood in the center.

Elaine said, "What's this?" An inscription in tiny letters fit into a curved line at the bottom—*On this path, let your heart be your guide. Rumi.*

Sam's eyes were withdrawn, and his mouth was set in a slight grin like a kid caught with something he knew was off limits. Elaine understood; you were vulnerable showing work to anyone. "I think I've lost sight of my path."

"You might be a little lost, but you'll get back on track." He fumbled with a napkin. The place had slowed down a little. Car horns echoed on Esplanade.

She glanced at the door to the front room, and her heart dropped when Peter walked in. "Shit." He glanced around like he was looking for somebody then went back towards the counter.

"What's wrong?" Sam followed the direction of her gaze.

"Somebody I'd rather not see."

"We can duck out the back if you want." He stood between her and the front door and put his hand on her back.

They slipped out onto the patio. "If you didn't think I was messed up before now I'm sure you'll have a better understanding."

"I don't know, there's people I wouldn't want to see right now. Let's walk." He led them down a side alley to Esplanade Avenue. They had to bend to avoid the heavy branches of the crepe myrtles that were full of wet blossoms. The street dead ended into a crumbling brick mansion that was covered with scaffolding. "Let's turn and go around the block."

"Are you okay?" Sam lit a cigarette and one for her.

"Thanks." She took the cigarette. "It's that guy Peter I used to date at school. Before you. I don't want to see him. I've gone out with him a couple of times. It's stupid. I'm not doing it anymore."

"You mean Peter Melancon? The prosecutor? Jesus, you gotta be kidding. Do you realize what an asshole he is? I mean he's a crook for one thing. He's got his hands in all kinds of pockets. And he's a coke head, too."

Elaine had stopped walking, which Sam didn't notice he was so busy ranting. "Hey, hey, hey, just stop, okay? I said I stopped doing it. Anyway, where do you get off? Are you filling in for Pappy? Or maybe my mom?"

Sam looked surprised for a second and then dropped his forehead into his hand and rolled his hand over his hair like someone trying to wake themselves up. "You're right. I'm sorry."

Elaine couldn't stop herself. "I know it's stupid, okay?"

"Look, please. You don't have to explain. I am not judging you; I promise."

"It sure sounded like it. But anyway, you're right. I need to be doing what you're doing, making art. All the stuff I used to do to ground me went out the window when I moved away from here. Now nothing works. I'm restless all the time. I can't get started on anything." She put her cigarette out on the sidewalk and stuck the butt in her pocket. "Your stuff is beautiful. It really is. I wanted to look more. Then he showed up." She kicked a root that had pushed up the sidewalk and cracked it.

"I took a woodworking class at Delgado to get me going. Maybe there's a class you'd like." They started walking again, and he lifted a crepe myrtle branch for her. "We can come back when they're less busy if you want to look more."

She felt demoralized that Sam knew about Peter now, and kind of pissed that he'd react that way. But it was hard for her to be angry with him. They ended up on Esplande again in front of the café near where her car was parked.

Peter was leaning on his Caravan with his arms folded across his chest in the position he always assumed when he feigned interest or compassion. He was wearing his jogging clothes and looked red and sweaty like he'd been running. A young man was talking and gesturing at him. The man seemed agitated and a little scared. His voice was high pitched and wobbled like he had little control over its highs and lows. Peter glanced in their direction and waved then continued to nod at the man who had not skipped a beat.

"Hey, man you not listening to me. I'm telling you they got three, four of them houses up in there all boarded up and 'less you burn 'em down you not gonna get them druggies outta there, no. And anyway, you can't just put all them guys outta business. What they gonna do then? You gonna get jobs for them? There ain't nothing here for them."

Peter kept a calm, neutral demeanor, as if this kind of thing happened to him every day, and finally put a hand on the man's shoulder. Elaine couldn't hear what he was saying, but the man quieted down, and Peter reached in his pocket and gave him some cash.

Elaine took out her keys and started towards her car, hoping to get out in time, but Peter was already making his way over.

"Elaine Landry, as I live and breathe." He offered a hand to Sam. "Peter Melancon. I don't think we've met."

They shook hands, and Elaine squeezed her eyes shut hoping the whole scene would disappear.

Sam said, "Is that guy okay?" The man Peter had been arguing with was leaning forward on a bench with his elbows on his knees. He was jiggling his knees like he couldn't control his nervous energy. "I overheard some of it. What neighborhood were y'all talking about?"

Peter said, "Oh, it's Mid-City, off Carrollton. Some property I'm trying to clean up around there, but that makes people restless." He studied Sam for a moment. "Where do you live, Sam?"

"On the lake. Little Woods."

"Ah. Another odd bird, like this one here. Nobody lives in Little Woods." He laughed his dismissive laugh. A noisy seafood truck pulled up behind the grocery store next door, making it hard to talk.

Peter said, "I don't want to keep you two from anything. Nice meeting you, Sam. Elaine, will you be at work tonight? I looked for you last night."

"Yeah, I'll be there."

"Okay, I'll see you then. Make sure there's an amandine for me, will you?" He smiled his most ingratiating smile, the fake one he used with everybody he met. Elaine saw a different smile sometimes, but that one seemed fake too, as if he had to try hard to make it seem casual and unaffected.

Peter walked lazily through the gathering of people outside the café nodding and waving.

"Did he just tickle that baby? He did the baby thing. When's the election?" Elaine tried to add some levity to the awkward situation. It was bad enough admitting to Sam that she'd been spending time with Peter, but for them to have to meet each other was grueling.

"The election's in October. He's been in trouble while you were away, not that it will make any difference in him getting reelected. He's got a lot of friends in high places."

"He was a sleaze in college, and he's still a sleaze." Elaine didn't want to have to explain what she saw in Peter. She didn't really understand it herself, except that it had to do with that bad side that let her escape her good-girl self. "He's taking it to new levels now he's got some power." She unlocked her car door and looked up at the huge clouds. "I was using him to escape, that's all. I've come to my senses now."

"I'm sorry I lost it. Your senses aren't my business. Thanks for coming." He kissed her cheek. "But if you do come back to them soon, let me know if any of them lead you my way."

He turned away towards his car, and she called to him. "Sam, your stuff, it's amazing. Congratulations."

He turned around and made a little bow.

She lit a cigarette in her car and reached up and pulled her hair on both sides, shaking her head back and forth and groaning. She had kept to her decision not to date for an entire year after Ethan. Her year was up and then some. She could tell she was warming up to Sam again and had to admit that she'd considered that might be a problem for her with him living that close to Pappy. Yet, to find out that he had not moved on by now and seemed ready to start up again with her, that was a surprise.

When Peter showed up at the café at the end of her shift that night, his eyes were already glassed over and red-rimmed. She had Leroy distract him, and she ducked out the back to her car.

On the way home she left her car windows open and let the warm humid air blow on her face. The pack of cigarettes she'd bought that morning she tossed into the parking lot dumpster. Pappy was still up so they split a beer and watched reruns of *Perry Mason*. After he went to bed she regretted the cigarettes but was not up for either diving into the dumpster or going to buy more.

When she went to put her apron in the laundry, the card from Alexander's gallery fell out of her pocket, reminding her of the statue in Audubon Park and the anonymous photograph. Her old Nikon was tucked away in the top shelf of her closet in a box of high-school memorabilia, yearbooks, corsages, and concert programs. She'd used the school cameras in college, so this one had been buried for years. She opened it up and clicked the shutter a few times, gazed through the lens taking imaginary pictures of nothing. When she went to bed, she could see the camera on her desk waiting in the pool of light that came in her window from the dock next door.

# 17.

## BAL DE NOCE

EARL GOT READY FOR HIS wedding day, a rainy Saturday morning in early spring. He was up long before the sun rose, pacing and worrying and praying for the rain to stop. When it was time, he dressed in the same suit his papa wore at his own wedding, and that he wore for his mother's funeral. Every few minutes he felt in his pocket for the gold band that his mother had worn all her life, afraid he would lose it, and either that or some other problem, like the weather, would ruin this day—Dolores would change her mind, and that would be the end of it.

His two brothers and some cousins met up in the front yard of Earl's house under the dripping trees to bring Earl over to Dolores' house. The whole family was going to walk to the church together like a parade; that was the tradition, and Earl wanted to do everything right.

The boys roughhoused with Earl and tried to get him to laugh, but he was too nervous to notice. They left the house and walked along the bayou across Redfish Street by the post office, along the block of oak trees on Crab Street, picked up Dolores' cousin at his house, and finally stopped in front of her house under the giant oak tree.

The only sound in the house was coming from Marie's babies. The quiet made Earl nervous. He climbed the steps and stood by the railing.

Dolores' father sat waiting on the porch with his pipe. He nodded at Earl and waved his pipe towards the door. "She's not ready yet."

She was standing in a beam of sunlight in the middle of the parlor with her head tilted back. Her dress came down below her knees—her maman's wedding dress; it had lace on the sleeves and neck and at the bottom. Through the screen, Earl thought she looked like an angel, glowing.

Marie traced over her sister's lips with a finger. "A little color for your lips. Mais, que tu es belle aujourd'hui! It makes me happy to see you in this dress." She pulled Dolores close to her. "Dieu te bénisse, Didi, God bless you, I hope that you will be well and happy." From the sound of her voice, Earl thought Marie might be crying like women do at these things.

Dolores turned her face in his direction when the boards creaked under his feet, and Earl moved back and turned his face away. When she came outside a few minutes later, he felt weak and had to steady himself on the railing. He tried to wet his lips, but his mouth was dry. "Is that you, Didi?"

She was wearing her mother's white Sunday lace veil—the ones they called a mantilla—that hung down below her shoulders. She had told him how wearing it made her feel close to her maman, more so than the dress, because she never saw her maman wear the dress, but the veil she wore every Sunday for Mass. The veil framed her pale face and brushed against her smooth neck, brown from the sun. Her eyes were brooding in their natural way, but with a nervous excitement, too, like the day she showed him the darkroom. She smiled and looked over his shoulder towards the woods.

Earl held an umbrella over him and Dolores as they walked to the church with their two families in line, collecting other people as they went.

*This is what I've waited for, this girl, this day, and our life together.* Earl wanted to believe in the happy dream of his life with Dolores, but deep inside he knew that he wasn't marrying any ordinary girl. Dolores needed things a regular girl didn't need. She had to have her camera, her darkroom, and her time and space. He was hoping that once they were busy with a family, those things wouldn't matter as much to her anymore. Away from Cocodrie, in their own home, they could grow up together, watch their children grow up, then their grandchildren.

The rain let up halfway there, and Earl stopped to close the umbrella. When they reached the church, Earl left her with her sister and joined Father Martin in front of the altar while everybody found their seats. The clear glass windows of the church were propped open with wooden sticks to let in fresh air, but not much light came in with the thick clouds, so the room was dim except for the candles on the altar and against the front wall.

Dolores walked the short aisle with her papa and stood next to him. Mass never seemed so long to Earl as it did that day. He got through communion and the vows in a kind of trance. He managed to get out the ring and kiss the bride without any problems, but before they could head out, the rain started pounding the roof.

The wind rattled the windows, and gusts slammed some of them shut like gunshot. The church grew dark and hot, and the candles made strange shadows on the walls. Dolores looked flushed, and Earl got worried. "Didi, ça va? Are you feeling alright?" She nodded, but she gripped his arm and dropped into a pew.

Father Martin said that everybody should sit and wait until the storm calmed down. "The bal de noce, the wedding dance, it can wait."

The back door of the church opened, and a woman stood in the doorway with the rain blowing behind her. It took a few minutes for Earl to make out that it was the traiteuse woman who traveled to the different towns doing her healing.

"It's Anna," said Dolores. "The one who came to see Maman."

Father Martin met her at the door. "Anna, get out of that rain." She used a cane and leaned on his arm.

"Did I miss it," said Anna, "did Didi get married today?" She was wearing a cloak that kept the rain off, but the scarf on her head was soaked, and her hair dripped water onto the pew. Father Martin sent one of the altar boys for a cloth and some wine.

"She got so old," said Dolores. "She looks like she can't see." Her voice sounded like she was seeing a ghost.

Father Martin sat Anna down in the back pew. She said, "Where are they? Can you bring them to me?"

The rest of the congregation had started visiting and talking, paying no attention to Anna, babies were crying, and little children were playing on the polished wood floors. Earl was impatient to move on to the party, but the sound of the wind and heavy rain beat down on the roof and the whole building shook with the thunder.

Anna touched Dolores' face and rubbed the edge of the veil between her fingers. "Your maman would be happy for you today. I felt her outside before I came in. She is still with us, with you."

Earl wanted to move the woman's hand away from Dolores. She was his wife now, and he needed to protect her from anything that might be a threat. This woman came back from the dead almost, it seemed, from that time when her maman was sick. At least they were married now, so nothing, a thunderstorm, or this healer woman, could make any trouble for them.

"How did you know she's still with us?" said Dolores.

"There's all kinds of seeing." She started to cough, and Father Martin gave her some wine while he tried to dry off her face and hair. The coughing stopped, and she reached for Dolores' hand.

Earl hoped she was done talking. Dolores had strange ideas already without having this woman stir them all up.

Anna said, "You have a special way of seeing. I knew that from when you were a little girl." She moved two bony fingers from her own heart to the lace part of Dolores' bodice. Her nails were yellow and brittle looking.

Earl had to stop himself again from moving the hand away.

She said, "Now is it time for the party?"

Earl laughed; he was so relieved that she was done talking to Dolores. The sunlight began to spread through the windows and into the church slow, starting in the front and making its way back, like somebody opening a great curtain, and when Father opened the door, everybody cheered. The clouds blew over, and the sun was bright again.

Earl was anxious about Anna showing up at the wedding, bringing up memories for Dolores, and sending her into thoughts of the sad times with her sick maman, and of the feux follets she would be leaving in the woods when they moved from Cocodrie. But the sunshine was helping him get rid of all the darkness Anna brought with her. He took Dolores' hand, and they led everybody outside. They had to stand as a couple and greet everybody as husband and wife. The music started across the yard where the tables were set up for the bal de noce.

"I am happy, Didi, are you happy?" Earl leaned close to her ear so she could hear him in the middle of all the commotion.

She looked up at him and nodded. "I think so," she said. "But we can bring my darkroom with us, yes?"

Earl was hoping for a different answer. "Will that make you happy?"

"Yes."

"Then yes. Somehow we'll manage a darkroom in New Orleans. I don't know how, but we'll do it."

"Time for the march!" Uncle Red lifted his fiddle into the air in a sign for the musicians to play the march music.

Earl's heart felt lighter with the music and the people lined up behind them, as though he and Dolores were being carried along by everyone's laughing and teasing—they weren't alone in this adventure. When the music changed to a slow waltz, everybody dropped back for the couple's dance. Earl didn't understand why the music for the dance had to be so sad-sounding with the crying fiddle and Red's voice: J'ai passé devant ta porte—I passed in front of your door. It didn't seem like a happy wedding song, but it was tradition. The only good thing about it was that he got to have Dolores in his arms during the dance, and she couldn't wiggle out of it. He'd never been able to get a slow dance out of her before. He was close enough to get the scent of her neck; close enough to feel in his belly and legs the longing for what would come later that night.

The party went on until well after dark long when the night animals started to come out and the crickets and cicadas went to sleep. People picked up their sleeping children from under the tables and kissed Earl and Dolores goodnight. Others were passed out in the corners from too much moonshine and beer. Earl's cousins led them on horseback to the houseboat where they would stay for a month while their house got ready in New Orleans. The boat was lit up with candles and kerosene lamps, and the flames were reflected in the bayou. When they were finally by themselves, they sat on the deck of the boat, holding hands.

Earl said, "I never knew what it felt like to be so happy." The crickets and bullfrogs, the whippoorwills and nighthawks seemed to be singing how he felt, like his heart was singing and them with it.

Dolores said, "Did you hear Anna say that Maman was there today? She's a little crazy, Anna."

A pair of alligators were doing their mating bellows, and it embarrassed Earl, but Dolores didn't seem to notice the sound of another animal's wedding night.

"She's crazy, but you know, I think Maman was there today. I could feel it. Earl, I'm afraid to leave Cocodrie, but I can't wait to take pictures in New Orleans."

Another case of nerves like that morning came over him when she said that. The thought of her wandering the city alone with a camera scared him. He was afraid she would not be alright in a big city, that she'd be better off staying in her small town with her people. But he was distracted and nervous enough thinking about the night ahead of him, and that pushed down everything else. When the moon came up over the bayou, they blew out the candles and went to bed.

# 18.

## ARNIE

J UST AFTER JULY 4<sup>TH</sup>, ELAINE paused at the top of the levee on the way to her car and inhaled the murky morning air. The white glare of the cloud cover hurt her eyes. Rain would come later and add to the oppressive heat with wafts of steam rising from streets and sidewalks. Welcome to Louisiana.

The gulls resting on docks were quiet and listless. The parking lot of the convenience store across the street had yellow tape around it with four police cars parked behind metal barricades. A few people from the neighborhood stood outside the tape. She crossed the street and approached one of the cars and recognized a couple of women from going to the store.

"What happened?" she asked a policeman. Thunder rumbled in the distance.

Two uniformed cops leaned against their car talking. "Robbery. Last night."

"Did anybody get hurt?" A cool sweat popped out on her forehead and nausea swept into her throat. Blood stains smeared the concrete a few feet away from her.

"Boy was killed." The officer threw his cigarette down and stepped on it. Two other cops stood nearby laughing and drinking from Styrofoam cups. One of them crushed the cup and threw it on the ground.

"What time did it happen? I live right over the levee. I didn't hear anything." Elaine spoke in the direction of the cop with the clipboard, and he averted his eyes.

"Two a.m. Right at closing." He seemed to notice her for the first time. "You live over there? I've always wondered about people living in those old camps." He grinned and lowered his clipboard, folded his arms, and looked her up and down.

"Can you tell me who it was? Who was killed? I know some of the kids who work here."

A young girl near her with a baby on her hip appeared to be listening to the conversation. Two other young kids sat in a grassy spot behind the girl. Elaine recognized three older guys who she'd seen sitting in front of the Tight Spot in folding chairs. They were huddled on the sidewalk away from the police cars.

The policeman sighed, "I can't tell you any names at this point. Some black kid, teenager."

"Was it somebody who worked here?" The yellow tape shook in a sudden gust, and it started raining. The parking lot was strewn with trash, empty cigarette packs, old Bic lighters, chip bags and candy wrappers. A blob that appeared to be a used condom.

"I don't know. Lady, this happens every day, five times a day, all over the city." His tone was a mixture of exasperation and nonchalance. "They kill each other over money and drugs and women. It's part of the culture."

She imagined that they reached the point of not caring anymore with all the violence they experienced, but their reputation with the black male population reflected the national trend, only worse.

"Shit." The young woman with the baby sidled up next to Elaine. "He don't care who it is. I'm wondering too, if it's Arnie, is that who you're thinking about?" She stood a foot taller than Elaine; her straightened hair was pulled back in a pink barrette, and her tank top was unraveling at the neck.

Elaine nodded. "Yeah. God, I hope it's not Arnie." Arnie's mother named him after Arnold Palmer, for some reason. He was a sweet boy, with long eyelashes and solemn eyes.

"He's a good kid, trying to get to college. Went to school with my brother." She shook her head and spat on the concrete.

The policeman added."There's lot of sad stories. This city is a bitch. Look, we have to get back to work here. You can look in tomorrow's paper at the police reports. That will give you the name, if it's released by then." He turned away to join a group of cops chatting by the front door.

The woman said, "There's talk that he got in some crossfire and the cops shot him by mistake. We need some help in this neighborhood, not more police."

Elaine had been on her way to the car to drive to Alexander's gallery and had gone to the convenience store for cigarettes. After what happened she needed one even more, but it would have to wait. Another hour anyway without smoking. She drove to the French Quarter and parked at a lot up against the levee across from Jackson Square. A heavy mist had settled over the river between rainfalls and a passing barge looked ghostly as only the very tips of the two tugs showed above the layer of white.

She took Decatur to Chartres Street and found the shop between a fancy antique furniture store and the Bottom of the Cup tearoom whose teacup neon sign had been there long before Elaine was born. A black wrought-iron gate with a grape vine design revealed a narrow brick alley leading to a typical open French Quarter courtyard. A noisy van parked behind her, and an older man approached the gate as a younger one started to unload metal serving dishes and plastic food containers.

Elaine rang the buzzer. "Hi, it's Elaine. From the Pontchartrain. You have some deliveries here."

Alexander's voice answered. "Come on back, Elaine. Prop the gate open for them if you don't mind."

As a kid they would visit the Quarter on occasion, get beignets, visit the wax museum. These mysterious alleys and courtyards used to fascinate Elaine. She would stop and stare into them from the sidewalk and had to be dragged away.

The temperature must have been ten degrees cooler once she got to the shady courtyard at the end of the alley. The surrounding brick walls were covered with trumpet honeysuckle and wisteria vines, palmettos, and banana trees. In the middle, a stone mermaid perched on a giant conch shell in a circular brick pond. The pond was bordered with dwarf azaleas and sweet olive trees. "Paradise," said Elaine.

Alexander stood in an open doorway of one of the buildings. "They're delivering refreshments for the Friday Art Walk. It's good to see you, Elaine. Come on in." They passed a bathroom and storage rooms on their way to the main part of the gallery.

"Go ahead and look around. I'll be right back. Let me show them where to set up. Can I get you some coffee?" He pointed her to a table next to the front counter.

She nodded and went to the window. "Sure, I'd love some." Across the street the upper balconies were draped with last year's Mardi Gras beads. A young couple leaned on the black iron railing and gazed down the street towards the Square.

She wandered past some generic tourist photographs, a couple of jazz fest posters and then came to an interesting wall where the photos were more artistic than touristy. In one photo, workers climbed up and down ramps unloading crates of bananas and sacks of coffee from a ship. Next to it was one of an old couple sitting on a concrete bench.

"Here you go." Alexander set a tray on the table with two bowl-like cups of café au lait and a plate of croissants. "How are you?"

She sat down and realized that she continued to feel nauseous from the morning's discovery. "I'm kind of shaken up. There was a shooting across the street from us last night. A boy was killed. They're not sure what happened."

"Oh no, I'm so sorry. Maybe you need something a little stronger." He went behind the counter and came back with a bottle of Jack Daniel's. He held the bottle over her coffee. "May I?"

Elaine smiled. "Sure, I guess so. Did those photos on this wall come from the same sale as the one at the café?"

Crumbs and flecks of chocolate clung to the edges of his lips. He wiped them with a cloth napkin. "Yes, there are two at the café, the ones you've mentioned. The Gumbel statue at Audubon Park, *The Meeting of Air and Water*, which you've noticed. There's another one. It's in my office so maybe you haven't seen it. I believe it is a building at the Zoo. My partner got them all at a yard sale a couple of years ago. Uptown on Valmont Street. Weird old house. There was no identifying information on them. So, Gary framed them. I think they are stunning. I had a couple of others, but they had a lot of water damage."

"The mystery photographer." She walked up to the photos on the wall. "The expressions on the faces of that old couple on the bench. The woman's looking straight at the camera—she's curious, intent, and he's off somewhere, worried or anxious. That could be the Zoo in the background. She had a way with a camera, whoever she was, and with the people in her pictures."

"She?" Elaine let Alexander pour a little more bourbon in her cup.

"I don't know why I said that. Seems like a woman took them. How old are they do you think?"

"Looks like they're from the 30s maybe. Same time as some of Bellocq's. There's an exhibit of his at the museum, have you been? Some Julia Cameron, too, and a couple by Sally Mann that actually remind me of these."

Elaine went back to the table. "Oh, I love Sally Mann." She was reminded of all the hours she used to spend in high school poring over photography books and feeling like she was floating inside the pictures.

"Tell me about yourself, Elaine. You said you used to take pictures?"

Elaine went through the sad story of her divorce and return to New Orleans. "I took a lot of photography classes and worked on the school paper and yearbooks. I wanted to go to art school, but my mom was against it. She was widowed when I was little, so I think she wanted to make sure I had something I could rely on for money. But the thing is, I hated my job, and I feel like I'll be unhappy doing most things unless I do what I'm drawn to."

"And you're drawn to…?" He leaned in closer and tilted his head towards hers.

Elaine felt his generous interest, and something shifted inside. She gazed at the pictures on the wall and remembered one of Sally Mann's that she loved—when she went inside it, it gave her that sense of being part of a larger universe—a landscape flecked with little points of light like fireflies. "I want to be a Sally Mann. I want to make something inspiring." Her breath escaped as an audible sigh. "Something hauntingly beautiful."

The sky rumbled loud enough to make the building shudder. They both looked out the wall of windows that opened to the street.

"Well, it sounds like you're halfway there. Most people have no idea what they really want, what their heart is telling them. Sounds like you already know."

"I don't think I did know until now. Must be the Jack Daniel's in my coffee."

"We could use some help around here. We just lost somebody who helped with framing and cleaning up, waiting on customers. Are you interested? It might not be as much money as the café, but at least you'd be around art. Or you could do both. Think about it."

"I don't need to think about it. I would love to."

Elaine walked back to her car with the photographs reappearing in her mind's eye like a flickering old film on a screen. From the parking lot next to the levee, she could see one of the great curves in the river, the same curve where the ship nestled in one of the pictures. She imagined the photographer standing there and wondered how violent the city was then, not even a hundred years from the end of the Civil War, in the aftermath of slavery. Arnie's life might have been different today, but maybe not much different. She said a prayer that it wasn't Arnie who was shot.

# 19.

## ANGELUS

DOLORES MADE THE SIGN OF the cross and pulled herself up by the metal bedpost. She was lightheaded in the mornings, but that bothered her less than her fear that the white feeling was coming back. It was there in the back of her mind, waiting. She thought being pregnant might have something to do with it.

The bedcovers were in a messy pile, and she was reminded of Marie's thick arms pulling at the sheets until they were tight then smoothing them down, shaking out the quilt, patting the pillows. The homesickness for Cocodrie came and went with the time of day. Mornings seemed the hardest after Earl left for work.

She dropped the bedclothes into the washtub next to the sink and lit the gas to heat water. Earl's cousin rented the three-room apartment on Joseph Street to them. It was only a few blocks from the river, so they could hear the ships going by. Dolores loved how the sound vibrated inside of her. The house was surrounded by oleander bushes and banana trees. Earl had said that the shed in the yard next to the clothesline would be perfect for the darkroom, but since she got pregnant, he seemed to lose interest in setting it up for her.

The sound of fall crickets reminded her of the bayou. She put the camera strap around her neck and walked into the yard to throw feed to the chickens. The weight of the camera against her chest helped her to feel more settled, not so anxious.

The sound of a cardinal lifted her spirits, and she wandered down the sidewalk between their house and the one next door to follow the sound. The sidewalk was overgrown with the banana trees. She stood under them, and a loud moan from across the street startled her, then a string of words that she couldn't understand.

A young man sat on the steps of the house across the street. He kept moving his hands in front of his face as though he was clearing off cobwebs. He moaned again and Dolores thought he must have the mind of a child like one of her cousins in Cocodrie.

Dolores walked closer to him and took some pictures. The milkman's cart turned the corner, and his horse clipped the street with a loud echo.

"Sorry to be so late, had to get a new shoe for Miss Alice here." The milkman opened a bottle and handed it to the man, who started smiling and stamping his feet. He turned to Dolores. "I don't know if his mama would want you to take his picture. Did you ask her?"

Dolores shook her head.

"But you can take one of me and Alice here."

She took his picture then picked up their milk and Earl's favorite, creole cream cheese, from the man and went back inside the house. The house was filled with smoke because she forgot to add water to the pot for the clothes. The pot was black. She decided to hang the bedclothes on the line to air instead of washing them, and then she would have time to get to the park to take pictures before she had to come home and cook dinner and take care of the black pot before Earl saw it.

When she was at the clothesline their neighbor came to the fence. "Going out again today?" she said to Dolores, pointing at the camera around her neck.

"Yes. I imagine so."

"Why don't you come have some coffee?" A little girl came up behind her and hid behind her skirts. "This is my little girl, Ida."

"Hello, Ida."

"Seems like you're gone all day, most times, with that camera. Like it's a job or something. After that baby, though, you'll be too busy for it, I imagine."

Dolores couldn't think of a response to her, so she went inside, made some lunch and left for the park. The people in Cocodrie had thought she was strange at first with the camera, but once they got used to it, they wanted their pictures taken, and they didn't say anything when they'd run into her with the camera.

The women in the park looked at her, too, like she was strange. One of them asked her if she was a newspaper reporter. Once she was there taking pictures under the big oaks and next to the islands of birds in the lagoons, she forgot all her worries. It seemed in those moments that the white feeling would never come back.

She went to the other side of the park close to the streetcars where she had seen a fountain with a statue. There were no children wading there and even the benches around it were empty. A plaque on the brick edge of the fountain said, *Meeting of Air and Water*. Although the statue above the water appeared to be floating in air, she was carved of metal. How could such grace be made of metal? She looked like a fairy or an angel.

Dolores lost track of time taking pictures of her until the Angelus sounded in the chapel across the street. Earl would be home waiting for her, upset. Dolores panicked. It was a long walk home, and by the time she got there, she felt sick and exhausted.

Earl was at the table with his head in his hands. He almost broke down in tears when he saw her. "I was worried. It's late."

"I'm sorry, I lost track. So many things to see."

"I know, I know." He made her a cup of tea and cooked a dinner of scrambled eggs and sausage. After dinner they walked around the block. Earl slept with his hands on her belly. Her thoughts swirled around the images on her film, imagining them in the darkroom. It was like that when she got started with something new. It stayed with her all the time she was awake and made it hard for her to sleep. If the darkroom had been set up, she would have left their bed and spent the night working on her pictures. Instead, she sat in the chair by the window looking out at the stars until she dozed.

# 20.

## TARPON IN LAKE PONTCHARTRAIN

SINCE HE'D MET AUDREY, EARL felt lighter, almost like he was weightless, instead of rooted to a wheelchair. A fog had lifted from his mind, and everything looked more clear, more alive. Old songs came into his head for no reason, and he sang along out loud.

"I didn't know you could carry a tune, old man. I could hear you all the way from my dock." Sam stood at the back door of the camp. "If I didn't know better, I'd guess that you got lucky in the past couple of days. I don't want to come in, I stink."

"All of us stink, boy, I'm not going to talk to you through the door." Earl was repairing a crab net near the windows while two fans in opposite corners of the room blew the warm air around. Working on crab nets always calmed him. "I may have to put on the air. You know that means it's hot."

Sam set a couple of bags onto the kitchen counter. "I completely forgot Elaine was here to do your shopping. I got all the usual stuff."

"Thank you, sir. Grab a beer. Sit down. She hasn't done it yet this week, so thank you. I appreciate it."

Sam put away the groceries and sat down with a Dixie beer. "I took a group out this morning. You won't believe what we saw."

"Yeah? What's that?" Earl adjusted the net in his lap, twisting the cord over the ring, under the ring, pull the knot tight.

"Tarpon. In the lake by the airport. Big ones." Sam looked towards the bathroom. Elaine shut the door and took the tiny hallway to her room with a towel over her head.

"There's no tarpon in this lake. You're crazy." Earl stopped weaving and sat back in his chair to rest.

"I found out the story. When they were building the lakefront airport, they dredged a big pit in the lake bottom to mine sand for fill during runway construction. Since then, they find big tarpons. There's a club now, Orleans Parish Tarpon Club."

"No kidding. I'll be damned. I'll believe it when I see it. Now I remember pulling a shark out of this lake once."

"Really, where?" Sam crossed a leg over his knee and gazed towards Elaine's room.

"The seawall. By the Seabrook. We hung it up in a tree and people kept stopping their cars and asking us where the hell it came from. I was young." Earl dropped the net into his lap. "Elaine, aren't you leaving yet?"

She came out in her yellow waitress uniform. "Yes, I'm leaving. So eager to see me go. What's up with that? Hey," she said to Sam. "I'm late."

Sam finished his beer and stood up. "Guess I'll go, too."

She picked up her purse and put her cup in the sink. "Why're you so grouchy?" She kissed Pappy on the forehead. "Have fun. See ya Sam."

"Wait. I'll walk you out. Bye, Earl."

Earl stayed at the front window to watch them. He wanted to make sure they were both gone since Audrey was going to show up any minute, but he was also curious how those two were getting along. It seemed like they were getting friendlier since the trip to Cocodrie.

They stood on top of the levee for a few minutes, deep in conversation it looked like to him. At one point Sam raised his hands in the air, then she laid her hand on his shoulder. Earl pulled up closer to the window. They sure could talk a lot. He was hoping Sam would do a little more than talk. Then Sam took her around the waist and pulled her close. The kiss wasn't real lengthy, but it looked like a good one.

"Thataboy, Sam. Nice going. Now get outta here."

As soon as they disappeared over the levee, Earl headed into the kitchen. He wanted Audrey to know he could cook, and he wanted to do something for her. They had visited four times, and he had not made any decent food for her. He grabbed the shrimp he had defrosted and peeled early that morning and poured oil into the heavy iron Dutch oven. The vegetables were out on the counter ready to be chopped for shrimp creole. It was a favorite of Audrey's. He got the roux started and added the onions and peppers, turned on the rice pot. The house soon began to heat up so he closed the back door and turned on the window air conditioner. The sailboats drifting in the distance were a sight he never tired of, that or the water that reflected dark blue in the sun.

He wasn't ready to let anyone else in on his sudden good fortune; he wanted to keep it close. It seemed like the most personal thing that had happened to him in a long time, not only personal, but special in a way that sharing would ruin it. It was too good to be true. Here he was 83, sick, without legs, and a beautiful and intelligent, funny woman wanted to spend time with him. What if she was doing it out of pity? How could she pretend so well to be interested in his stories, and then to be willing to share her own with him if she didn't at least think he was tolerable? He wasn't going to question it.

The rich smell of the vegetables and the roux filled the little camp. He was excited to be cooking for someone other than Elaine. He felt like a young man: no aches, no pains, no whisperings from his legs. All excitement and anticipation. The fear of disappointment, of failure, the things he remembered feeling so long ago, was that with Dolores? All the times he had tried to please her, to make her happy. The thought sent a slight wave of despair through him, but he brushed it off. It was like being given a new life, a prize on one of the daytime game shows. Don't screw it up, old man.

"Boy, it sure smells good in here." Audrey wore white creased pants and a light green flowered blouse. The room danced when she walked in.

"Sit, Audrey, lunch is almost done." The steam hit his face as he stirred.

"Well alright I will. I'll just set this pie over here on the counter. When I was a girl, my mother baked cakes. She worked at a baker's and baked cakes. I got so I hated those cakes. People would forget to pick them up, you know, or there were mistakes, and she always brought them home for us to eat. All colors of cake and icing. To this day I can't stand to eat cake. Pie is what I like to eat."

Earl shook his head back and forth slowly and made sympathetic sounds in the back of his throat. "I never cared as much for cake either, me. Too much sweet. Not enough substance. Here sit down at the table. I'll get some French bread."

"Let me do something."

"Okay, you can slice the bread and butter it." The shrimp sizzled when he tossed them in. "Did your mama live a long life then?"

"Smells good. You're a good cook, I can tell."

"Better taste it first."

Audrey spread butter thickly onto the slices of bread. "Mama had a hard life. She had me when she was real young and then Daddy died right away. Everyone in town were miners in Sack City, Kentucky. But it wasn't the mine killed him, it was his heart. Bad hearts ran in his family. His Daddy died of it too when he was young. Mama was left with us, and she was doing real good with the bakery and all, then she met a man. He was a monster. Oh, I hated him. The way he talked to her and pushed her around. We'd hide under the beds and fall asleep under there sometimes. They never came in to look. She started drinking because of him. Drinking and smoking. She was never the same."

"That's too bad. I'm sorry to hear that." Earl scooped the shrimp Creole into a serving bowl.

Earl set a bowl of Creole in front of Audrey and watched closely as she took her first bites.

"It's delicious. You are a good cook, you weren't lying."

She seemed to be telling the truth. He didn't think she was the type to tell tales.

"Earl, I was wondering this morning, what does Elaine do during the day, I mean besides the housework and so forth? She has a job?"

"She works at a restaurant at night, and she's starting a new job at a gallery in the French Quarter. I don't like her wandering around there much. But she always liked to wander around. Takes little notebooks, writes things down. Draws. Been doing that since she was a little thing. Once I looked at her notebook and it was full of lists. Names and phone numbers, street names, flower names, breeds of dogs. And drawings to go with the lists. She won awards in high school for her drawing."

"She spends a lot of time by herself then."

"I've been hoping that she gets back with my neighbor, Sam. They used to go together, before she married somebody else. Now she's divorced and going around with a married man who she went with in college. Well, her mother and I think so, anyway. Sleazy guy, even back then, before he was married when they went together. I didn't like him. I don't like the way she looks when she comes and goes after being with him. But what can I do? Charlotte, that's her mother, she's upset. Thinks Elaine has lost her way."

"Well, of course she is. She wants to see her daughter married and taken care of and having babies of her own. That's what mothers want. Charlotte has had a hard life. First, she lost you in a way. Then she lost her mama young. Then her own husband. She probably goes around waiting for the next shoe to drop."

Earl sat back in his chair. "I never thought of her as losing me. I mean she didn't lose me. She lost her mama. She struggled trying to take care of her mama like the rest of us, which was bad, but I was there. I didn't leave. She was close to me when she was a girl, then we drifted apart as she got older, and it seems like she's always fighting me about one thing or another."

"You didn't leave, but for a little girl, you were her knight in shining armor. You were the one making it all okay and safe. Even if her mama had problems; she depended on you and you were there. And you were still there after your accident, but now you were vulnerable too. She lost her mama then she lost the daddy she knew. When that drunk left my mama, I was so relieved, but I was mad at her. At least he was there to help us take care of things. Once he was gone, and she started to drink, I had to take care of her. It took me years not to be angry with her. Wasn't until I tried to raise my own children and take care of a husband, too, that I realized how hard life can be."

"You think Charlotte blames me for her mama's problems?"

"Well, I'm sure she doesn't know it, but it may be lurking there behind her eyes. Maybe you could try talking to her."

"Talking to her?"

"When was the last time you talked about her mama, or your accident or how it affected her?"

"Well, I…" Had they ever talked about it? Now that seemed impossible, but, no, he didn't think that they ever had. He didn't grow up in a family that believed in talking. Audrey stood up to reach over and adjust the collar of his shirt.

"There. You was tangled up back there."

She sat back in her chair. The lines of her face were soft and relaxed. Her arms rested on the arms of the chair, her long fingers dangling over the edge. If he didn't know better, he'd swear he felt a once familiar longing below his belly.

"We've never talked about it," he said.

"Well, that's not so unusual, but it's something to think about. Especially now when you and Charlotte both have Elaine to consider."

"Elaine?"

"How this affects her. What she can learn from it," said Audrey.

"How did you get to be so good at stuff like this?"

Audrey laughed. "Washing lots of dirty dishes and loads of laundry. Gives you plenty time to think."

They went outside to watch the sailboats come and go from the marina. It was always busy on Saturdays. He put his arm around her shoulders and pulled her close. He had always thought that inside he'd felt no different from when he was young, like he was the same person, just in an old body. But having these kinds of feelings again, he never in a million years expected it would happen.

Earl said, "This is quite a surprise, having a woman like you to put my arm around. Like tarpon in the lake. Who would have thought it?"

"Well, I certainly never thought I'd feel this again. A good man with his arms around me so I can let go, not worry about a thing. You are a good man, Earl, I hope you know that. You think I'd be here if you weren't?"

He pecked her cheek. "Well, I know it's not the sex and my good looks."

# 21.

## BITTER HOPE

THE COLD CRISP FEBRUARY AIR shook Earl awake. He lifted the box of darkroom equipment and groaned, not that it was so heavy, but since he started working in New Orleans, muscles he never knew he possessed ached every day. He would get used to it. He found work on one of Huey Long's state road projects. Every day he did the road work until mid-afternoon, then went to a construction site of the Hotel Dieu hospital where he apprenticed with a joiner in hopes that he could move into that work instead of the hard labor of highway construction.

He opened the door to the shed as a blue heron passed above him, the wingspan so wide that the bird seemed to be flying in slow motion. Earl felt a pang of longing for home. It was a Sunday, too, such a nice day in Cocodrie, a little extra to eat, and the luxury of a nap after lunch, or a game of cards on the back porch.

He set the box on a wooden shelf he'd built and stopped to sit down, rubbing the back of his neck and forehead. Dolores had become withdrawn since she got pregnant. He had waited on this darkroom hoping that the pregnancy would make her content like he'd heard it did with some women. It was a foolhardy hope. Dolores was nothing like other women, that became clearer every day. She had good days where he felt she was really with him, especially after she took pictures the day before. Excited and full of energy. That might last a few days, then the opposite mood took over, and she couldn't get out of bed.

The contents of the box had not suffered from the move. Everything he remembered from the old darkroom seemed to be there. He laid it all out on the counter and checked to see if the water was running and the light functioning. Maybe the darkroom was what she needed.

He stepped out for a smoke in the sunshine and a neighbor appeared at the fence. "Looks like you got yourself a biscuit in the oven, hey Earl?"

It took Earl a few minutes to figure out what he meant by the remark. "Yeah, that's true. Coming in a few months."

The man's wife came out and said, "She'll have to stop taking those pictures after that, I imagine." She tossed a pan of water into the bushes. "She feeling well, your wife?" The woman hustled up to the fence. "I don't see her out hanging her clothes lately. Although I do see her leave in the morning with that camera. I thought, you know, maybe she's going to the doctor or something, till I saw that camera. Now is that her job, taking pictures?"

"Yep, baby's due in two months. We're very excited." Earl pushed his cigarette out on the bench and stood up.

"Must be nice to have so much free time, go off on her own like that, like somebody in New York or something." The woman dried her pail with a cotton sack.

The man said, "Dorothy, get in the house. Good day to you, Earl."

Dolores was off at that moment, somewhere with her camera, alone. In Cocodrie, she'd done that every day; people thought she was strange, but she was Dolores and they loved her. Earl hadn't thought about how she might be looked on by people in the city, a woman alone wandering around with a camera. He was so busy working, cooking at night, cleaning up, and even going to the market sometimes.

He waited with his newspaper for her on the front stoop. Her figure appeared a block away, he could tell by her straw hat, walking with careful steps, gazing around her, always.

Her smile captured him the way it always had, maybe because it wasn't offered easily, and the lecture he was about to give went away with the breeze. Her cheeks were pink from the sun. She looked thin, but healthy, the baby only a small bulge below the camera.

"You had a good day, Didi?"

He had put on some rice, and they worked on supper together, her chopping onions and peppers while he fried the meat. "There were children in the park," she chopped the onions slowly into tiny bits, "children with problems. Their arms were short, or they had a leg brace, other things, but they were beautiful. Those things made them more beautiful."

Her dark hair fell around her flushed face. She kept pushing it away with the back of her hand. Her voice was quiet and rushed, as though it took some effort to get the words out, but with excitement behind them.

He told her about a man he'd met at work, with five children, who worked three jobs. He told her that a long piece of metal fell from the second floor of the building, but no one was hurt. "The noise was something." He told her he saw a pair of blue eggs in a tiny nest inside the crook of a crepe myrtle, and four kittens sleeping on a pile of newspapers.

She told him that he should have a camera and take pictures, too, because of all the things he noticed.

"It's you makes me notice. I see the way you notice, and then I do, too."

Their walk after supper was short. When she had her good days, Earl began to hope each time that they would last forever. It was easy to forgive the times she came home late or had no supper ready because of the darkroom. He believed she would grow out of the homesickness, or sadness or whatever it was made her go away into herself. When the bad days came back, and she had trouble even getting up in the morning, he worried all the time, was afraid to go to work, and started to think about moving back to Cocodrie. If his sister Grace ever left New Orleans or couldn't help them anymore, he'd have to go back. Sometimes he wished he'd never taken her away.

# 22.

## BELLOCQ

"E.J. Bellocq was born in the French Quarter in 1873. He was known as a dandy in his youth, but as he grew older, he became more of a recluse. He's best known for not his commercial, but his personal photographs of the hidden side of local life, notably the opium dens in Chinatown and the prostitutes of Storyville."

The guide had an annoying nasally voice that Elaine found distracting. He also displayed a total lack of interest in anything on the tour. The girls in the photographs looked young enough to be in grade school. That was disconcerting enough, but the make-up and poses added to the exploitive feeling. Elaine couldn't help being drawn in by the melancholy mood of the pictures, the Spartan furnishings of the rooms, and the broken atmosphere with cracks on the walls, the mirrors and the ceramic washbowls. It was as though the fissures were intentionally placed to imply the brokenness of the subjects. She knew not to judge sex work as something morally wrong, but these girls looked like kids.

"Why are some of them masked?" a woman asked.

"No particular reason," said the guide, "perhaps to hide their identities."

He continued, "Many of the negatives, as you can see, were badly damaged. This caused much speculation. It looks as though they were damaged deliberately. You can see some of the faces have been scraped out. There is a suggestion that the destruction may have been done by Bellocq himself since some of the damage took place while the emulsion was still wet. Now if you'll follow me."

Rain drummed on the roof of the building. The cloud cover added shadow to rooms already dimmed to protect old photographs. Elaine felt sickened by the scratched-out eyes and moved on to the next room and an exhibit of early glass plate photography. She had always loved the glass plate photos from the late 1800s, they were so heavy with the past.

The room stayed quiet except for a few single individuals; the group seemed to have moved on to another part of the museum, so she was able to spend as much time as she wanted with each picture. Sally Mann's photos were mixed in with Atget and Greene and Le Gray. Most of her photos were shot with an antique view camera from the early 1900s—she had to duck under a dark cloth to take the pictures. The camera had a hulking wooden frame, accordion-like bellows and a long brass lens. Elaine always imagined the bellows opening with a creaking sound and a puff of mildewy powder.

Elaine read the exhibit information about how Mann had learned how to use the complicated glass plate process and set up scenes of the aftermath of Civil War battles near her home in Virginia. The glass plate is coated with a substance called collodion, which is susceptible to scratches and damages, then dipped into silver salts and loaded into the camera. The process is so fast that the plates have to be processed immediately, so she carried a darkroom in her car. She used damaged and uncoated lenses which created flares and distortions.

Elaine found the melancholy effects startling, especially in the archaic landscapes illumined by eerie, distorted light. Hiding inside southern bayous, swamps and fields were glimpses of shadowy figures, ghosts of soldiers in the abandoned battlefields, or hints of their presence.

One of the images in the exhibit was titled, "Battlefield, Chancellorsville (Rever's Bend)." It had a curved path winding through thick black masses of trees identifiable only by their collective shape against the gray grainy sky. The darkness of the image is offset by a luminous horizon in the direction that the path is leading. There was a quote from her with the photo: "This one picture offers a way out of the gloom, as if around that bend there might be some forgiveness or some peace or some way towards redemption and understanding. Despite the dark edges and the glowering sky, there's a numinous glow just around the corner."

The picture was intriguing, and moving, in light of the quotation, and Elaine felt the same longing she'd had in her talk with Alexander to create something moving and beautiful herself. She could not help thinking about Arnie's senseless death—mentioned in the back page of the Metro section that week—and that the gloom of the Civil War battlefield was present in 20th century America. Yet this picture was optimistic, and that aspect of it stuck with her, not about the Arnies of the world, but about the persistent lifeforce—even in the midst of something as gruesome as that war.

A speaker announced that the museum was about to close, so she headed to the store to buy the book of the exhibit. There was one more compelling photo by an unknown local artist who had experimented in the 1920s with damaged negatives. The results were similar to the collodion process in the other room. The distorted image of a female figure had a tragic quality, blurred and hazy, with only the upturned face and hands illuminated. The entire picture was covered with flecks of light, a night sky filled with tiny sparks, like the one she remembered by Sally Mann, except this was not one of hers. It reminded her of the feux follets Pappy talked about, the lights in the woods.

A warm rain hit her face at the front exit, and she was irritated with how far away she had parked. She headed down the main sidewalk, and of course the rain got harder. A van idled at the curb next to the lagoon. Peter sat in the driver's seat facing her way. She had successfully managed to avoid him at work the past couple of weeks since she saw him outside the café with Sam. Either he hadn't shown up when she was working, or she hid from him with the help of Leroy and Alexander.

Peter opened the car door and gestured to her to come over. "Get out of the rain."

"What are you doing here?" she asked him.

"Hey, beautiful. How are you?" His windblown blonde hair had grown out over the edge of his suit collar. His eyes looked like he was using something, and he was agitated. "I had a meeting here. A late luncheon type thing. I saw your car, so I waited."

"I'm beginning to think you're stalking me," she tried to protect her new book from the rain and held it close to her chest.

"Come in out of the rain. Maybe I followed you. Maybe I had a meeting. What difference does it make? I'm here. Get in. I can take you to your car."

She climbed in. "Okay, my car is behind the building a couple of blocks towards the tennis courts."

He started the car, and they went deeper into the park. "Did you enjoy the photographs of jailbait in there? Bellocq?"

"Jailbait?" She wiped her wet face with her hands. "What a disgusting way to look at it."

"That's what we'd call it nowadays." He parked near the carousel which was closed for repairs and surrounded by wooden barriers.

Elaine had loved the carousel as a kid, and even in high school they'd hang out there, but abandoned and dismantled, it looked depressing and even scary. The animals and figures seemed grotesque.

"My car is over by the tennis courts. Opposite direction."

"Let's have a drink first." He took a flask out from under the seat, drank some and offered it to her.

"Peter, please, just bring me to my car." She tried to open her door, but it was locked. "Can you unlock the door?"

He unbuckled his seatbelt and made a lunge towards her, grabbing her around the shoulders trying to kiss her. His mouth came down hard on hers, and she pushed on his chest, struggling against the tight seatbelt. She finally hit him on the side of his face with the heavy book.

He heaved over into his seat. "Jesus, Elaine. What the fuck?"

"Yeah. What the fuck?"

"I'm sorry. I thought you were still into this. You used to like our little car escapades. Look we can go to a motel next time. I want to make things up to you. I realize I didn't treat you very well." He rubbed his face where she'd hit him. It was turning red, and a small cut opened on his cheek. He brought the flask to his lips again.

"Listen, if you want to do something nice for me bring me to my car, but also check into this. There was a shooting at the store across the street from our camp, and a young kid was killed. A kid I knew that I saw all the time. He was so sweet; he always had a big smile. He was getting ready to go to college. He was shot. It was a robbery."

"Yeah, that's too bad. You know these kids get mixed up in all kinds of shit and shoot each other. That's the way they are, nothing you or me can do to change that. They're making this city a total war zone." He lit a cigarette and took a long drink.

"What? But that's exactly what you're supposed to do. Change things. Change the process. Justice not brutality. Work against the stereotypes you seem to subscribe to. Jesus, you're not the guy I knew a few years ago. Working for the Southern Poverty Law Center in Alabama. Doing gang mediation." She tried the door again. The rain came down harder, and a pile of construction debris flew around in the wind.

"Youthful idealism. Nothing more. You're living in a fantasy world. You always have been."

He started the car, jerked it into reverse and drove towards the tennis courts stopping behind her car. "I guess you've taken up with that peasant fisherman. Good luck with that."

She shivered inside her car as the rain washed across the tennis courts, and the street began to flood. What had prompted her to ever get involved with Peter Melancon again? She must be crazy, and now it would haunt her. Well, maybe not, but it did almost ruin her visit to the museum.

The book kept her company while she waited for the rain to let up. She went back to the old glass plate pictures and realized they brought back the same sensation that often came up since she'd returned to New Orleans—being pulled back in time, as though the ground held thoughts and memories of people long dead. She'd never felt that anywhere else.

# 23.

## FRENCH QUARTER

*Dolores:*

*It was nice to hear from you. I'm happy you have moved to New Orleans. I will include directions to my studio on Chartres Street. You can get off the streetcar at Canal Street and walk the rest of the way. My wife would love to meet you also.*

*-A. Dozier*

EARL DID NOT WANT ME to do this trip alone. We have only been here a few months. We took this trip together first on one Sunday after church. He rode with me downtown. We walked along the river. He said no camera that day, but I came back a different day with my camera. Then Mr. Dozier invited me to meet him, and I went back alone again. Earl leaves very early for work, and this time I did not tell him I would go. I know he worries about me all the time, and he doesn't like me roaming the streets with my camera. He says that women should not do that.

The streetcar on St. Charles is painted red, dark green and brown. I can't describe the sound it makes. Squeaks and rattles and moans then when it stops it shakes as though it will explode. Castles line the big avenue on the way to the French Quarter. Fairy tale castles with turrets and balconies, red and green roofs, and fancy gardens with sculptures.

The ladies on the streetcars dress up in narrow skirts and leather shoes. They stand holding onto the straps unless a gentleman offers the seat. The ladies on the block where we live, they seem more like Marie and the other women, with big skirts and aprons, outside in the gardens, or hanging clothes.

My streetcar stopped at Canal Street, the biggest street I've ever seen. It runs into the river and is wide with more streetcars running back and forth in the middle of it. Automobiles and delivery vans, carriages, more streetcars, and more and more people. I climbed the river levee to get away from the noise and took careful pictures of the ferry crossing the river, and the ships at the docks. Ships lined up at the dock, and men squirmed to carry boxes and crates down ramps onto trucks. Black men were climbing up and down the ramps carrying bananas and sacks of things I could not recognize. There are faces and faces, in doorways, on the curbs, men playing music, black women with white babies, old men smoking, beautiful ladies with white gloves, artists drawing and painting next to the iron gate that surrounds a big church.

I had to watch how many pictures I can take because it costs money for film and paper.

Along the river I found the market that goes for blocks and blocks with people selling vegetables and meats, all sorts of food, kitchen things, expensive coffee beans and China tea. There were chickens and doves in cages, and the smell of fish mixed with the smell of the coffee beans. All noise and color.

I followed Mr. Dozier's directions away from the market, and the streets became quiet. The buildings there are very old, made of red bricks and black iron railings on balconies. There were fancy ladies sitting in the park with umbrellas and children in pushcarts. I passed by important looking men standing with cigars in doorways talking together. I took picture after picture, too many. It seems that there are stories behind every face and doorway. No one seems to mind me looking at them. I think they like the attention like people did in Cocodrie. An old woman was hunched over a baby carriage carting a dog the size of a baby's toy. There were flowers around the dog. Two men played cards at a wood bench outside a bar, and they spoke in a different language and wore turbans and colored scarves.

I stopped at the square where the cathedral stands and spent a long time there watching the artists. Earl rushed by them when we were here. They have portraits and landscapes hanging on the fence and a few of them were painting alone, but others had people sitting for drawings. There was even a woman painting, a beautiful woman with brown skin. I wanted to stop, but I was afraid to be late, so I turned onto Chartres Street, and there was the sign, "Bottom of the Cup Tearoom, Psychic Readings and Tarot Cards." In the window of his shop next door was a smaller sign, "Dozier's Photography."

The pictures on the walls of his studio were of weddings and families, babies and portraits of old couples or men in suits. Two of the photos were from Cocodrie, one was of the old man cypress tree that hangs over the water, the other of the fais-do-do where everyone is eating crabs and oysters. He showed me the room where he works and the darkroom in the back. We had tea with his wife who is big with a baby. He gave me some ideas when he looked at my photos.

He wanted to give me some film, even though Earl likes me to pay him. Then he pointed me down the street to a place where they have photographs and paintings on the walls.

I left Mr. Dozier feeling excited and tired out, but I could not help lingering at all the shop windows selling gloves and hats, or flowers or dresses. The door to the gallery was open, and a man sat at a counter. He told me to come in and look around, then went right back to his newspaper.

I went through one time, then again stopping longer at each picture, then another time, stopping even longer. The man looked up from his newspaper more than once and said if I needed help to ask him. I was afraid he was getting angry with me, but I could not stop looking. I had never seen pictures like these even in magazines. They were old, from before Papa was born, when they only had glass plates. A woman took some of them, Julia Cameron was her name. A woman photographer showing her pictures in a gallery.

Another one was of a young woman half dressed in an upstairs room with a view of a balcony like the ones in the French Quarter. I didn't like that her eyes were scratched out. The ones I could not stop looking at were very much not perfect. They had shadows and smoke and patches of too bright light. Not perfect, but beautiful and filled with feeling. I asked him how they did that, and he said they were mistakes, damaged in the darkroom or the plates.

He said he would be closing soon, did I want to buy something, and I remember that Mr. Dozier said I should show him my pictures. He laughed when I asked him but agreed. He seemed surprised, but then he looked and looked, and I got worried because I noticed the shadows outside on the sidewalk. It was getting late, and Earl would be upset. The man took the one of the statue at the park that is called *The Meeting of Air and Water*. He said if anyone bought it, he would send me the money.

It was dark when I got home, and Earl seemed ready to cry, but he listened, and I told him everything that I saw that day. He is the only one I can talk to.

# 24.

## RALLY

ELAINE HAD GONE FOR A run along the levee and was standing at the stairway to the camp stretching and trying to cool down in air that was anything but cool. The harsh light and suffocating heat were keeping people inside their air conditioned spaces. Over the lake, towards the Gulf, mountains of clouds rose, like rooms in a terraced garden. The clouds seemed overwhelmed with rain, yet lately they would push off in the early afternoon and offer no respite from the heat.

The convenience store was quiet with only a couple of guys smoking out front. An eerie calm had settled over the area in the three weeks since Arnie's shooting. Arnie's death was tragic in so many ways, but after three weeks the uproar over the injustice had already begun to die down, so the neighbors decided to have a rally to support Arnie's family and raise people's awareness in the city of the violence in East New Orleans. People were already starting to set up chairs outside the Tight Spot where the rally would take place.

She showered and dressed and took her camera outside for some shots of the street and the ruins of the camps on the lake as she made her way down to the rally. By the time she got there, grills had been set up with chicken and sausage starting to sizzle. People were gathering, and Fats Domino blasted out of the juke box.

"This is quite an event," she said to a wiry old man that looked familiar. So many people in New Orleans looked familiar to her.

"We decided we're not gonna let police come in here killing and escalating the violence. We gotta assert ourselves here, establish a presence? You're Earl's girl, right? I remember you."

Elaine shook his hand. "Yeah. I'm Elaine. You're Mr. Edgar, right?"

"That's right. Yeah, we invited the city councilman, Alvin Tousley, and somebody from the DA's office. We'll see if they show up." He stood up and offered her the wooden stool he'd been sitting on. "Here you sit."

"No that's okay. I'm going inside. What do you mean establish a presence exactly? You mean like this rally?"

"To start with, yes, community gatherings. But maybe we start policing a bit ourselves. Stop things before they start, that kind of thing. It's been successful in other cities. We're talking about that."

"That's interesting. You mean like Neighborhood Watch?"

"Something like that. Ida's keeping track of meetings, you just check with her. We gonna have a festival soon, live music and food on the street, you know? Get folks out."

"The city people haven't showed up, hunh?" Cool air hit her legs from the dim interior of the bar.

"Yeah, you know them guys, not enough media to make this have any sex appeal. I know your grandpa real well. He's doing alright?" He sat back down and wiped the sweat off his forehead with a red bandana.

"He's doing fine, went fishing just this morning." She looked around at the crowd with the passing thought that Peter might be the city's representative coming to the event. He acted so weird at the museum, she wondered if he was following her around.

"Alright, that's good."

"Is it okay if I take your photo?" she asked Edgar.

"Sure, sure."

Elaine took a few shots of the outside, then went into the dark coolness of the bar. Before she had settled onto a wobbly barstool a glass of beer landed in front of her. "Hey sweetie, how ya' doin'?" Ida's face was flush, and she wore a big smile.

Elaine admired people like Ida who showed the signs of some wear and tear in life, a redness and sadness in the eyes, but who had smiles for everybody. Ida always made Elaine feel like she was being hugged when she saw her.

Elaine said, "Fine. You? You're a sight for sore eyes yourself."

"Hah! That's not what the old man says. What ya think of all that outside? It's different, hunh?"

"Yeah. I bet it was your idea to invite somebody from the city, wasn't it?"

"They need to see for themselves, come into the neighborhoods. I'm tired of feeling like we fell off the face of the earth. What you gonna eat today?"

Elaine said, "Oysters. Butter and lettuce. And can you…"

"I know, you like the little devils well done. Gotcha. How's Grandpa?" The cook sidled up next to Ida at the bar, sweat pouring off his forehead, and reached under the bar for the Coke dispenser. Ida gave him the order. "Half a oyster loaf, well, butter and lettuce."

"He seems good, better mood than normal. He mentioned a visitor. I think he's happy, but he hasn't given me any details. Did you send somebody over?" Elaine set her glass down on the coaster.

Ida smiled and wiped her face. "I don't want to divulge anything I shouldn't. He'll tell you when he's ready. That's all I'm gonna say. And it's all good, nothing you oughta be afraid of." Ida took a long drag from an extra lengthy cigarette and pulled it out to reveal a large red lipstick ring on the filter. "How's your mama? Y'all getting along okay?"

"I guess so. She's always after me to go back to school. And she gets all mysterious when I ask her about my grandma."

"Maybe there's memories she doesn't want to revisit. You know, there's always things in a life that are hard to remember. Like me and my Joey." Ida took another drag of her cigarette. Her voice wavered. "I mean it's been, well, I guess it's been sixty years now. My little brother, died in the hospital. Meningitis. He was just a baby, two years old, and he died all alone. At Charity. They wouldn't let none of us in to visit him. Maybe because we were poor, I don't know. I cry every time I think of that baby alone in that place."

"God, that's awful. I'm sorry." After sixty years the memory was fresh enough to bring tears.

Ida reached up to her eyes with a clean corner of her apron.

"You knew her, didn't you? My grandma?" Elaine remembered that Pappy met Ida when he was first married. They'd been neighbors at some point.

"They lived next door. I was a little girl when your mama was born. They had a nice yard. Your grandpa kept it real nice. She had long hair, Dolores, long and dark, wavy at the ends. She was peculiar. Moody and always with that camera." She paused and took a drink of water. "After she died, my mama helped, you know, took your mama sometimes. I got to know Charlotte; she was very quiet. Then after your grandpa moved out to this camp, I didn't see them much until we opened this place. Then he'd bring you over sometimes. You were a pretty little thing."

"Was Dolores sick for a long time before she died?"

"Sick?" Ida wrinkled her eyebrows together and tilted her head like she didn't understand the question. Then she looked up, and Elaine felt someone standing next to her.

"You must be Ida. I'm Peter Melancon." He reached his hand over the bar. "The DA's office sent me over here. We are concerned about the crime in this area. We're going to do everything we can to prosecute someone for that shooting." He gave Ida his fake smile. "May I have a shot of bourbon, please, and a Dixie draft. And bring another of whatever this lady is having."

Elaine felt her body stiffen. "I have to go, Ida. I'm sorry. Can you make my sandwich to go?"

Peter put his arm around her. "Not leaving already? Have a drink with me, Elaine?"

His eyes were already red rimmed and swimmy, and they had a vacant look at the same time. Maybe he was stoned and drunk. Elaine stood up and tried to move away from him, but there was somebody sitting on the stool next to her, and people had crowded around the bar.

"You two know each other?" Ida set the drinks in front of them.

"Elaine and I are old friends. We went to school together."

"We appreciate you coming, Mr. Melancon." More customers came up to the bar, and Ida left to take care of them. "I'll be right back."

"I was hoping to see you, Elaine. I've missed you. I wanted to apologize for the other day. I was out of line. You're not at the café when I stop by lately, or else you manage to avoid me. We can still be friends."

He was leaning in close and gripping her arm. "I don't think so, Peter."

"Oh, come on, Elaine, we had a lot of fun together." Peter downed his bourbon and signaled to Ida for another one. He closed his fingers firmly around her forearm again and put his lips to her ear to whisper. "I'll make it up to you. I promise."

Elaine pulled her arm out of his grip and backed away from the bar into some people. Sam was making his way towards her from the door. He was smiling until he noticed Peter.

Peter said, "Sam, nice to see you again. Can I buy you a beer?" He motioned to Ida with his empty shot glass.

Ida filled Peter's glass. "Sam, I was about to tell Mr. Melancon about the shooting. He's from the DA's office."

Sam stepped in next to Elaine, forcing Peter to move over. "I know who he is."

Elaine sat back down on the barstool, relieved to have Sam's body between hers and Peter's.

Peter said, "Well, seems like we have a party here." He downed the second shot and held up the glass to Ida. "The incident is being fully investigated. I want everyone to know that. The perpetrators are still at large."

Ida put a beer down in front of Sam and gave Elaine a to-go bag. "We all knew the boy. Knew his mother. She works at the dry cleaners, worked there for twenty years. We heard that what really happened is he tried to stop something going on, some kids causing trouble, and when the police got there, they were quick to pull out their guns."

"You understand I can't say much about an open investigation." Peter propped himself up on the bar. "However, there may have been some crossfire that he became involved in. Not a deliberate shooting."

A few patrons stepped up behind Peter. They were people who lived in the neighborhood, Sam acknowledged a couple of them, an older man, two young women including the one she ran into the day Arnie was shot, and three middle-aged women. Elaine was happy to see it was a mixed crowd with as many black neighbors as white ones. That was not common, in her experience.

One of the women said, "You know as well as me, you're not going to find the ones who tried to rob the place. The problem is we need some presence here, not police running around with guns. More than that. Community centers for these kids. Jobs. Job training."

The others spoke up in agreement.

"Sounds like y'all don't have much faith in our criminal justice system. Again, there's a full investigation going on. If we find that any impropriety took place, we'll get to the bottom of it. I'll make a note about your ideas, the community center and so on."

The music got louder–Dr. John, "Right Place, Wrong Time"–and some cheering started outside. The group continued trying to engage

Peter, but they got distracted when the city councilman showed up and went to talk to him instead.

"I really need to go." Elaine said.

"Stay, Elaine. Have another beer with us. You work around here, Sam? What do you do?"

"Fishing tours." Sam lit a cigarette. "Elaine let's go sit at a booth."

"Ah. A fisherman. Nice. Like to fish myself. Very relaxing. Good profession. Is this why I haven't seen you in a while, Elaine? This fisherman?" He put his hand on her arm.

Sam gripped Peter's wrist, and Peter lost his balance swaying onto the man sitting next to them.

"Sorry, sorry." Peter waved apologetic hands to the man and reached into his pants pocket. He laid some bills on the counter. "I need to go talk to these folks outside."

Peter weaved toward Elaine again and leaned over like he was going to kiss her cheek. Sam took a step forward, and Peter stepped back, lost his footing, and fell. Elaine even felt embarrassed for him.

A couple of guys helped him to his feet and headed towards the door. "Let's get you some air."

"Yeah, yeah. Okay. Wait a minute." Peter turned to face Sam. "Don't let her go, Sam. I should have tried harder to keep her. She's worth the trouble." He held Elaine's gaze for a few seconds then pulled his arms away from the guys on either side of him. "I'm going, I'm going."

He stumbled once on his way to the door but seemed to recover right away and started shaking hands as soon as he reached the outside crowd. Elaine sighed. She put her elbows on the bar and dropped her head into her hands.

"Well, at least he appreciates you. I'll give him that." Sam put his arm around her. "Are you okay?"

Elaine nodded. "I feel sorry for him now. I've known him for a long time. I hope he gets his shit together."

Sam said, "If he keeps making an ass of himself like that, I don't think his campaign will go well."

Elaine hadn't seen Sam since their kiss on the levee, and she felt sick that he had to see her with Peter pawing at her like that. "That was icky."

"Yeah, I'll say."

"He's acting weird. He's never been this bad." She told him about what happened outside the museum. "I hope this is the end of it."

"He still comes by the café?"

"I manage to avoid him. But I think I'm going to quit. Alexander wants to give me more hours at the gallery."

Ida set two more Dixies in front of them. "Well thanks for getting rid of that guy, Sam. What a worthless pile of doo-doo that one is."

Elaine said, "He told me that hoping for change was youthful idealism and 'these people' will keep killing each other for nickels. So, he's a drunk and a racist and a hypocrite."

"And a prosecutor. Nice combo." Ida slid some peanuts their way and left.

Sam's food came, Elaine took hers out again, and they ate for a few minutes without talking. Most of the crowd was moving outside. Through the door Elaine could see a sax and upright bass setting up to play.

Sam set down his po-boy. "Listen, about the other day. On the levee. I don't want to rush you. I'll give you some space, okay? No pressure."

"I don't feel rushed, Sam, it's just that are you sure you want to take a chance on me? I mean after I left you high and dry last time? And you've seen what a mess I've been since I got back. I guess I'm not sure why you would keep trying."

"You heard what the man said, she's worth the trouble. You sell yourself short. And me. I know you're worth the trouble, and I trust that." A cheer went up outside from the crowd. Sam took a drink. "I just don't want to push you. So, you're warning me off then?"

"I don't know. Maybe. Rebound and all that. But the first time, when I left here, it wasn't about you. I just wasn't ready, and you were so eager to settle down. I had to get away from New Orleans, from Mama. Then I met Ethan, and it seemed like the right thing to do. But he was all surface, and I don't want all surface anymore. I want real. Like you."

"So, you're not warning me off?" He smiled behind his bottle of beer. "I'm a little confused."

"I mean, you live from your heart, you know? Miss Pearl said I need to live from my heart."

"Sounds like a wise woman. But it's also wise to take our time, agreed?"

They clinked glasses, and he leaned over to kiss her.

The kiss lasted long enough for Elaine to feel the rush through her body. "Well, that's not going to help us take our time, is it?"

# 25.

## SARA

A WOMAN STOPPED ON THE STREET to talk to me when I sat on the stoop in the morning sun softened by the early clouds. Her face was so bright and happy, but with dark, still eyes. Words followed her dancing hands. She had a beautiful heart, I could tell, and we both had growing bellies.

She asked why I take pictures, and I said that the camera makes me forget I am there. It's like I am hidden, and the world happens through it in front of me. It becomes something apart from me, a living thing, seeing in its own way, things I do not see.

We had tea almost every day, and she let me take picture after picture of her. I used different lenses and light, and in the darkroom, I did things to make effects with her arms and hands, her eyes and neck. One day she was so happy that she took my hands and danced with me in the backyard under the oak trees. She said that we were dancing with our babies; she was so happy about her baby. But the neighbor came out and we ran back inside laughing.

We used to pull up our bodices to see each other's bellies. Hers was dark brown with the navel up, mine so pale next to hers. I told her that I tell the baby to stay in there longer, that I need more time, and she laughed at me. She couldn't wait for hers to come, to make her man happier with her, she hoped. To make her happy, too. "I want something to love, Dolores, something that loves me more than anything in the whole entire world. Something that's all mine."

From the change in her face when she spoke of him, her man was not good like Earl. He sounded stern and mean. Her house needed to be just so, and the food just so, and her clothes just so. And it pained me because I had never known anyone so happy and free, except when she thought of him. She didn't want him to know we were friends. I had never had a friend like her, except for Earl.

She showed me where her house was, but we had to meet at our house in case he would find out. She said for me not to stop there, or go by, that people helped him to watch her. But at least when I saw it, I could imagine it at night when she is there asleep. The neighbors might tell her man that she has a friend, and he would not like it, so she comes to me. One evening before she left, she kissed me on the lips. She had a light heart and dark skin, and I have a dark heart and light skin. We were opposite sisters, but the same.

We took the streetcar to the big park one day to feed the ducks. We walked arm in arm and people stared at us, maybe because she was black, and I am white. We lay on a blanket near the lagoon and ate bread and cold fried shrimp.

She said, "You are so strange, Dolores, I talk and talk and you smile and take my picture. But you don't talk."

Sara went on to tell me about her ten brothers and sisters who lived in a little town upriver. How she met her man one night at the diner where she worked before the baby. He worked offshore on oil rigs, and she never knew when he was coming home so she had to make food for him and keep the house clean. We lay on the ground with our bellies pointing to the sky and counted the leaves above our heads.

She said, "Trees are like you, quiet and still, and they watch and listen deeply, like you do."

I told her all about Maman and the feux follets. She laughed about the lights in the woods. "There's no spirits out there. That's your imagination. My mama told me about those lights too, but she said they were the devil's temptation. They call to you from the darkness, made of light to trap you; you go close, and they pull you in. She said they call you to do bad things, take you away from your children and from what you're supposed to do, take care of your husband and your children."

One afternoon in the darkroom I found the feux follets in the dancing pictures of Sara. They looked like sparkles on the paper, and Earl said that something happened to the negative or maybe my lens is damaged like that picture at the gallery downtown. But if my lens was damaged, the feux follets would be in all my pictures, not just the ones of Sara. I liked the little sparks and the bright patches that appeared and could not wait to show her.

But five days went by, and Sara did not come. I thought maybe her time was there for the baby. I had to hold myself back because of her man and her neighbors, so I would wait on the stoop after Earl left for work. One evening I was so upset that Earl agreed to walk down there with me to her house. We took an umbrella because there was a cold rain. I found the house on Octavia Street, the blue house. The rain stopped, and a woman come out to sweep next to the blue house, but Earl and I stayed across the street. The evening paper delivery boy on his bicycle passed us. The woman with the broom looked at us then she went inside, and we crossed the street.

Earl said, "The house looks empty. Are you sure it's the right one?"

We went up the walk that ran alongside the shotgun house. It was overgrown with banana trees taller than us. We stood and looked in the windows. The house was abandoned. The first room had an old couch, the second a bed with a bare mattress, and in the kitchen a wood table and two chairs, and a two-burner gas stove. There were no signs of life, and papers and trash had collected in the corners. On the wall, the only thing left in the front room, was a photograph of Sara that I gave her a few weeks earlier.

The baby started to pain me, moving, and kicking, maybe because I was upset and cold from the rain, shivering and crying. Earl put his arm around me, and at home he fixed soup and covered me with blankets. I felt empty, like when the white feeling comes, and there is nothing left for me in the world.

———◆———

Earl came home from work the following week to find the dishes undone, the bed not made, and chicken on the stove in the skillet half cooked. The weather had been cold and windy, with icy rain showers. He had never felt such a pain in his throat. He reached for his handkerchief, wiped his eyes and nose, and called her name. When she didn't answer he went out to the darkroom.

Cold rain splattered his face on his way to the shed. When he saw the closed door, an angry fist formed in his chest. She spent all her time in that room with the door closed, shutting him out, shutting the world out. He had not married her so that she would hide herself away in the backyard, forgetting all about him all day, not even noticing if he got home.

He pushed open the door, knowing that even the late afternoon light could ruin anything she was doing. "Dolores! It's supper time, I am tired and hungry, the food is cold sitting out on the stove, and the house is a mess!" The smell of chemicals filled the little shed.

She turned around and dropped the soaking pan. "Close the door."

"I'm not having my wife traipsing around all day taking pictures then spending all her time alone in this dark closet. Damn it, Dolores. Now get back in the house. This can wait until tomorrow." Earl sneezed and wiped his nose with the bandana that he wore around his neck for work.

He realized that he had never used that tone with her before, and he regretted it as soon as he saw her face. She had been even more withdrawn since her friend disappeared without a word, and he knew she missed her.

He dropped into a chair by the door. "Didi, I'm sick and I'm tired, I need something to eat, and I need to see my wife. Please come inside now." He held out a hand to her. She came over to him and stood with her arms at her sides like she was afraid to touch him.

Affection had never come easy to her, but he had thought that over time she would get better. It didn't come easy for her to comfort anyone or take care of anything. When he looked back, he recalled that he had never known her to have a pet like other girls, a kitten or a dog. It made him worry about the baby, but he had heard that taking care of babies came natural to women, so he thought she would learn in time.

Earl finished making the dinner. The wind whipped through the cracks in the house. "I know you're sad that your friend is gone, but you go out all the time with that camera, or you're in the darkroom. The house is dirty, dinner is not ready when I come home, and you rush off to that darkroom all hours. I want a wife to make a home for me while I'm gone all day. To be here when I'm home."

Her face was flushed, and her eyes seemed almost frightened which he could not bear.

He went on. "I want you to be happy, I'm sorry I talked to you that way. It's just, I'm working so hard, for you, for us, and I need some help."

She picked at her food, lifting her eyes off the plate and down again. "I'll do better."

After that evening, she was home more often at suppertime. Sometimes there was food and other times they cooked together. If the dishes had piled up in the sink, or the bed had remained unmade, Earl overlooked it. She still went out during the day with the camera, but he thought it would be a mistake to stop her now from doing that. Once the baby was born, she would have to stop, but he was too tired and busy to give in to his worry. As long as she was there at supper, and listened to him talk about his day, he felt content. They would sit on the cold nights by the wood stove, and he would read to her from the newspaper.

But as she grew bigger and it got closer to the time for the baby, she seemed to withdraw even more into herself. She even said that now she sometimes felt like she had as a little girl closed in the room with her sick maman. When he asked her to describe it, she used the French word, crainte, or would say that it felt white. She would stare out the windows at night, saying that she missed her mother and started to mention those lights in the woods again. She got anxious sometimes and said that the room was getting smaller. She didn't have the desire to go off with her camera during the day anymore. More often than not, Earl came home to find her in bed.

After two weeks of this Earl contacted his sister, Grace. "Is this normal for a woman about to have a baby? I can't get her to eat much of anything. She is always in the bed. I don't know what to do. She won't say much, either. I can usually get her to talk about it, but not now."

Grace came from Cocodrie a few days later. She went into the bedroom and sat on the edge of the bed. "Eh, chérie, tu dois manger. You must eat. For you and the baby."

Dolores nodded. She cooperated more with Grace than she did with Earl, and she let Grace feed her some soup.

When Dolores slept Grace and Earl sat in the warm kitchen with the fire going in the stove. Grace said, "You know she was always pampered. She's frail. Once the baby comes, she will know what to do. She'll be fine."

"What if she's not? What if her maman's sickness, what if that was in her head, and now she has the same thing? I never knew what was wrong with her maman, did you? But she was strange, I know that."

"I heard things." Grace was a big woman with fair skin and red hair. Her thick arms rested on the table, her strong hands clasped together. "That there was something wrong with Adine, with her maman in that way. Even when she was young, they say. But Earl, if that's so, you come back home with her. We can take care of you there better."

The last thing Earl felt like doing was going back to Cocodrie. He had a good job working on all the new roads Huey Long was building around the city, and he had a chance to have another job on a building site on the weekends. They were going to be able to have more for themselves, a bigger house with a real washing machine, a bathroom inside.

Earl left his sister with Dolores and sat on the front stoop to smoke. His head drooped and his long arms hung on his knees. The bellow of the ships on the river a few blocks away echoed his melancholy. A cold fog floated above the surface of the street. His memories of Dolores lying next to him in bed with her dark hair around her face, a content smile on her lips, made him choke with tears. It had been a long while since he had seen her that way.

# 26.

## LIKE A LITTLE CHILD

CHARLOTTE HUSTLED INTO THE HOUSE with her usual brisk efficiency. Earl had determined before she came that he would be patient with her fussing over him, and that he would take Audrey's advice and talk to her.

"Well, I wouldn't have come over if I'd known she wasn't going to be here. Why didn't you tell me?" Charlotte's light, curled hair fell onto her forehead, and she pushed it back with the back of her hand. She had on one of those blouses with the little white and blue checked squares that made him think of picnic napkins. She unloaded plastic containers of frozen food, a carton of eggs and a quart of milk. He had so many people bringing him food lately that the icebox was full.

"There's no room in here," she said.

"I didn't know she wouldn't be here." He leaned in and helped her move things around. "I'm glad though. I wanted to talk to you alone."

"You didn't mention that she and Sam were, well, getting close again, either. That's a surprise."

"No, I didn't." Pappy chuckled then coughed. He took his white tobacco pouch out of his pocket. She stared at it, and he put it away.

"I wish she talked to me. I'm always out of the loop. I don't like her working late nights at that bar." She pushed her hair back again, tucked the shirt into her blue cotton pants and went to the stove with a container.

He took his coffee to the table. "Well, she doesn't talk to me either, if that helps."

"I wish she'd start on those graduate school applications. She did very well in business school. I don't know why she doesn't go someplace like Chicago or Atlanta where she can do something with that degree." She poured something from a container into a saucepan.

"Charlotte, she just got home, why are you trying to get rid of her? Besides she hates marketing, she hates business. She wants to do something else."

Earl cleared his throat and sought for an image of Audrey to shore him up. He dove right in. "Did you blame me for what happened to your mother?" He paused as she turned towards him from the stove with the spoon held in mid-air. Figuring out people's emotions had never been easy for him, but Audrey had made him more aware of it lately in their conversations. His daughter seemed like a little child in that moment, her eyes soft and pained, her lips parted, and her body tensed. If he'd tried this sooner in his life, he might have discovered a lot more about the people he was with. "I know how hard it must have been for you as a girl with her the way she was."

She lowered the spoon slowly into the pot. "Blamed you? I don't know." The wind seemed to go out of her sails. Her determined sense of purpose melted out of her, and she seemed thinner inside her clothes.

He said, "You were so young. I was so caught up in my own problems with your mother and trying to make a living. It was all so crazy then. I wouldn't blame you if you were angry, upset with me, upset with her. I just want you to know I'm sorry. That's all. I'm sorry." He brushed his forehead with the back of his hand and reached again for his pouch.

"We never talked about, about her, about anything really, not even about the end." Charlotte covered the pot and turned down the heat.

"I guess that's what people do. They just go around mad at each other. That's what Audrey says, anyway."

"Audrey?"

"She's a woman I met recently. We visit sometimes. I'll tell you more about her another time. But my point is, you and I, we grew apart, Charlotte, and I regret that, I do. Pour me some coffee."

Charlotte poured the coffee, and they moved to the living room. She opened the blinds of the big picture window that opened onto the porch. "It must have been horrible for you, living with her. I never appreciated that until later. I imagine in some ways it was a relief when she died." She was facing the lake, and her voice trailed off at the end.

Earl shook his head then blew on his coffee. "The first time I really felt like I lost her was right after Francis died. She went into shock, and I had to have your Aunt Grace take care of her so I could work. The neighbor lady helped too. She was pregnant with you of course. And I worried about that all the time. That she wouldn't be able to take care of you. That a new baby would destroy her. The first one nearly did. I didn't realize how much giving birth can rile things up for a person like that. If I'd known, I would never have… But she came around again after you were born. She even started taking pictures again and we got the darkroom working. Her pictures were different after that. Darker, I guess. She walked around the park and took pictures of people. Suffering people. Damaged people." He paused and glanced out as a sudden breeze pulled up little white caps.

Charlotte stared down at her hands in her lap. "I hated that wall with all pictures of scary people."

"Then when you were about three, she had a breakdown again. I came home and found you crying, and she was in bed. Laying there staring up at the ceiling. I couldn't rouse her. That's when she went into the hospital. That's when they did the treatments."

"Treatments?" She looked up.

"Electric shock treatments. I know it sounds horrible. That's what they did, still do for all I know."

Charlotte shuddered.

Once he started talking about it, everything poured out. "And it had some effect. For a long time, she seemed better. Not exactly herself anymore, but she could take care of you, she could take care of the house. She stopped taking pictures. Then after a year or so, she went back to the way she was before the treatments. And I refused to do that to her again. That's when I realized I had to have somebody to help take care of you. And I had to watch her. And I just let her be. That's when she started painting."

"Painting? She painted? I didn't know."

Earl rubbed his head with his open palms then his eyes. He reached into his pocket then took his hand out.

"Papa, let's go outside so you can smoke."

He looked up at her in surprise.

"You go ahead. I'll get us some more coffee." Charlotte nodded towards the door. Pappy went out on the back dock.

Charlotte came back out with the coffee. Pappy rolled a cigarette. He let out a long exhale. "Thank you, Charlotte."

"Where are the paintings? Did you keep any of them?" She sat down next to him.

"No. There are no paintings. You see, I let her be. We all did. Grace helped take care of you. I made sure you were safe. At first, we tried to watch Didi real close, but it was impossible. She wandered around the city, much more than before, all day sometimes. She went to the park and went for canoe rides in the lagoons. She walked everywhere. People thought I was being sloppy, that I didn't care anymore. But I read something about that kind of sickness. About leaving people alone and not expecting the same things out of them as you do out of normal people. So, I didn't. I tried to watch her when I could. Got other people to help keep her safe. And she was for a long time. She always came home at night. And she always waited for Grace to come over before she left the house." He had a pleading tone to his voice.

"What about the paintings? Why aren't there any? What were they like?" Charlotte leaned in closer to him.

"The first time I knew of her painting I walked into the shed, the one that had been a darkroom. We'd gotten rid of the darkroom by that time. I kept household tools and old cans of paint in there. I went in to get something, a screwdriver, or, I don't know. She'd painted on the walls; every square inch of the walls and the ceiling was covered. Even the workbench. She used small trim brushes and used up all the paint I had in there. It was something."

"You mean she just covered the walls with paint? No images or anything?"

"Yes, yes! All kinds of images! Fish and water and boats and birds, trees, and vines. Woods like back home and little lights, sparkles of green and gold in the woods. Like she'd had it in her all that time and knew exactly what she wanted to paint. It was beautiful."

"Really? But why didn't you give her canvas or something?"

"We did, we did. She didn't want canvas. She painted on stuff she found; cardboard, old wood, newspaper, walls, cans, anything. I gave her paint. She painted and she wandered. That was the happiest I'd ever seen her. Every now and then she'd come home from the park exhilarated, full of life, like a girl again."

He looked out at the lake, and when he turned back, Charlotte was crying. "Like a little child." Charlotte sobbed and quietly wiped her face on a Kleenex.

Earl had only imagined her being defensive or angry with him, not the broken child in front of him. He was at a loss as to what to do. Audrey would have known, but he felt helpless. "I'm sorry," he said again, but his words sounded empty to him.

The buzzer sounded in the kitchen. "Oh, I forgot about the food." Charlotte jumped up and went inside. When she didn't come back right away, he followed and found her staring out the kitchen window holding a couple of plates in her hands.

"Lottie? We have to forgive her. Like you said, she was like a little child."

She turned around, "No one's called me Lottie for years."

She leaned down and kissed him on the cheek. "Thank you for telling me all this."

"How do you feel? Are you going to be alright?" He felt like he should have anticipated her reaction and made a plan to deal with it. But it didn't work that way, he guessed. Planning is for making a meal or building a cabinet, not talking about things like this.

Charlotte set the plates down. "Would you like a beer?"

"A beer? I'm not sure what's got into you, letting me smoke and drink, but I won't say no. I'll have one if you do."

"Let's go outside."

The heat was building up, but there was a nice breeze rustling up the water. One by one seagulls landed on the dock and preened like it was some kind of planned gathering. Mullets jumped in and out of the water at their feet.

"The question is, should we tell Elaine about her." Earl felt like he had to go one more step. "She's asking all those questions. It doesn't seem fair."

Charlotte shook her head. "Maybe you're right, but let's wait a bit. Give me some time."

He nodded.

"Now, tell me, who's Audrey?"

# 27.

## FRANCIS

DOLORES STOPPED IN THE SHADOW of a streetlamp and rubbed her back. Her back was aching from the weight of the baby. The light in the French Quarter had been pearly from the fog. She had spent too much time there. The fog had rested on the river, and the freighters floated out from it like ghost ships. The streetlamp went on above her head and the windows glowed in her house a few feet away. Earl was already home.

She leaned against the lamppost for a labored breath. The hard place on her belly where his head lay pressed on her lungs. *Stay a while longer, I need more time.* Earl lifted the curtain aside and turned his head up and down the street. A sudden sharp pain made her double over and drop her camera case.

Earl opened the door and warm water poured down her legs as soon as she sat down. "Lie down in bed. I'm going to get Grace."

The birth took the whole day and into the next one. Grace said Dolores was holding on, fighting it. They named him Francis after Earl's great uncle. Earl cried when he held Francis for the first time and kissed her face and thanked her. He brought Francis to her at night and whistled as he cooked for them. He sang their wedding songs to the baby.

The baby consumed her, mouthful by mouthful. He sucked with such ferocity that it frightened her. His eyes were cloudy and dark without emotion. He stared at her relentlessly. All she wanted was to be alone.

The day that Grace left Dolores began performing all the tasks of cleaning, nursing, diapering, and cooking. Days seemed like long empty stretches of white space. Sometimes the hours ticked by as she went through her routine, and when Earl returned, she had no idea where the hours had gone or what she had done with them. She had not fallen in love with this strange creature as everyone told her that she would.

One afternoon she held him and walked under the crepe myrtle trees, sweat dripping between her breasts. The clustered pink flowers held rain like tiny cups. When she shook the branches, water fell in cool droplets onto her face. It smelled fresh and powdery. Her arms began to ache; Francis had fallen asleep.

That day she went to bed and could not get up. Everyone seemed like they were puppets, not real people, but things with no substance. Earl's face came into and out of view. Figures came in and out of the dim room and moved like shadows with no face or voice. The baby tugged, warm liquids were spooned into her mouth, Sara and her mother came to her in dreams. Sometimes the room felt cold, other times she burned with heat. Once she tried to will her feet to move; when nothing happened, it terrified her.

One morning the sharp sound of a cardinal penetrated the emptiness. She went to the window. A breeze brushed her arm. Birds jostled the holly bush fighting for berries. A male picked one and passed it on to his mate. Dolores laughed. Grace came to the window and embraced her. When Earl came home, he buried his head in her lap and sobbed. Later they told her that it was January—she had been in bed for two months.

Several weeks later, she left Francis with Grace for a doctor's appointment. At the last minute, she pulled her dusty camera bag out of the closet and made her way to the streetcar. The February day was warm and sunny. The sweet olive scent seemed to come from heaven. Huge magnolia flowers hung from branches over the sidewalk. The mixture of the smells made her giddy.

The doctor was pleased with her color and weight. "Mrs. Rizan," he said as she buckled her shoes, "a new baby can be exhausting. Drink a lot of milk and eat red meat. You will continue to stay as strong as you are today."

On the streetcar a baby started crying near her. Her breasts throbbed and spots of milk dampened her blouse. She got off at her stop heard Francis wailing half a block away. When she got home, he seemed heartbroken. He clung to her, ate greedily, his tiny hands clutching her fingers, her dress, the cross hanging at her neck.

# 28.

## WINDOWS ARE LIKE PHOTOGRAPHS

E VERY SATURDAY MORNING AT SEVEN before her shift at the library Charlotte went to a novena to the Blessed Virgin at St. Raphael Church. Her companions were older women from the neighborhood who had being doing the novena for over forty years. She enjoyed the constancy of the ritual, the repetition of the prayers, the sense it gave her of Mary as the ever-present Mother, a mother she could rely on.

There had been an alcove in her parents' bedroom with a blue and white wooden statue of Mary. Her rosary was painted gold. Later Charlotte learned that Pappy had built it for her mother. That area of the room glowed from the votive candles filling the alcove. Charlotte would sit outside the door of the bedroom if it was open and watch her mother kneeling in front of the statue.

It was Charlotte's turn this month to take care of the Mary Chapel, dust the marble altar, discard the withered flowers, replace them with fresh ones, and replenish the supply of votive candles in their crimson glass holders and black iron sconces. She waited until the novena was over, the women had hobbled out, and the priest left for his duties elsewhere. This quiet time alone in the cool dark space of the church was consoling.

She emptied the collection box where patrons deposited money in exchange for lighting candles. This day it seemed particularly heavy, and she wondered what kinds of burdens people were laying before Our Lady. She opened a new box of the white votive candles and began replacing the spent ones. Today Charlotte did not find much pleasure in it, nor did she receive any consolation from her duties. Her moodiness made her want to hurry through what should have been a prayerful task.

Talking to Pappy had brought up so many emotions and memories, and she was at a loss as to how to deal with them. She wasn't used to letting things bother her. Instead, she was very good at doing the opposite by ignoring them. But maybe ignoring them was not the best way, because it seemed that the painful things might teach her about herself, the parts that were hard to face.

Her memories of Cocodrie were vague. Visits had been infrequent, and her grandparents had died when she was a young child. She did remember roaming around while the grown-ups talked, and her mother wandered with the camera.

She hadn't looked at her mother's photographs in many years. She remembered faces, faces and more faces. Weathered fishermen, weary mothers holding babies, disabled children, old worn-out faces. Her mother had given so much time to faces when in real life she had seemed so disconnected from them. The other pictures were lonely: downed trees after a storm or a flooded sidewalk with a muddy doll. Never just a beautiful flower or line of trees, mostly dark things. Dark people. Dark children.

She emptied one box of candles and realized that she would need another, so she slipped back to the vestibule to collect more. A slow rhythmic thud from the marble floor of the church grew louder. The sound startled her until she recognized the grunting breath after each thud. One of the church ladies, Edith, who had missed the novena that morning was making her awkward way down the aisle with her walker toward the Chapel. Charlotte watched her lean on the walker and lower herself with a groan onto the leather kneeler at the foot of the statue of Mary. "Edith, how are you? We missed you this morning."

The woman took a moment to catch her breath. "I'm just fine, Charlotte, and yourself?" Edith wheezed, and the sound bounced off the Chapel walls with a hollow echo.

"Fine. Here's some new candles." Charlotte began replacing the different sized candles. "Did you want to light any today?"

"Always. Always." Edith reached into the front pocket of the large men's work shirt that she always wore.

"Edith if it's not too personal, do you light your candles for the same thing each time, or is it always something different?"

"Always the same, Honey." She leaned over carefully, and the coins rattled into the metal box. "It's Jimmy's wife, Natalie."

"Is she ill?" Charlotte lifted a bunch of droopy flowers from a brass vase.

"She's sick but it's not normal sickness, you know." She tapped her forehead. "It's up here."

The flowers dripped water onto the floor, and Charlotte knelt to wipe it up with a cloth.

"It's the depression. She takes medicine for it. She was fine until she had the baby. Then it was like a dam burst. They say having a baby can do that. With the medicine she can cope, thank goodness, but I don't think they'll have another one."

Charlotte stopped wiping the water and sat down on the step.

Edith lifted a wooden stick from a vessel filled with sand and lit it on a burning candle. "Some people have a harder time living than other people." Edith made the sign of the cross before lighting each of three candle wicks.

Charlotte went to another bunch of withering flowers. Dozens of white rose petals had fallen. She cupped them into her hands, their edges bruised and brown. A profound sadness came over her, her head throbbed, and she brushed her eyes with the back of her hand. It was not like her to cry like that.

Edith's eyes closed over her folded hands, and she murmured a prayer. Charlotte finished up with the flowers and brought everything back to the closet where she kept her supplies. Edith was preparing to leave when Charlotte came back. Charlotte wanted to ask more about Natalie, but Edith stopped for air and pointed up at the heavens. "It's that storm, Charlotte. It's gonna be a bad one."

"Good-bye Edith. Be careful."

Edith paused and lifted one hand to wave, too winded to speak.

Charlotte cleaned up and started to leave the church through the side door but decided instead to go out by the big doors at the entrance. Both sides and the front area above the doors were lined with large clear glass windows instead of the usual stained glass of most churches: three rows of rectangular windows on each side and five double rectangles above the doors. Each one framed a particular view that changed with the time of day or year. Some of the trees were bare in winter, most stayed robust and green. In summer, flowering vines covered the fence. Today the clouds allowed only a dim, moody light, but at times the entire narthex glowed with sunshine.

"Like photographs," she thought. As she stood there watching, the view changed with shifts of shadow and light or slight currents of air.

Charlotte felt exhausted at work, and she couldn't figure out why, except for the sadness that she couldn't seem to shake. Even her co-worker noticed.

"Aren't you feeling well?" she asked Charlotte.

Charlotte was not only unaccustomed to having feelings, but she was also definitely not used to sharing them with people, especially at work. But something urged her to open up.

"I had a long talk with my father the other day." They made tea and sat by the big window that looked out onto St. Charles Avenue.

Charlotte loved the library with its walls of glass and dozens of nooks to read and be quiet. "About my mother."

"Your mother passed, right?"

"Yes, when I was little." Charlotte could tell that this opening up was new, her body could tell, it felt foreign to her head, her lips, her stomach. "She had depression. Or some kind of mental illness."

"Oh, that's so difficult for children. I'm so sorry."

Charlotte looked at her, surprised, not at the words themselves, but the effect they had on her. She felt a wave of gratitude, and something she would have called love, but never expected. Her tears were close to spilling out. "Yes, it was difficult."

Janice passed her a Kleenex and poured more hot water over her teabag. "What was it like, you said you were little, but you have some memories?"

By the time Charlotte left to go home, a huge weight had been lifted from her. She poured out a glass of Merlot, took out the Britannica and read every article she could on mental illnesses, their symptoms, and treatments, current and past. A link to a different article led her to read about Virginia Woolf, Van Gogh, James Baldwin, the list went on and on of famous writers and artists who had struggled with mental illness. Like Edith said, life was harder for some people than it was for others.

# 29.

## DARKROOM TRAGEDY

OLORES KNEW THAT HE COULD tell that his mother was agitated. He would not take her nipple but kept flailing and whining. She set him down on his blanket on the floor, and he started to wail. She picked up the breakfast plates and put them into the sink, turned the diapers over that hung on the drying rack by the heater, and went into the bedroom and made the bed.

One day the week before, Francis had fallen asleep and Dolores thought about going to the darkroom, but she'd been afraid to leave him. He usually slept for at least an hour in the mornings, sometimes longer. He had been awake often the night before, but she did not want to go lie down and nap with him using up all her free time. Her mind was on the darkroom and negatives she had processed the day before. She had climbed under the covers in the bedroom, removed the film and wrapped it in dark paper and developed it in the tank in the kitchen.

She longed for Francis to sleep for just a few minutes. He continued to cry so she picked him up. "Shhhh. Tais-toi, petit." The solid wood rocker that Earl had bought for her creaked on the wooden floor by the backyard window. Dolores tried singing to him. «Dors bien, pauvre petit bébé; dors bien. Les chattons viennent de te voler. Dors bien, pauvre petit bébé.»

She had not been in her darkroom since the baby. Only a month ago she finally started walking with him and taking pictures. The day she woke up and the white feeling went into the background, she had gone out the next day. With the camera in her hands every day she began to feel connected again. Connected to herself, and Earl and Francis, and to the world.

Finally, his lids began to close. She moved him into his bed in the other room of the house and covered him with a quilt. *Give me just an hour, only one hour.* She kissed his damp forehead then closed the door and retrieved her leather camera bag from a hook by the front door. She put a shawl around her shoulders at the last minute. A cool spring rain had started to fall.

She entered the quiet stillness of the shed. Bottles lined the shelves, covered in dust. The room retained the faint odor of chemicals. Her heart pounded against her chest. She shut the door and closed the dark shade on the one small window that looked out on her neighbor's yard. Men's work shirts were hanging on the line, and the neighbor ran out to grab them in the rain. Dolores pulled the string for the red safelight and her breathing relaxed in the dimness. The world outside fell away.

She cut the negatives apart to put them into the enlarger and prepared the trays with the different liquids she would need that were already in bottles on the shelf above. The first negative in the enlarger was of Francis. When Francis' face appeared on paper in the tray, she smiled at his perfect smile, round head and deep eyes. That something so beautiful could have come from her seemed impossible. Then she frowned realizing that she needed to get back, he had been alone, how long? She had no idea. She made another print of the same negative adding a bit of light to the background of dark foliage in the park. Once the finished pictures were hanging on the line to dry, she pulled the string and left the shed without cleaning up and rushed to the house worried now that she would find him inconsolable.

Dolores felt relieved at first not to hear any crying when she approached the house. Francis lay in his crib, the blanket pulled over his face. She sensed something not right in the room and hesitated to touch him. Gently moving the cloth, she noticed a bit of blood around his nose and lips, his head thrust back slightly as though he tried to look back at the door. So pale, like thin fine china. He rolled slightly with her weight on the bed. His lips were blue, he was not breathing. She grabbed him and ran out into the yard praying no, no, no, to the Blessed Mother, no, not this, not this. A cold sickness gripped her stomach. She ran down the street with him to the man at the corner. In his truck she prayed and rocked, prayed and rocked, images of her baby cousin came to her, the day that he had gone under in the river for too long and came out blue without breathing until her Papa pushed the air back into him and he began to breathe again. She kept repeating out loud, "Please, please, please, please, no, not this, not this," clutching him to her, and saying the Hail Mary over and over. "Je vous salue, Marie, pleine de grâces, le Seigneur est avec vous, Vous êtes bénie entre toutes les Femmes.»

He had been dead before she left the house. They said it was not her fault. That it could happen to babies, especially boys, sometimes in the first six months. No one was at fault. At the hospital the priest said it was God's will, and Dolores threw herself upon him beating his chest.

A tight knot of self-hatred grew in her, blocking out any grief, anger, or regret. Grace tried to console her. "God took him, chère, he took him to a better place. He takes babies all the time, yeah. Every woman I know, she's lost a baby. Now you'll have other babies, you know? You will have other babies." But Dolores didn't want other babies.

Her sleep was never sound, more like a restless journey in and out of wakefulness, a constant stream of images without respite. Sometimes she would leave the bed at night, when the world seemed more forgiving, and she would walk the street, or sit in the yard and look up at the stars. One night, two months after the baby's death, she picked up the beating stick that Grace had left out after beating the rugs and bedspreads. It was a solid stick of sturdy oak, polished from use. She brought the stick to the shed. She had to push the door hard as it was swollen with humidity.

The crack in the open door let in light from the street. The shed smelled of damp and mildew and chemicals. Her pans and bottles were as she had left them that day, the day Francis died. Even the paper from the picture she had worked on sat in a metal pan, the developing fluid evaporated and the paper a dry hull. The two prints she had made of Francis hung on the line. She battered the bottles first, then the pans, and the red lights. The chemicals and glass splattered over her hair and dress. The enlarger shattered with one loud blow. Earl stopped her before she destroyed her cameras. She collapsed against him.

# 30.

## ELEVATED

THE SMELL OF COFFEE WOKE Elaine, but when she opened her eyes, it was still dark. Light came in under the door, and a low voice came from behind it humming a tune. She closed her eyes and huddled under the blanket again, sensing in her body the absence of Sam in the bed, and longing for him again. Their decision to take things slowly had not worked out.

She called to him, and he opened the door a crack and talked in a quiet voice like he didn't want to wake her when clearly it was too late for that. "I'm sorry. I forgot to tell you, I'm taking Earl fishing this morning."

She patted the mattress next to her, and he came and rolled her body into his. He kissed her, and it was one of those full body kisses like you're falling, and there's nothing there but the kiss.

"Are you okay?" he brushed her hair back from over her forehead. "I mean with everything, with last night?"

"My hair is one huge tangle, but yeah, I think so. You?"

"I know we'd said slow, but it seemed right to me."

"We're not twenty anymore. It seemed right to me too."

"Good. You can sleep. It's only five."

She closed her eyes and felt his lips on her forehead.

A couple of hours later she stood making coffee in Pappy's kitchen. A whole morning for herself and her new book from the museum. Since she'd stopped working at the café, she felt more comfortable in her own skin, more connected to the person she thought she was, or wanted to be. Being around Sam helped, too. He seemed to recognize the things in her that she'd always thought were the best things, even if they got buried sometimes, like the past few years.

On the way out to the back porch with her coffee she almost tripped over a dilapidated cardboard box in the middle of the floor. The box was overflowing with crumbling newspapers, and what looked like layers of waxed paper. Further investigation revealed dozens of photographs.

She leaned back against the sofa and leafed through the photos. They were not the typical family pictures of babies and little kids, Christmas trees or vacation shots of groups or kids at pools or campsites. They were professional looking, composed, artistic, taken by an experienced photographer who used a darkroom to experiment with many prints of the same negative. They ranged in subject and place. There were portraits of disabled children, old people, workers, pregnant women. They were posed, but not touched up in any way to make the subjects look a certain way, as though the photographer came upon them on the street and clicked.

She didn't recognize anyone in any of the pictures. She'd seen family photos before, of her as a baby, some of her father and his family, of her growing up and a few of her mother when she was little. These were different.

The people were mixed in with some landscapes, trees, houses in New Orleans, the river, the streetcar. As she got further down in the box, the photographs looked much older and were in bad shape. They were smaller, commercially processed from a less sophisticated camera, and of completely different subjects, a group of people eating crabs in a kitchen with newspaper clippings on the wall and a picture of the Virgin Mary pointing to her bleeding heart; kids climbing mountains of oyster shells, fishermen mending nets, people dancing, statues of Mary. Then it switched to New Orleans, ships docked at the wharf, a boy sitting on steps of a shotgun house drinking out of a milk bottle, a paper boy on a bike.

The name, Dolores Couvillon, was written in a child's handwriting on the backs of some of the matted prints. Elaine felt blindsided by all of it. Her grandmother had indeed had a darkroom, had been a professional photographer, and this had been kept from her for all these years.

The photos never seemed to end. At the very bottom of the box, a brown envelope held dozens of proof sheets. Most of them were photographs that she'd already come across. The last two sheets were portraits of a pregnant black woman. She looked peaceful and happy, and in some she had her eyes closed and was dancing under some low flowering bushes, her arms curled gracefully in the air. At first glance the next two sheets looked water damaged. They were hard to see so Elaine grabbed Pappy's magnifier. It was the same woman smattered with tiny specks of light like fireflies, or she was faded out with bright patches of light, or she was blurred and ghostly looking. Like the photo she'd seen at the museum.

The very last contact sheet was stuck to the bottom of the box. She pried it loose and there it was, the statue from the fountain at Audubon Park. It might not be the same person taking the picture, but it looked like it. It was hard to believe.

Elaine met Pappy out on the dock after Sam dropped him off. She had planned to confront him, but he looked so exhausted and vulnerable that she toned down her reaction as much as she could. She had taken out her book from the museum to compare the pictures and showed it to him.

He took the book from her hands and closed it to look at the cover. "One of her pictures is at the museum? Well, I'll be."

"'I'll be'? That's all you can say? And look at this one. It looks a lot like one hanging at the Pontchartrain." She moved next to him and held out the photo. "Could that one be hers too?"

"The statue at the park. By the zoo," he said. "Possibility. The man who first gave her the camera. He had a gallery around here. She kept in touch with him for a while. Maybe they got circulated somehow."

Elaine tried to control her emotions that were bouncing from shocked to hurt to angry. "Unbelievable. What made you finally show this to me? All that time in high school when I was into photography and art. Begging Mama to pay for equipment, for drawing classes. For art school. She never said a word. And discouraged me from all of it."

Pappy sighed and wiped his face with his handkerchief. "I need to lie down. I know you're shocked and I'm sorry. Your mother was afraid of all your dark moods. Your depression. Even hurting yourself. Charlotte had to grow up with a disturbed mother, and it has been hard for her to go back there and revisit it. Hard for both of us."

Elaine felt a sudden deflation, a release of air and energy. "You mean like she was schizophrenic or something?"

"We can talk about this more later. We don't know. But I was hoping you could put these into some kind of order and protect them from any more damage. I might be finally getting too old for these fishing trips." He headed towards his room then turned around at the hallway and looked at her. "Don't blame your mother. She's the one told me to do this, to show them to you. It took a lot for her to do that."

---

Elaine gathered up samples of the photos and took them to the gallery with her. She was due to work that afternoon and into the evening for the Art Walk. She let herself into the front gate and when she entered the shop Alexander and Gary stood close together talking in low voices. Gary touched Alexander's cheek with an intimate gesture.

She had assumed they were lovers but had never seen them behave as a couple in the gallery. She made some noise, so they'd notice her.

Gary said, "Elaine, greetings. Your former boss here is insisting I get a haircut before tonight's big do."

Elaine laughed. "It looks fine to me. Anyway, I need both of you here right now."

"Oh dear, what's up?" said Gary.

She started taking photographs out of the portfolio and laying them on the table. "My grandpa left these for me to find this morning. My grandmother took them. Some of them look very much like the ones you found at that estate sale that have no name on them. I don't know how we can tell, maybe you can tell, if they were taken by the same person? How do you figure that out?"

They leaned over the photos. Gary went to the drawer of the counter and came back with a magnifying glass. "There are a few different ways to tell. The obvious things like subjects, locations, time period. Then you can check the specific type of paper and processing techniques. Different paper, different ways to treat the paper, some of them soaked the paper with the solutions, others just brushed it. They could use toners. These are regular gelatin silver prints."

Alexander switched to a different pair of glasses and lifted a couple of Elaine's photos by the edges. "There are a lot of similarities. It looks like the same kind of camera. She used a wide-angle lens for this one." He held an image of the peristyle at City Park. "And that's what was used for the picture of the wharf up there. Gary, why don't you grab the light from the back?"

Elaine handed him another one. "Look at this one. It's not exactly the same, but it's the same scene, isn't it? The same wharf with the ship in the background?"

"The subject and composition of it alone tells me it's the same person that took the photograph." He held the light at different angles, straight down, and across horizontally. "Yours has some damage. Look."

Gary came back with a powerful lamp, and Alexander turned it on and squatted so his eyes were level with the photo. "See there's a bit of surface damage there. And here." That abrasion is from mold. But neither one has any discoloration or frilling around the edges. She used a toner, I think, you can even see a deeper blue-black color," he pointed to the ship's hull, "here, and over here on the smokestack. That is probably due to the toner. The toner preserves it too." He took off his glasses and leaned back in the chair, smiling. "This is exciting. How many of these do you have?"

"Dozens," she said.

Alexander said, "Great. I think we should do a show. And you should curate."

The photographs covered the long table like a patchwork quilt. "I can't believe it."

Gary said, "I don't know about the one at the museum, I haven't seen it, but the image in your book does look like it could be hers. I'd have to get them to let me look at it out of the frame. Let's celebrate in the yard for a while before people start to come in." He went to the caterer's table and picked up a bottle of Merlot and an opener. "You didn't know anything about these photographs or your grandmother?"

Elaine replaced the photos carefully. "Not until today. He asked me to put them in some kind of order for him." She followed them outside to the courtyard in front of a banana tree with immense green and brown leaves and purple flowers and fruit. The cast iron gate framed a view of Chartres Street that included part of the building across from them and its balcony, a streetlamp, and on the bottom level dozens of lights glowed in the framed window of an antique light shop.

"He said my mom was afraid to show them to me or tell me about her because she was mentally ill. I guess Mama blamed it on the photography or something because she discouraged me from doing it, and she kept all this from me." The wine felt especially calming. Elaine hadn't noticed how tense she'd become during the day. An old woman leaned over the balcony of the building across the street, and Elaine almost leaned forward anticipating her plummeting over the side. She took another big sip.

"He said she started with a Brownie that a photographer in Cocodrie gave her when she was young. I did know about that. He told me that when we went to Cocodrie." Elaine had forgotten about the Brownie, but not about the darkroom they'd talked about. "And he also said that the guy had a studio down here somewhere."

"These were taken with something a lot more advanced than a Brownie, maybe a speed Kodak. And they are in New Orleans, did she end up here?" He refilled her glass.

"Yeah. They moved to New Orleans later and I think my grandpa gave her another camera at some point. Anyway, she had her own darkroom. One in Cocodrie, and I guess one in New Orleans after they got married and moved."

In the distance a slow blues on trumpet started up. A young couple walked across their view through the gate and sat down on the curb. They were drinking from a paper bag. It seemed like the set of a play with scenes and characters moving in and out.

Gary said, "Well, it became more than a hobby for her. You said the one who gave her the camera had a studio down here? What was his name? Maybe we can find him if he's still alive."

Elaine put her hand over the top of her glass when Gary tried to pour more. "I should stop, I have to work." The wine worked on her so that she started seeing everything through the gate as though it was a camera lens. The couple got up and moved away, and a woman who looked like a dancer glided into the shop across the street.

She said, "I'm trying to imagine what she was like, and how she felt about her subjects. How she worked. I have to study the pictures. I'm already seeing details in them on the second or third glance that I didn't notice at first."

The phone rang and Gary went back inside.

Alexander said, "And remember that the finished photograph can reveal so much more than what is apparent to the photographer."

"What do you mean?"

"Things just show up. Some of those details you see could have appeared out of nowhere so to speak. Unseen by her. Julia Cameron thought it was a spiritual revelation."

"Maybe it's the wine," she said, "but it feels like I've been looking at a series of photographs," she gestured to the street, "through the gate. The gate is the frame. And each image seems, what's the right word? Weighted."

"Weighted?" he asked.

"Each one is a dramatic moment. High stakes. I mean that's what photos do, isn't it? Like poems or paintings? They take something ordinary, like that trumpet player walking by, and frame it, something from everyday life, and then it becomes more than ordinary. It becomes…"

"Elevated." Gary had returned and was standing behind Elaine's chair.

The sun had started to slide behind the buildings leaving the street in shadow. A cool dampness moved in off the river and a breeze picked up in the courtyard. The images continued to enter and exit the frame then became livelier as the three of them continued to watch the street until voices came from inside the gallery. They went in as dusk settled over the French Quarter.

# 31.

## CRAINTE

THE WHITE FEELING ALWAYS COMES and goes, but with the baby, it was always there. He was always there needing me, to eat, to live, to breathe. He was so helpless. His eyes were on my eyes every moment of every day. When he looked at me, I felt he could see inside of me, and that he wanted all of me for himself all the time. His eyes followed me around the room, the house, everywhere, and he grew unhappy if they could not find me. I felt suffocated by them. When he took my nipple, his eyes would latch on to mine, and he pulled and pulled until I felt empty and exhausted.

I cried because I missed Sara. I prayed that she was somewhere safe with her baby. When I had Sara with me, I told her about the white feeling. "What is the white feeling?" she asked me. I said that it was like being afraid all the time. Like the world is so big that you cannot imagine being so small inside of it, disconnected from it, untouched by anything. She asked, "What color is it? Is it only white?" I had never thought about it before, except to say that it is white, and the French word, crainte, in English I think dread. Empty. Long days without time, like I felt sometimes when Maman was sick, when I was in her room drawing. I feel trapped with no way to escape, and even light hurts my eyes. Nothing can move me, nothing beautiful or happy or filled with grief. I feel nothing. Not the clouds I usually love to watch, or the cardinals singing in the pecan trees, the ships on the river, or an old man's face. Nothing moves me.

And when the baby came, the white feeling came back, even more than before, and he was always there needing me. Everyone watched me all the time waiting for me to feel something, Earl, Grace, the neighbor with her little girl baby, Ida. I could tell they were waiting for me to change somehow and come back to the world.

One day the white feeling went into the background. Earl and Grace, they were so relieved. I went to the window when a cardinal sang, and it was as though I suddenly could hear again, see again, feel again. The fear of it is always there, that it will come back anytime, uninvited, but this time I could see the color of the sky again. I could hear the birds. And I wanted to show all of it to Francis.

So, during the day when Earl went to work, I would take Francis with me and walk. I covered him with an old coat of Earl's on rainy days. I figured out how to tie him to me with a sheet, and then started to take the camera too. Someone gave us a baby cart with wheels.

I took many pictures during that time with Francis in the cart, reflections of clouds and branches on the sidewalks, shadows of all kinds of things. Trees, leaves, the statues and fountains, the arches where the seals lived at the zoo, the bridge shadows in the lagoon. I loved shadows. Earl finished setting up the darkroom, but one day while Earl was at work, I left Francis for a few moments and when I came back, he was not breathing. I started to scream, and something kept screaming in me and has never stopped screaming.

We put a white dress on him and laid him out like the baby in Cocodrie that I took pictures of. I took a stick and destroyed everything that I could get to in the darkroom before Earl stopped me. I almost destroyed the cameras, but he saved them.

# 32.

## WALKING ON BROKEN GLASS

"Try to get him to leave before I get back. It's not going to make hurricane, but the winds will be high. You shouldn't be out here." Sam put the last of the darkroom equipment into the back of the van. "I'll move the van to the church where it's higher ground. It should be okay there. You don't have any of the photos here, do you?"

"I left them all at the gallery. Don't you think I've tried? He refuses to leave, and it's hard for me to manhandle him. I can't tell him what to do. Did you talk to him?"

"He's never left for a tropical storm, he says, only hurricanes."

They were on top of the levee. The storm in the Gulf was inching its way closer and the lake had started to look as angry as the sky. Waves rolled into the shore. The sky was a swirling mass of greenish gray and yellow clouds. The wind on Elaine's legs felt hot and sticky.

Sam put his arms around her, his chin grazing her hair. "I'll be gone a few hours. My mom should be ready by the time I get there, I hope. Sometimes she forgets things. Then it's about an hour here from there. When I get back, we'll get him out of here even if it means me carrying him to the car."

"Audrey said we should go to her place. By the way, she said you were a good man and that I should hang on to you." Elaine had met Audrey finally after a couple of months of clandestine meetings.

He laughed. "Glad she approves. I didn't know you needed any reassurances."

"I didn't, but she offered. She's cool. She had these ideas about why New Orleans is such a hard place to leave and then come back to."

"Like what?"

"That there's so much ritual here, everybody eats the same things, plans their lives around the same events; it's easy to fall into that instead of having your own life. So maybe that's why I felt like I had to leave. It's interesting anyway."

"Not everybody, but I guess it's true for the most part."

Pappy appeared out on the deck and waved to them gesturing to her to come inside.

"I love you," he said. "I'll see you in a few hours."

"You know we're about to be in the middle of a tropical storm here?" Pappy asked when she walked through the door. "What are y'all doing out there?"

Rain started to touch the windows with a soft patter. Elaine said, "Maybe it won't get too bad."

Pappy said, "It was supposed to go farther west but it turned at the last minute and it's coming in here. It's not a hurricane, don't worry. Time to get out the cards. We're going to be stuck here for a while. Sam go get his mother?"

"We should have gone to Audrey's like she asked us to. I should call Mama again. I've talked to her a hundred times already. She's so worried."

"Don't call your mother. She worries, that's what she does. I've been through this before. There aren't any trees to fall on us. The winds will be around 50 or 60. Nothing major." He went to the stove and mixed coffee with hot milk in mugs. "Come get these. Let's watch it come in on the sofa."

Pappy pulled up to the table. "We're gonna make gumbo. Seems like a good day for it. Why did Sam wait so long to go get his mother?"

"She had something to do and told him to wait. I hope he'll be okay. It looks like it's getting worse fast." The light disappeared from the house like a large blanket had descended over it. The gentle patter turned into a loud pelting with cracks that sounded like nails hitting the glass. With the haze and rain, you could only see a few yards out.

The back dock started swaying with every gust of wind, and the house trembled. "50 or 60, hunh?"

They watched the weather for a while then started cutting up the vegetables for the gumbo. By early afternoon the camp was pitch dark. Once the gumbo was on Earl dealt the first hand of hearts. They'd been playing for almost an hour as the camp filled up with the smell of the roux and shrimp and okra. A loud crack of thunder boomed through the house.

"Jesus," said Elaine.

Earl made the sign of the cross. "Sacré bleu, that was loud, yeah."

Elaine realized she had him captive at this point, so she went ahead and tried to get him to talk about Dolores. He had been evading her questions since the day he gave her the photos. The idea of a showing at the gallery seemed to make him nervous. He wouldn't comment on it. "Do you think Mama is ashamed of Dolores? She seems angry with her."

Earl scratched the stubble on his cheeks. "Ashamed? I don't know. I think she has trouble forgiving her for not being there for her when she was little, but she's getting there. Dolores had trouble forgiving herself. And I don't want you to be that way about your life. Everybody has their own suffering, and you learn from it. That's what it's for, but you don't dwell on things. They'll eat you up."

"But it wasn't Dolores' fault. I mean she was sick."

"Still a lot of people, most people don't understand that. Think everybody needs to be the same way, be able to hold a job, raise children, make a lot of money. None of that stuff is really who you are anyway, but people don't see that."

"Well, if you're not all that stuff, who are you then?"

He tapped his chest. "It's the stuff in here that nobody sees. That's who you are, that's the important part. It's not out there. I'm going to check on the gumbo."

He lifted the lid of his large soup pot and stirred. The rich smell of the gumbo escaped in a cloud of steam as a hefty gust shook the camp. Buckets of rain seemed to batter the windows. He said, "You hungry? It's ready."

She moved the cards out of the way, and he brought the bowls to the table one at a time. Elaine began spooning the gumbo into her mouth slowly. "Did you forgive her?" The wind and rain roared.

"What? It's damn loud in here." He tore off a hunk of French bread and dipped it in the hot soup.

"Did you forgive Dolores?"

He took a few bites. "No. No I didn't. Not then. Now I do. And I hope she can hear me at night when I tell her so." The lights blinked with an irregular rhythm then went out. "There it goes. Get the lamps. I cleaned them last night and left them in my room."

Elaine came back with the kerosene lanterns, one in each hand. "I guess I just don't understand what she did that was so awful. I mean what could you not forgive her for? Is it too personal? Did she have lovers?"

"No! God, no. It was nothing like that." He shook his head hard and fiddled with the wick in one of the lamps. "She was distant, she would go to bed for days. And then there was Francis."

"Francis?" A weird wailing sound whipped around the camp. "Is that the wind? What is that?"

Pappy set the now lit lantern on the coffee table, and weird shadows started to flicker in the room. "It sounds like the whole god damn roof is vibrating. Must be some loose pieces of tin."

She said, "Dammit, I should have made you leave."

"Elaine, who has ever been able to make me leave in a storm? What makes you think you could have?"

She went into the kitchen for a beer and settled back down at the table. "Who was Francis?"

"Francis was our firstborn. He died. She left him during a nap and went into her darkroom for a while. When she came back, he was dead. It was nothing she did or didn't do. Now they have a name for it. I can't remember…" He ran a hand across his forehead.

She said, "SIDS?"

"Yeah. That's it. Babies just die suddenly, nobody knows why. That's what happened. She had a very hard time getting over it. Stopped taking pictures for a long time. Hardly went out or talked. Then your mother was born."

"That must be devastating. I didn't know about that. Of course, I didn't, I didn't know about anything. But I'm not buying that Mama was afraid to tell me because she thought I'd be like her. There's got to be more to it." A loud ripping sound tore the air above them, and rain started to come into the room near the sliding glass doors.

"We lost a piece of roof, dammit. Get the bucket from under the sink and put it over there, will you?"

She ran to get the bucket, but the rain fell from different spots. "Do we have any more buckets? The rain funneled around the door frame into a series of smaller streams. "What if we lose more of the roof?"

"We'll use every bucket and pot we have. We may be looking up at God's sky eventually." He said this as though that would not be such a bad thing after all. "Just say a prayer or two. I don't think we'll be getting much sleep tonight. I sure hope Audrey is okay. And Sam."

They tried to play cards, but Pappy became more agitated with the rain coming in and the incessant wind. He kept moving around the room from the table to the back deck.

Elaine said, "I think you should stay away from the windows. There could be tornados too. Don't you have a battery powered radio?"

He asked, "What good's that gonna do? What if they tell us there's a tornado?"

"Then we will go into the bathroom. That's what you're supposed to do. Where's the radio?"

"In the skinny cabinet in the kitchen. Damn. I should know better than to listen to those goddamn weathermen. None of them any good anymore. Jesus Christ!"

In a flash of lightning the big picture window in the back of the camp blew in, and the whole camp lurched like an earthmover had pushed it off its pilings. Several feet of the wooden dock came to rest on the floor. Glass flew into the room with the wind and rain and some of it reached Pappy.

Elaine screamed and ran to him. His bloodied hands covered his eyes. She saw glass pieces in his hair and larger ones on his lap. His forehead was gashed on the left side, and the back of his head was bloody. Elaine guided the chair into the bathroom and reached for towels to press onto his head.

She shut the door to close off the terrifying sound of the wind and rain coming in. "Are you okay?" The darkness was profound. She fumbled for the matches that they kept on the back of the toilet. In the dim light, she tried to see the cuts on his head and hands.

"We have to get you to the hospital."

He continued looking at his hands while she tried to wipe them with a wet washcloth and hold the towel on his head. Elaine lit a match. The blood clotted in his hair, dripped down the side of his face and stained his white T-shirt. Elaine kept wiping his hands with wet washcloths and rinsing them out. She started shivering. "Pappy hold this on your head. Take some deep breaths."

"I'm fine." He gripped the armrests and tried to breath deep. "That's a lie. I need a cigarette. Can I put this towel down now?"

"Wait. Let me see." She held another match close to his head. "I can't see anything with this, dammit."

"There's a candle in the cabinet there. One of those religious ones from your mother." He waved his hand toward the linen closet.

"I'm afraid there's glass in there. We're going to wait in here until the storm slows down and I can get you to the hospital. I'm afraid of tornados."

His hands settled in his lap, showing only specks of blood. She put his arms into the robe and wrapped it around him and held onto him. She felt their breathing come together, and both of them grow calmer. "I'm useless in a situation like this. But I think you should stay warm. Are you warm?"

"Yes. I am. And you're doing fine. We'll stay here for a while. Why don't you put some towels down on the floor and rest?"

"Are you sure you're okay? You seem like it, but I'm afraid."

"I think I am, honey. A little shook up, but my head doesn't hurt, and my breathing is fine. I've been through things before; I'd tell you if I thought something was wrong. Get some rest."

She huddled close to his chair with her head resting on his blanket. It seemed like the noise was starting to quiet down. The words of the rosary came back to her, and she muttered through them. After the third decade she began to doze.

# 33.

## THE LITTLE DOLL

T SEEMED THAT SHE HAD only begun to walk again and to feel colors and birdsong when she realized there was another baby. When she knew, when she first recognized the sensation, she had been combing her hair in the bedroom mirror and had dropped the shell comb Earl had given her. Fear and dread came into her belly; la crainte again, and a cold gripping. She had said no many times aloud and shook her head as though she could make it not be true.

After some time, she started to walk again, and walking helped the feeling. She walked to the river and took pictures again, but they were different now. She was attracted to faces, especially faces that betrayed the pain of life. Old, lonely men on benches by the park, wrinkled and weary women. One day children from the home for incurables came to the park, and she asked and took pictures of the disfigured, sick, disabled.

She began to have nightmares of Francis and afterwards could not help going over and over again, seeing him on the bed, in the white dress, feeling her empty arms. Earl asked her to talk to him, but he was so happy with another baby, she hated to say that she was afraid, and more certain that she did not want the new one, or any other one.

When the little girl came the white feeling returned and stopped the milk from coming. She did not want to hold her or take care of her. This baby would not be hers. She would not do that again.

Then she grew into a beautiful little doll. When the baby looked at Dolores, it was not the same as Francis. They had separate selves, she, and Charlotte, as though the baby understood the distance there. Earl put the camera again into Dolores' hands and took the baby as much as possible so that she could go out alone. He rebuilt the dark-room, and she was in the darkroom every night when he got home.

They went on like this for a time, and Charlotte grew older. She drew a picture of a figure consumed by fire and said that it was her mama. The eyes were dark circles. The picture frightened Dolores, and she threw it away. The feeling came back, and she went to bed again. She remembered that Sara said it was those lights in the woods, that they were bad and make people do bad things. They took her into the camera, and away from Earl and Charlotte. But without the camera, she felt that she did not exist.

They took her to Charity Hospital. She told the doctor that the white feeling came so strong everything else was blocked out. The doctor did something that Dolores could not remember to make her better. After that she went home and could take care of Charlotte. The feeling became like a white seed in the back of her brain that might blossom at any time. For a while it stayed as a seed, but she did not want the camera.

Earl put away the darkroom and instead she painted. She painted on any surface she could, the walls of the shed, newspapers, sidewalks. She didn't like the limits of the canvas that Earl brought home. The painting made her feel like she was back home in Cocodrie outside under the dripping cypress trees or by the edge of the bayou with the sounds of the birds and bugs and the smell of heat and water and rich earth and fish and the colors of the sky next to the bright spring green of the cypress and the purple flowered vines. And that's what she painted.

She painted the woods at night, the moon dipping its tip against the water like it was liquid itself. She filled the darkness with feux follets. When she painted, she left this world and went to another one, as if you walked out into the river and let the dark water surround you, cover you in darkness. Everything behind you would disappear.

The seed blossomed again, and the painting stopped, and Dolores grew weary of it. Weary of the struggle and the treatments. She was afraid that God could not forgive her for not being able to take care of Earl and Charlotte. For not being able to love them. She was not sure what it meant to love something except to take care of it, and that she could not do. God had abandoned her, and yet another baby was coming.

# 34.

## LIKE SATCHMO

AN OPPRESSIVE SILENCE WOKE ELAINE some hours later. Her body was curled at the foot of the wheelchair in a mound of towels. The beginning of daylight shone under the door. A fishy salt smell from the Gulf filled the room. Earl groaned. She held onto the sink and pulled herself up, tipping over what was left of the candle. "Pappy," she jostled his arm. "Pappy," she said, louder.

He opened his eyes and winced in pain, reaching up to the back of his head. "Ouch, that's a doozy."

"Does it hurt a lot? It's not bleeding but it's ugly. How are your hands?"

"Scratched up, that's all." He reached for his tobacco repeating a seventy-year-old habit that was stronger than any disaster. "Should we go survey the damage?"

"Shouldn't we wait a minute and make sure you're okay first? Let me get you some water at least."

He said, "We have to go out sooner or later. No point in putting it off. He pushed himself forward past her and the door opened against some resistance. "Chair fell on it." The chair tipped over and clattered with a hollow sound.

She stared at the scratches of dried blood on Pappy's hands. The wheels of his chair crunched on the glass. "Oh my God," she said.

"Hell, that had to be a tornado did this. Picked up the dock and threw it right at us."

The gauzy curtains hung on the sides of the opening where the window had been. They hung in a heap, wet and filthy, draping against what appeared to be a five-foot segment from the end of the dock that angled halfway in and out of the house on the sodden rug. The shards of glass strewn across the room sparkled like glitter.

"A tornado. We're lucky to be alive." She felt her legs start to give way and gripped the back of the drenched sofa.

"Well, it's not good, but I thought it would be worse, much worse." Pappy shook his head. "That's something." He took out his tobacco pouch. "We can handle this. Make us some coffee, Laney. You'll have to use the little propane stove." He stopped rolling his cigarette and turned toward her. "You okay?"

She hugged her arms. "I'm worried about your head. And I'm thinking how crazy you are in the middle of all this chaos to say that even though we lost a wall of the house, it's not so bad. If I wasn't so worried, I'd laugh."

"You're still young. If you'd gone through all I have in my life, you'd know real tragedy when you see it. This ain't tragic, it's a damned annoyance, that's all." He touched his head. "I won't argue with you about a doctor. But I'm not going anywhere without some coffee. I hope Audrey's alright." The surface of the lake was dotted with white crests from a leftover breeze that swayed the curtains. "It's going to be a beautiful day."

"God, what happened to Sam?" she said. "He was going to come back here last night. His camp looks fine, just some debris on the dock. How is that possible?"

She spooned coffee into the top of the white enamel pot and put the kettle on the back burner. The sun broke through a crack in the clouds and caught the glass shards on the floor, turning them bright orange. Earl's hand came to his mouth and lowered again, the smoke curling up to the holes in the roof.

"It came in faster than they thought. He probably couldn't get through. He'll show up today."

Elaine took some bottled water into the bathroom and tried to wash up. The sun already began to intensify and sweat trickled under her shirt. Her reflection looked pale with dark circles under her eyes. She drank two glasses of water, brushed her hair and teeth and hurried into her room to change.

Pappy called, "Laney, I hear it boiling."

She tossed her soiled T-shirt on the floor and took a clean one from a drawer, slamming it shut. The framed photo of Dolores on top of the dresser fell over and the glass cracked.

"I'm coming." Elaine rushed Earl through his coffee. In the now bright sunlight, sparkles of glass reflected in the crusted wound on his head. They ate cookies and bananas, and she forced him to drink water and take his pills.

"Sam's place looks okay from here," Pappy said as they maneuvered the first zig-zag of the convoluted ramp. "That's the damnedest thing that dock coming through the door like that. I can't wait for him to see it."

They stopped at the top of the levee. The awning at the convenience store had collapsed onto the gas pumps. An LP&L cherry picker was parked at the corner working on a transformer. People were out on the sidewalks and in their yards picking up limbs; chain saws had already started to whine.

"That had to be a tornado. Look at that awning and the roofs, that tree on Jandy's house. It goes in a path."

"Look over at the Tight Spot. The sign's down." He pulled the chair up to the van and unlocked it. Before she could protest, he'd shimmied up to the edge, braced his arms on the seat backs and monkeyed his way into the van. "What? Didn't think I could do that, did you? Sam won't let me. Don't tell him." He chuckled.

"Would you please take it easy? Jesus. Buckle your seatbelt."

She shut the door and sidled into her seat and put the key in the ignition. "I wonder how Mama is." He didn't answer. "Pappy?" In the rearview mirror she saw his head slumped over onto his chest. "Pappy?"

The left side of his mouth drooped even more than usual, and a thin line of spittle dripped out from the scar he'd had since he was a child. "Did something happen?"

He shook his head and looked down at his left arm. "Can't move it. This arm."

"Relax, Pappy. We'll be at the hospital in a minute. You're going to be fine."

Two blocks from the Tight Spot, a group of firefighters stood outside their trucks in front of a building with fallen electric wires. An ambulance was parked next to them.

Elaine pulled her car up and jumped out. "My grandpa, something's wrong."

One of them opened Pappy's door without waiting for her invitation. "How long has he been like this?"

"Just a few minutes. It just happened, he was fine and then…"

"Has he ever had a stroke? Is he diabetic or hypoglycemic?" He fired questions at her. "What's his name?"

"Earl Rizan. He's not diabetic. I don't know about the other thing. He has congestive heart failure; I know that much."

"Has he ever had a stroke before? Anything that would leave him weak on one side?"

"No, no I don't think so. I don't know." She felt helpless.

"Mr. Rizan." He took Pappy's pulse. "Did he complain of a headache? Was he talking normally before this?" He called to the paramedics to bring the gurney.

Pappy groaned, "Lane."

The firefighter said, "Get the oxygen ready." They lifted him out of the van and onto the gurney.

"I think he's trying to say my name. Elaine." She started crying.

"She's right here, Mr. Rizan. Mr. Rizan, can you smile for me sir?" Earl attempted a crooked smile. "Does that look normal to you, Elaine?"

"It's always a little crooked because of his scar, but that looks a little droopier." She stood back and let them take him to the ambulance.

"And he was talking normally before this?" He repeated his questions. "Any complaint of a headache?" He asked her again.

"He was talking fine about the storm damage then I looked back, and he seemed confused. Then he said his head hurt, but he said it in a weird way."

"Okay. Mr. Rizan? Puff up your cheeks, sir. You know like Satchmo. Like Louie Armstrong."

"Good, good. Okay, let's start the oxygen."

Elaine climbed in and sat near his head. "Why did you ask him to do that?"

"East Jefferson okay?" He fitted the mask over Earl's face while another one pricked his finger for a blood sample and checked his blood pressure.

"Yeah." Earl began reaching around on the sheet they'd put over him like he was looking for something. "What is it?" Elaine leaned closer to him and placed her hands on his chest. Pappy grabbed one of her hands with his good one and held tight.

"His cheeks didn't puff out the same amount. One side was off. Mr. Rizan can you raise that left arm, sir? No." He reached for his radio and alerted the stroke team at the hospital. "Elaine, I think, he's your grandfather, right?" She nodded. "I'm pretty certain he's had a stroke. But we'll get him there fast and that's the best chance for successful treatment. I just have a couple more questions for you."

Elaine stared at the breathing mask and Pappy's closed eyes behind it. His tenacious grip on her hand surprised her. "What will they do at the hospital?" The firefighter gave her a tissue.

"Probably do an MRI to determine the type of stroke and then administer a drug. It's very effective in most cases." He went on to ask her about Pappy's health and medications, and the events of the past hours.

They had to pry her hand away to get the gurney out of the ambulance. His eyes were closed. A team of people met them at the entrance to the ER.

"They'll take over now. Take him in for an MRI." The firefighter took her elbow and walked her over to the window. "You okay?"

She nodded, "Thank you."

"Yes, ma'am. You can check him in here." He walked away from her and went outside.

The hospital felt humid and warm, maybe on generator power. She watched the doors close and the gurney carrying Earl disappear and waited a moment before going back to the front desk to fill out paperwork.

In a half hour she was finally able to call her mother. "Elaine, stay right there. I'll be over in a few minutes. Sam called me. He went to the camp and saw what happened. I'll call him back, he's at his brother's in Kenner. I'll tell him what happened."

Elaine stepped outside into a small seating area that opened onto the street. A dozen sparrows were fighting in the bushes next to her, and mourning doves cooed from somewhere above her head. She sat on a bench and felt like it was someone else's body sitting there, and that her body was still standing a few feet away. A thin layer of grit was embedded into the layer of sweat on her arms, and she picked at it with a fingernail. The street glistened and a steady drizzle fell, the sun had disappeared again; palm fronds and branches covered the street and sidewalk. The palms in the center of the yard were silhouetted against a green-gray sky, and their fronds made a scratchy sound brushing against each other. It felt desolate, like a science fiction landscape. She leaned her head back and felt herself falling asleep.

# 35.

## CONFESSION

DOLORES PICKED UP HER SHAWL and went to the door. Earl was stretched out on the floor with his long legs filling up the room. He and Charlotte played a game with wooden blocks he had made for her. The blocks were shaped so that she could build castles and towers, fences and barns. There were horses, cows and birds, even a unicorn. This day they had built a tower with steps for her wooden horse to climb.

The look of them together on the floor, so easy and relaxed. She recognized the familiar sense of being apart, of not belonging there or anywhere.

He looked up when he heard the door opening. "You're leaving?"

She said, "I'm going to church."

"Are you coming right back after Mass?" There was that look on his face, of being removed from her, left out of things, the little sadness of it.

"Yes." The door was open by now, and she stepped halfway outside.

"We could walk with you then." A hint of hopefulness in his voice. "Go to the park and wait for you."

She felt again the tearing apart, of self from self, who are they and who am I. "Another day?" she asked. She gave her camera sitting on the table by the door a longing glance. Lately she'd tried to take pictures again, but was afraid to be gone for too long, and could not seem to find the same energy anymore.

He went back to what he was doing with the child. "Another day."

Outside she stepped down off the porch, the shawl over her head. In the pocket of her skirt, she held her mother's rosary, saying the prayers as she walked. "Hail Mary, full of grace." Grace. God's grace. Mary filled with God's grace. Was this something you could feel inside? Or was it only its absence that you could feel?

She looked down at her arm as it brushed against a crepe myrtle branch leaving water and blossoms behind. The bright blossoms fell in a shower to the ground. She lowered her eyes and moved aside to let a young woman holding a baby pass on the narrow brick sidewalk. She could see grace there in the two faces side by side, the woman and the baby. "The Lord is with thee." Both kinds of grace. God's grace and the other kind. The grace of a dancer. Or a heron stepping in shallow water. A dance on the edge of the woods. The woods back at home. Back in Cocodrie. Where it seemed, she had left God's grace behind. There was a pull to that place as though she'd find mercy there in the woods.

The blocks went by. "Blessed art thou amongst women." She did not feel blessed, not inside, not where the grace was supposed to be. Her hand went to her belly and the new baby that grew there, and she felt afraid. Mansions made a circle around the park and a brick path ran in front of them. Orange trees blossomed in December. "Blessed be the fruit of thy womb."

At St. Charles Avenue the noise and activity began. Streetcars and buses. And the Church of the Holy Name of Jesus. Solid red brick with white trim and newly planted palm trees. She waited on the park side staring at the building. It did not look like Jesus could be inside most buildings, especially this one. Or grace, either. But she hurried across the streetcar tracks and found the office in a small building adjacent to the church. A middle-aged woman sat at a typewriter. A long hallway went back to other offices. The priest was not in sight. The woman asked how she could help her. Dolores looked back into the dark hall. The Father was with a couple but would be out soon. Would she care to wait in the sanctuary?

She stepped into the back of the church. Everything was bright and gold and white. Shiny and new. Carvings and statues painted all colors. She almost left, but she came upon a statue of Mary hung high on the wall behind a stand of red and blue candles. "Pray for us sinners. Now and at the hour of our death." She had to reach up to touch the edge, such a quiet statue. The stone felt rough to her hand, and the face so peaceful. She closed her eyes.

She heard the swishing of his robes and felt a cool shadow over her. She pulled her hand back from the statue.

"Hello," said the priest. "What can I do for you today?"

A puzzling question. There was an accent. His hands hiding in his robes.

"How can I help you, child?" He glanced at his watch. "I'm sorry, but I do have to hear confessions in a moment before the Mass."

Confession. Pray for us sinners. Confess to this man?

They stood together in the alcove. "I don't know how to love," she said.

"I could not hear, what did you say?"

His breath touched her cheek. She repeated what she'd said because she didn't know how else to say it.

"You do not love, you do not love whom, you do not love your husband, is that what you mean?" He leaned in closer.

She shifted to look at the statue. "Not like she loved."

"Please sit down here." He sat next to her, in a pew, the robes touching her arm. She hated leaving the protection of the statue. "Well, of course, no one could love that way, Mary was filled with the Holy Spirit to allow her to carry out the life that she had to carry out." She nodded. "But why do you think you cannot love? Do you have children? Surely you love them?" He smiled. His face so large. His smile, knowing, joking.

She shook her head. "Pray for us sinners."

"Yes of course, what is your name, dear? I don't think I've seen you at Mass here before?" His face was so close that she could smell his cologne.

"I sit in the back." She said and swayed a bit suddenly in the pew. "I am so weary."

"My dear, perhaps you are ill? I can go for some water?" He started to stand.

"No, no." She reached out and touched his robe. "I am weary of life. Yes, of the child. I'm not sure that I can." She let her hand drop from his arm then reached up and touched it again. "Can a woman be more than a wife and mother? Can she love something else as well? As much?"

"I can't imagine what that would be, how a woman could, unless God forbid you mean another man?" His voice trembled. "A woman's glory is in her love for her children, her husband. Nothing else should come before that. You understand this? It would be a grave sin, to love something else or someone else more. And I'll tell you why. It would take her away from her main purpose in life, to care for her family, to make them happy, to make her husband happy. It would be selfish, yes, so yes, I believe that it would be a grave sin."

Now unto the hour of our death.

"A woman's glory is her home and her family. You understand this?"

She nodded. Again, her hand went to her belly.

"And if you have something that takes you away from this glory, some temptation, God forbid it would be another man." He paused and cleared his throat. "I believe that you should pray that you have the strength and courage to put your family before that, all of that." He stood up next to her, his face dark against the colors of a stained-glass window above his head. Angles of black keep the color from bleeding out.

"You must come and confess dear. The sacraments will give you strength. And perhaps you should see a doctor, um, did you say your name? A doctor for this, this weary feeling that you have." He stood up, and she felt dwarfed next to him. "The confessional is in the back on the right. I must go prepare. First let me say a prayer for you."

His hand heavy on her head, she closed her eyes, the Latin flowed over her like a balm. A moment of grace. "Amen."

For a moment she felt peace, and the swirling sensation paused.

Walking home, she understood that she would have to put away her camera and the darkroom, even the painting, for good. She could not have that and a family because once she started, she fell into it with her whole self and had nothing left for Earl or Charlotte and now another baby. It consumed her. The musky smell of the lagoons in the park reminded her of home. She longed for Cocodrie. She sat in the park until late afternoon and watched the night herons nesting.

# 36.

## REVELATIONS

"Elaine," Charlotte shook her gently. "Elaine, it's me."

"I must have dozed off." Elaine jerked awake.

"You must be exhausted after all you've been through." Charlotte pulled a light sweater closer around her arms and nodded to an elderly woman entering the hospital carrying full plastic grocery bags.

Elaine wrinkled her forehead and looked around the courtyard and at her mother, then her body tensed.

"I checked on him at the desk. He's asleep. He's stable. The doctor is going to be here a bit later to talk to us. He had to go see to someone else."

Elaine slumped over and put her face in her hands.

"You did a good job." Charlotte put her arm around Elaine, gave her a quick hug then let go and moved over on the bench. "I'm proud of you, Elaine."

Elaine wrinkled her forehead at Charlotte, then started crying. Charlotte sat up straight. "Is he gonna be okay?" Elaine whispered in a hoarse voice.

"I think so. They think so. He'll need some rehab. It was a little stroke. We were lucky. And lucky you were there." She reached over and touched Elaine's arm, stroking it once.

"I wonder if the storm brought it on. The camp, you should see it, it's ruined." Her sobs became stronger.

"I'm sure it can be repaired. We'll see, we're not going to worry about that right now." Charlotte sprung up and brushed off her skirt. "Should we get some coffee?" Elaine started wiping her nose on her T-shirt. Charlotte reached into her purse and grabbed Kleenex. "Then we'll go back and talk to the doctor." As they made their way through the sliding doors into the lobby Charlotte pressed a hand into the small of Elaine's back.

More activity animated the ER and the lobby. They went to sit at the café near windows overlooking a lush courtyard garden with ten-feet-tall banana trees and elephant ears whose leaves were as big as a small child. People waited on benches under the shade of dark pink and white crepe myrtles. Children played in the dirt under the trees. All waiting for news, the normal flow of time stopped by illness.

"What happened exactly? How did he cut his head? He is so damn stubborn!" Charlotte opened a cellophane wrapped ham and cheese sandwich and put it on a plate in front of Elaine.

Elaine gulped down coffee and started on her sandwich. "I tried to get him to leave, up until the last minute. But he wouldn't leave. We thought we did okay. I mean we had a few leaks, but then the big picture window in the back blew out. It must have been a tornado. A piece of the dock came right through it. It's still there on the floor." She relaxed back into the seat and the story poured out of her.

"If I had waited much longer, I know I wouldn't have been able to get him out of the house. Not the way he was, so confused and unsteady."

"You really kept your head. He can be stubborn and then he gets angry and belligerent. Like a toddler."

"Yeah. It's weird to be taking care of him. I guess I've never really thought of him as old. He thinks of himself as young and able bodied. Maybe that's why he's survived so well through everything." They stopped talking and watched a child in the courtyard climbing one of the crepe myrtles while his parents were deep in conversation. Elaine's coffee had black grounds floating on the top. The sun at that moment opened onto their table like a wedge of light in a dark room. Then Charlotte and Elaine both spoke at the same time.

Elaine said, "I wanted to ask you…"

"Elaine… I, no you go ahead. I think I can guess what about." Charlotte looked down at the table then directly at Elaine. "Go on."

"Pappy told me you had a brother who died. Francis. When he was a baby. I didn't know that."

"No, I never told you." Charlotte shifted in her chair, crossed and uncrossed her legs. "I wasn't even born yet."

Her mother gazed out the window as the parents discovered the boy in the tree and helped him to get down against protest. As soon as they set him down, he began chasing a moth, trying to catch it in his hands. Elaine asked, "Well, how did he die? Was it SIDS?"

"We don't know exactly. What difference does it make? Maybe it was SIDS. They didn't even know about that then. Anyway, people didn't talk about things like that in those days. I didn't even know for a long time."

"Well, don't you wonder about it? Didn't you want to know how it happened? Who found him, Dolores?"

"No, I don't want to know. Somebody said she was outside when it happened and then she came back in and found him dead. They said she was never the same after that." Charlotte looked away as she tore at a paper napkin with her long fingers. Her fingers were long and thin like Earl's.

"I guess you don't get over something like that, imagine the shock. I'm sure she blamed herself. I just don't know why you'd leave a baby alone like that." Charlotte's eyes became vacant.

"Mom, that kind of thing can happen if you're standing right there. They don't even know these days why it happens. She could have gone out to hang some clothes or something."

"I know, I know. You're right." Charlotte fumbled with the spoon on the table.

"Do you think that's why you're so hard on her? I mean you hardly ever talk about her and when you do, it's almost always negative. I don't remember hearing nice things about her growing up." Elaine leaned forward in the chair with her hands wrapped together resting on the table.

Charlotte leaned back. "You didn't know her. You didn't have to grow up with her. But I understand more now than I did," she paused. A couple passed them. The man had an arm around the woman who was weeping. "I understand more than I did when you were growing up. I can see that she was a very sick person, and she would have been sick whether she had a camera or not, in fact the camera probably helped her more than anything."

"You thought it was the camera that made her sick? And if I was interested in that stuff, I would end up like her."

"I was afraid to tell you. I could see you gravitated that way. I blamed the photography for everything."

"Was she that terrible?"

Charlotte breathed in deeply and looked into Elaine's eyes for a moment. "My memories are blurred; the years get mixed up together. I remember her in bed with the shades down. Or in the kitchen doing one task after another, like a wind-up doll, her eyes down on her hands. It seems like her eyes were always down, as though she couldn't bear to see, really see, anything, as though it was painful to have to look at the world. Ironic, isn't it, considering she was a photographer? That's what they do, right, they look at things, closely, they want to capture their view of it all. But at some point, she must have stopped looking. She stopped looking at me, that's for sure.

"There were times when she was there, when we could talk to her, when she could see us, and she wanted to see. But that was when I was really young. I hardly remember it. We were always so careful. Always so cautious because we knew that at any moment she could change, and we never knew why, what would make her go to her room, close the door. I used to sit on the floor by her door, I memorized every shape in the grain of that wood. I waited, so quietly, for her to stir, hoping she'd come out. She usually didn't. I drew pictures while I waited. I wanted to show them to her. After a while I gave up. I stopped waiting."

Elaine's voice wavered. "It sounds so sad. I'm so sorry." Her eyes were red from fatigue and anxiety.

Charlotte reached across the table and squeezed her arm. "You're exhausted from yesterday. Maybe we should talk about it later. We can go see how Pappy is doing. See if the doctor has been yet."

"I was just thinking how hard it must have been for Pappy."

Outside in the courtyard the kids started climbing the crepe myrtle trees. One of the dads picked up a child and practically tossed him into the tree. "One time she was in her room, and Daddy, Pappy, came home whistling. He had ice cream for us. He picked me up from the kitchen chair and held me high in the air. I remember I was laughing, and he did it again. Then he walked over to the big picture window. The sun was going down right behind that magnolia tree, and it lit up his face. It's so strange how I remember all of this." She tore her napkin up into small pieces.

"Did something happen?" asked Elaine.

"His face changed. He looked towards her room and set me down. He went into her room and things got quiet after that. It was like it went from a happy house to a dark one. And I blamed her, of course, what did I know?"

"You were too little to understand all of it. You must have felt, I don't know, discarded. Did she ever get diagnosed with depression or something?"

"They used to call it manic depression. A lot of famous people had it: Virginia Woolf, Van Gogh, Hemingway. I learned about that later. But people didn't talk about things like that then. Nobody talked about it. It was swept under the rug. She had shock treatments and spent time in the hospital. She took medicine. She'd go away for what seemed like months and months, maybe it wasn't that long. Then she'd come back. And you know the tragedy? She'd come back, and we'd got so used to her being gone that we hardly noticed. Somebody would say, Charlotte, your Mama's home, aren't you gonna go see your Mama? By then, I'd be playing I didn't even want to see her anymore. I got so used to it. I gave up trying. They told me I was bad not to want to see her, my own mother, but I didn't care."

The same man outside held the child upside down while a little girl next to them cried.

"I've always worried so much, too much, that you'd be like her. You know, it is hereditary, manic depression, now they call it bipolar, if that's what it was, and I was terrified that you might be the same way. But even if it is hereditary, a lot of other factors go into it." She picked up a clean napkin, wiped her eyes, and got up quickly with her cup. At the coffee station she grabbed more napkins and filled her cup. After she sat down, she added the cream and sipped. "Still, it was no reason for me to keep all this from you. I'm sorry if I held you back from activities and things. I understand better now, and I should have told you about her. I'm sorry."

The courtyard had emptied out, and a quiet calm replaced the noise and activity. Clouds moved in again, and a soft rain fell.

Elaine rubbed her face with her hands. "I understand. I'm just so tired right now." She watched the family that had been outside enter the building and get in the cafeteria line. "I know it was hard for you to talk about this."

"Long overdue. Let's go back to his room. I'm starting to get anxious."

When they stood up, Charlotte put her arms around Elaine and held her close for a few seconds. Elaine softened her body and rested it into her mother's, long after Charlotte tried to pull away.

# 37.

## THE RIVER

SHE WOKE TO THE SOUND of the ships' bellows on the river. The deep call always spoke to her in a way she could not explain, like an embrace or an invitation. That day it was a call as though from inside her to go to the river. The river was a divine place, bigger and more powerful than anything she knew. Lately she had been thinking often about its dark water.

She knew that the priest had to say what he said to her, about duty and her calling as a woman. It was his duty to say such things. She had had good days since then, and other days where the white feeling came back. She went from day to day, week to week, not knowing, and she would say, *Today I can manage, at least today.* Today is a good day, the feeling is held back, but I am weary of all of it. The headaches, the white feeling that stays there ready to blossom, the fear of it; weary of what they expect, of their disappointment, of that look in their eyes when they are watching and waiting.

She put on one of Earl's heavy cotton shirts against the chill of the humid air. She rolled up the sleeves that hung beyond her hands, and the smell of Earl and tobacco and woodsmoke was comforting. Charlotte and Earl slept, and Charlotte's lips were pursed in a pout, her hands balled into fists. Earl's sleep was always like the dead, so exhausted from work all day and then at home. She whispered thank you to him.

The wisteria flowers along the side of the house were like purple cups filled with dew. The moisture seeped into Earl's shirt when she brushed against them. The paper boy passed on his bicycle and handed her the paper. "River's rising," he said. "We might be in for some flooding."

The headline of the Item-Tribune read: *Flood Stage Reached at Memphis. Surge Seen in New Orleans.*

If she had doubts before that, they disappeared. Another ship horn sounded in the cold air, low and mellow, three short bursts and one long one. Her palms rested on the open paper in her lap, and she called to the boy to wait. The milkman had left change under the metal milk box, so she gave him a nickel.

She eased open the front door where her camera sat gathering dust on a table. It was loaded with film, but it had been weeks since she had used it. She hesitated a moment then closed the door, drawn to the rushing river.

The fog hung low on the streets. She crossed the splintered train tracks and slipped between two warehouses onto a large open platform above the water. The river was churning, and violent waves hit the shore leaving limbs and debris behind.

The blurred hulk of a ship headed downriver, and its horn blast vibrated in her belly. The willow fronds along the bank seemed suspended in mid-air, their trunks obscured by the fog. An object had become tangled in the fronds, something dragged down the roiling river from up north.

She climbed off the dock and onto a grassy bank that led to the willows. As she got closer, the object became clear. It was a piece of fancy lace, large enough to be a lady's shawl. It seemed to have been placed there on purpose, waiting for the moment it might be needed.

She made her way to the swirling water and took hold of the lace, wrapped it around her shoulders. Another bellow called, and the wake from the ship met her as she walked towards it, her feet sinking into the thick sandy mud until the water overtook her, and all became dark.

# 38.

## THE PHOTOGRAPHER, 1988

S AM'S BREATH WENT IN AND out with a slow easy rhythm. Elaine followed the soft curve of his eyelashes, the smooth line of his cheeks, and his full lips. He had fallen asleep every night with one hand on her belly since they found out about the baby. Neither one of them was known for their great planning ability, so that it happened this way, seemed to fit. She kissed his dry lips.

His eyes opened. "Hey. Those owl eyes of yours are kind of scary in this light."

"Sorry." She rolled over onto him.

"I'll take it," he said.

A while later he brought a blanket with her coffee on the back porch. The lake air had become crisp and cool with the fall, and the water was more often covered in white caps.

"I still get a bad feeling when I look over at the dock." Pappy's shattered dock was white with gulls, but that didn't make it any less sad looking. "Do you think we'll be able to do anything with it?"

"We'll do something. It won't be like it was." Sam put his feet up on a chair and leaned back on the glider. "After we find a place and get more settled in town, we can start thinking about it."

"I guess it couldn't last forever, out here on the water." The city was waking up behind them, but it was still quiet enough to hear the birds in the trees along the street start singing.

"Hey, it's not over yet. We'll still have these, until the next big storm anyway." Sam refilled her cup. "You think he likes it at Audrey's? He lived alone for a long time."

"When I went yesterday, he was outside on the patio with the newspaper. She brought him coffee and a fresh cinnamon roll with the sugar dripping off it. I'd say he's pretty happy there."

Sam laughed. "It's been quite a couple of months. So, you're at the gallery today?"

"Yep. Alexander has a surprise for me. I have no idea what it is."

⸺◆⸺

Elaine got to the gallery early before the French Quarter had fully revived after a typical chaotic Friday night. She loved being alone there in the morning with the door to the courtyard open, and the sky visible above the banana trees. The iron gate to the street would always feel like a frame to her that she checked from time to time for new scenes.

She cleaned the floors, dusted the shelves, and made the coffee they fixed for guests. She went to the back room to work and laid out another series of Dolores' photos that would not be used for the show. Pappy had found a folder with family pictures, the ones that had never been kept from Elaine because they were normal everyday pictures. She wondered how she hadn't noticed that they were more than average. Now that she knew everything, she could look at them with different eyes.

There were not many of Charlotte, which seemed strange. It hurt Elaine to think of her mama as a neglected little girl, and she started to cry which happened more often lately. In one of them Pappy was holding her in his arms, he was smiling, but Charlotte gazed straight at the camera with a frown. There weren't any with Charlotte smiling; she always looked sad or angry.

Alexander's voice came from the street, and the iron gate opened. He and Gary were with another man that she didn't recognize. She met them at the door.

"Elaine, I want you to meet someone." Alexander stood back while the man used his cane to get over the brick steps. He was wearing an old-fashioned wool hat with a wide brim, and he took it off when he came in. "Adrian Dozier, Elaine Landry."

Dozier held his hand out to her. "I can't tell you how pleased I am to meet you. And how thrilled I am that you're doing this showing of her photographs."

Gary tapped Alexander on the arm. "Look at her face," he said with a silly grin. "Come sit down Mr. Dozier. I'll get you some coffee."

Elaine took his hand and closed her mouth, which she realized had been hanging open. His grip was firm, his skin transparent and wrinkled around the jutting knuckles. "I had no idea how sneaky y'all are," she said. "You could have told me over the phone who the surprise was."

Gary said, "We could have. But we didn't."

Dozier said, "I knew her in Cocodrie when she was a girl." He continued holding her hand. "My you do favor her. The same eyes and hair."

"You gave her the camera, the Brownie."

"Yes, an innocent gesture, yet I knew something might come of it. It was one of the first Brownies. She made quite a few pictures with it before she moved on."

Alexander said, "Elaine we have a private showing to get ready for. Would you like to go to the back where it's quiet? I thought you might like to look over some of your grandmother's photos with Mr. Dozier."

Elaine guessed that he had to be at least five to ten years older than Pappy, so closer to ninety. Many of the photos were laid out on tables in the back room where Elaine had been working on them, trying to decide which ones for Gary to frame for the showing. It made her nervous that the opening was only a few weeks away, and she was responsible for writing a biography and the information cards about each picture that would be part of the display.

Dozier said, "Some of these I recognize." He leaned over the table with his face close to the photos. "I had forgotten her, for many years, after I moved my studio to Baton Rouge. I did portraits then, more commercial stuff. But when I started out, I travelled all over south Louisiana. I could see the life of those people would not survive forever. I wanted to preserve it. I had my little boat." He chuckled. "What foolishness, but what a wonderful adventure. That's how I met her. I knew right away that she was a talent."

"How did you find us?" Elaine sat close enough to smell a lavender soap or after shave.

"I saw the advertisement in the paper for the opening. I remembered the name, Dolores Couvillon." He continued to look through the photos. "I kept in touch with her for a few years and then lost the connection. I wondered about her often. Such devotion she had, even at the start. As though she were born to look through a camera lens."

"You saw her after the time in Cocodrie? Where?"

"Yes, I met her right here on this street at my studio. She met my wife and showed us some of her newer prints. She was pregnant. She was quite distant and wary of us. Shy, maybe, as she had been as a girl. I think she was eager to get home, or maybe to go take some pictures. A few days later, I saw one of her photos hanging at a gallery, nearby, with a price tag. It was the fountain at Audubon Park."

Voices reached them from the gallery as the door opened. Alexander brought in two cups of coffee on a tray with cream and sugar.

Dozier said, "So kind of you. I'm a bit fatigued from my journey. It is a long way from Baton Rouge now. Though it never seemed like it before." He sipped his coffee. "I never understood how, for someone so shy, she was able to get such natural portraits. These, for example, these faces. How did she make portraits like this? This couple on the bench, her head leaning on his, his eyes on the lens. How did she get them to feel so comfortable? It was a gift."

"I've had the same kinds of questions since I started learning about her. She was more than just shy. I don't know if you knew it, but she was mentally ill, depression or manic depression, no one is sure."

"No, I was not aware of it, although now that I look back, it makes sense with what we know now. She had a strange way about her. Being around people was a challenge. Except with…"

They both said it together, "a camera."

"Ah, here it is. She won a contest with this one." He held up the picture of the child in the coffin. "It was a competition Kodak had for young people. You could look up the journal, really it was a newsletter of sorts, but they published the photo in there, it might be hard to find. But you see that's how she won her first real camera. A big step up from the Brownie. Oh, I almost forgot." He reached inside the pocket of his linen jacket.

"Looking through my journals and mementos I found these." He handed her a small bundle of stamped envelopes bound with a faded ribbon. "Letters that she wrote to me. She would send me her film and I would develop it for her and send it back. Sometimes she wrote me letters. Not many. But I thought you'd like to have them."

Elaine held the brittle paper in both hands. "I never thought I'd have anything of hers. I mean other than the photos. She actually wrote these." The handwriting on the envelopes was neat and childish.

"I thought you could use some quotes maybe for the opening."

"Yes, yes, that's a great idea. Thank you so much."

Dozier leaned back in his chair and gazed up towards the lights. "She was an unusual child. Well, in those days children grew up fast, worked so hard, married so young. She was fast approaching womanhood. I was young myself, barely twenty." He gazed again at the table. "I've never met anyone who felt the way she did about the camera, about the possibilities of it. As though it was the most important thing in her life."

"And that was a blessing and a burden, I guess. Did you know my grandfather too?"

"Your grandfather? No, well, I wonder, I remember a boy back then. Followed her around like a puppy but from a distance. Always whittling something."

"That sounds like him."

"It's wonderful what you're doing here, showing her pictures."

"I can't wait to look at these." She held up the letters.

"I read them all over again after I found them. Her writing can be difficult, you know, English was not her first language, it's what they learned in the little school they had access to at that time. She asks questions about the craft, but she also talks about it, about how it made her feel to take pictures, about how she saw things. I think you'll find it illuminating." His hand shook on the handle of the coffee cup.

Elaine said, "Thank you so much for giving them to me."

"Of course. I wish I could do more. I've wondered about her so many times, if she kept it up, if she had a family. Seeing you is like seeing her again. You've made an old man happy. My son should be here now. I don't last as long as I used to. Call me anytime if you have any questions. I hope to see you at the opening."

# 39.

## ADVENTURES OF THE PINTAIL

"YOU DOING OKAY OUT HERE, Hon?" said Audrey.

"Yes ma'am, sure am." Earl felt weary. It was the first time he'd been anywhere for any length of time except doctor's appointments since the storm and his stroke. He hadn't been to the French Quarter in as long as he could remember. People looked different, but it was the same really. Elaine's laugh reached him from inside the gallery.

Audrey said, "I'm glad to see Charlotte came. That will mean a lot to Elaine. But I think you've had enough. We need to get back home and fix some supper."

Earl still wasn't used to having a woman cooking for him and taking care of him, much less of sleeping with one and having his toothbrush on her bathroom counter, but he was adjusting easily.

"This was a good thing, Elaine did," said Audrey. "Good for everybody."

Earl nodded. He felt more at peace than he had in years. "The strange thing is that I didn't even know I was bothered by all that happened with Dolores, until Elaine came along and started churning it all up. I guess it needed to be churned."

Sam walked out of the gallery to the sidewalk.

Earl said, "You had enough of all that in there?"

"You're still letting him smoke?" asked Sam.

"Watch it, boy."

Sam handed him a plastic cup of beer.

Audrey said, "He gets four smokes a day, that's it."

"She's a mean one, Sam. These women, you got to keep 'em in line. I know you realize that. Haven't seen you with a smoke lately."

Sam said, "Had to quit, boss's orders. Babies and smoke don't mix."

Earl laughed. "You look like a kid, boy, at a Mardi Gras parade. If I didn't know better, I'd say you were verging on happy."

Sam looked down at the sidewalk. "Maybe so. I've seen you smiling a lot lately yourself."

"Now you have a baby, you think you'll get married?" asked Earl.

"You'll have to ask her that. She's gun shy. At least she's living with me now. That's something. I don't know if she asked you yet, but we thought we could fix up your camp into an art studio. How's that sound?"

"Good idea, as long as you keep my workshop in the back."

"Agreed," said Sam. "Would you two like to stroll a bit and look at the other galleries? Things are going to shut down soon."

Earl waved his hand. "You two go. I'll sit and listen to the music."

When they left, he took the opportunity to roll another cigarette. He leaned onto the left arm of his wheelchair and smoked. He had not listened to much jazz in his life, but one thing he enjoyed was a muted trumpet. The bass player was a young girl who looked like a child next to the instrument. When the music started, he teared up and reached into his pocket for his handkerchief. "Damn." Since his stroke he'd cry for no reason.

He closed his eyes, the late afternoon sun felt good on his face. Earl felt a hand on his shoulder.

"You're Earl," the man said.

"Yes, sir, all day. I can't see you with that sun behind you. Do I know you?"

"Adrian Dozier. Maybe you remember me." He lowered himself slowly into the chair next to Earl and leaned a cane against the brick wall.

Earl leaned back and squinted at the man. "Can't say that I do, no. I'm sorry."

"I'm the man who gave Dolores her first camera. Adrian Dozier."

Earl lowered his head and reached his hand out to him. "Elaine told me she met you. I never thought I'd see you again. You saw the show? It's something, how she ended up taking all the pictures. I bet you didn't know what you'd started. You weren't much more than a kid then, were you?"

"I was a kid. On a great adventure. In a beat-up old shrimp boat with a car engine." They both laughed. "But you're right, I knew she would have talent, but I had no idea she would take it this far."

A group of people crowded around the trumpet player and some of them started dancing. It occurred to Earl that he would never know what Dolores would have ended up like without a camera. It was foolish to think in that direction, but with the man right next to him, the thought crossed his mind that it was a blessing and a curse, the camera. Maybe if it hadn't been that it would have been something else that she attached herself to. He would never know.

Dozier said, "I have something for you."

He took a book out of a brown bag and handed it to Earl.

Earl said, "*Acadians of South Louisiana: My Adventures on the Pintail.*"

Dozier said, "The Pintail. That's what I named that bucket I traipsed around in."

"No kidding. Look at that. That you standing on the deck? Who took that?"

"I had a buddy with me for a while, but he got tired of it. By the time I made it to Cocodrie, I was going solo."

Earl opened the book. "This must be Dulac. The schoolhouse. Here's Floyd's store in Cocodrie. The church." He held the book up closer to his face. "You got my daddy in here, too." He grabbed his handkerchief again. "My cousins. This is something."

Earl felt his hands shaking and rested the book in his lap. "You have a lot of her in here."

"I'm afraid I took quite a few pictures of Dolores," said Dozier.

It happened so long ago that she seemed like a stranger in the pictures, but there was also a tug of recognition and something else that reminded him of the times a memory came back of a dance or running on the bayou. "She used to sit like this all the time, with her head resting on her knees just staring into the distance. Here's one at a fais-do-do. On the dock. Ha, that's me next to her, whittling."

"I admit, I'm a little embarrassed. You have to remember, I was young, nineteen. She captured my attention. She was so serious about things for someone so young. The way she looked at things. When she'd look in my lens it felt like she was taking my picture sometimes, instead of the other way around. I never forgot that."

Earl lingered on certain pages, and his lip trembled. He wiped his forehead with the back of his hand. It was getting dark and harder to see the pictures. Earl closed the book, and the trumpet started playing a slow blues that Earl felt would break his heart.

Earl said, "I didn't trust you at first. A lot of us didn't, and I was very protective of her. But you were good to her, over the years, all that film, the darkroom. I appreciated it, even if I never told you."

"You were her champion, I could see that. And I imagine it wasn't always easy."

Earl was relieved when the trumpet switched to something less melancholy.

Dozier said, "I think I was a little in love with her."

"I was jealous of you more than once, but I never once suspected you of anything other than kindness towards her."

"I'm grateful for that." He reached for his cane. "My son will be waiting. It's been a pleasure."

"Yes, sir, it has." Earl held up the book.

"No, that's for you. Share it with Elaine, when you're ready, and her mother." He groaned and stood up. "I hope you'll forgive me for falling for your girl."

"I'm honored for her."

Dozier nodded and headed towards the bar on the corner.

Earl pressed his fingers around the edges of the book. The young man grinning on the cover didn't look all that different from the one who'd been sitting next to him. And really, he wasn't all that different from what Earl remembered. It was funny how bodies gave out on you, some people's faster than others, but something inside stayed the same through all of it; a spark of something never changed. Maybe it was true, something lasts even after you leave all this.

# 40.

## A WAY OF SEEING

*January 27, 1925*

*Dear Mr. Dozier:*

*Everything changed after the darkroom. I'm so happy to have it, I want you to know that, and Papa told me to write this letter to you to say thank you for everything. Seeing the way the picture comes out on the page and changing it this way and that. It is something that I almost can't believe.*

*At the start, I spent all my time in there. I would take the pictures and run in there to work on them as soon as I could. Then I noticed something didn't feel right. Something changed in me. The way I looked through the lens. Instead of it being a part of me, it was part of something else, part of a thing, like any other thing that I had to do. To make something, to finish something, like a job, or one of my chores. I got separated from the doing. Because when I'm separated from that then the doing becomes a thing in my head that I'm figuring out. Then I'm not seeing from my heart, and it feels bad, empty, like when somebody dies.*

*So now sometimes I take the camera out with no film in it. Then it's easy to see from my heart and take in what I see instead of figuring out the best way to make a picture. Because somebody told me that it's not about seeing more of life, but of seeing it with more of yourself.*

*I hope I always remember that. It seems like grown up people forget it sometimes they get so busy.*

*Thank you for everything.*

*Sincerely,*

*Dolores Couvillon*

## THE END

# NOTES

Cocodrie is an unincorporated fishing, shrimping and crabbing village in Terrebonne Parish, Louisiana, home to the Louisiana University Consortium of Marine Studies. CoCo Marina continues to be up and running. I am grateful to the people of Terrebonne Parish for the use of the name and location for this novel. I apologize for the lack of accuracy in certain descriptions of landscape and architecture and some historical details. The surname, Couvillon, is common in Avoyelles Parish, and was not a common name in Terrebonne parish. I took liberties for the sake of fiction.

Efforts to restore the Louisiana coastline are ongoing. Coastline restoration is about more than saving land and wildlife resources. As with all threatened coastal communities globally, the restoration of precious coastline refers also to the preservation of longstanding cultures, traditions and languages that will be lost along with the land. The Acadian and Native American presence in south Louisiana represents a unique and fascinating feature of United States cultural history.

Louisiana Public Broadcasting aired a segment as part of their regular program, La Veillée, in April 2024, called *Cocodrie: Autrefois et Asteur; Cocodrie: Then and Now*. Will Mc Grew, founder of Télé-Louisiane, an organization dedicated to the preservation of French and native

Louisiana culture and language, interviews long-time residents of Cocodrie about the differences between life in the early 20<sup>th</sup> century and now, and the effects of coastal erosion on the livelihoods and culture of the population of the region.

https://youtu.be/SFc8bV0XMXo?si=R7iEbHTWmFHmLp4T

The character of Adrian Dozier is based upon Theodore Fonville Winans (1922-1992), a photographer who traveled around south Louisiana documenting the lives of the Cajun people. The photo on the cover is by Winans. He operated a portrait studio in Baton Rouge until his death. The story of his encounter with Dolores is fiction. I am grateful to Winans' son, Robert and grandson, Fonville, for allowing me to use his photographs and to build my novel around a character based upon him.

*Adventures of the Pintail* is my fictional name for Winans' journal written during his travels around Louisiana. The title of his journal is actually, "*Cruise of the Pintail*," by Fonville Winans, edited by Robert Winans, LSU Press; Illustrated edition (September 26, 2011).

The folk story, "Feux Follets," is taken from Barry Jean Ancelet's book *Cajun and Creole Folktales: The French Oral Tradition*, copyright 1994.

Some of Dolores' musings about photography are taken from quotes by Annie Leibovitz, Diane Arbus and Julia Cameron. Sally Mann is a celebrated American photographer who resurrected the collodion process in many of her photos including Civil War battlefields, southern landscapes, and family portraits. Here is a link to her photo mentioned in the novel:

https://www.getty.edu/art/mobile/centr/mann/stop.php?id=369583

This photo is from 2002. I took liberties with the timing of her photos as she did not begin the Civil War project until the 2000s. I am grateful to her for her work and inspiration.

# GLOSSARY OF FRENCH TERMS (IN ORDER OF USE)

**Feux Follets:** A Louisiana Acadian term that translates as 'crazy fire.' It is popularized by the Cajun Folktale mentioned in the book. It can also refer to the will-o-the-wisp, a flame like phosphorescence caused by gas from decaying plants in the swamp, or swamp gas.

**Veillée:** The word veillée indicates a visit, by friends or family, but is also used to mean a wake with the body after a death.

**Traiteur/Traiteuse:** A healer in the Acadian culture who uses prayers, herbal remedies and touch to help the ill and dying.

**Pauv' p'tit bébé:** Poor little baby.

**Acadien, Cadien, Cajun:** Acadian. The name given to a group of French settlers from the area of Canada now called Nova Scotia, originally termed French Acadia, who were expelled from their land in the mid-18th century by the English in what is called the 'grand dérangement.' Many of these families found their way to Louisiana as there was a vibrant French community thriving there. The word "Cajun" is a shortened form of "Acadian".

**Folle:** Madwoman. Crazy mad.

**Fais-do-do:** The English translation is 'go to sleep.' Indicates in Acadian culture a dance party usually held on Saturday nights in which the parents let the children climb under tables and chairs to sleep while the party went on into the night.

**Sacré Bleu:** Translates to 'sacred blue', originally Sacré Dieu, which was considered to be taking the Lord's name in vain, so was changed to Bleu which rhymes with Dieu.

**Crainte:** Indicates an ongoing state of fear and apprehension.

**Bal de noce:** A wedding dance held in a dancehall before the public.

# ACKNOWLEDGMENTS

Many have contributed to this novel over the years. These include all the iterations of my writer's group from the Loft in Minneapolis, who read every chapter more than once. Also Tom Andes, Joseph LaCour, and Bill Lavender for reading, editing and proofing. Dan Duke started the novel off by giving me a book of Winans's photographs many years ago. All three of my brothers—Joe, Brian and Ken—helped with questions ranging from Louisiana history to the French language, from fishing to photography. I am especially grateful for their love and support. Thanks to Ralph Adamo, who published my first short story and gave me hope. Thank you to Daniel, Mara and Mikey for their love and inspiration; to my mother, Marjorie, for inspiring me to write; and to John, who gives me solid ground to stand on.

# ABOUT THE AUTHOR

Sharon LaCour grew up in New Orleans and her writing takes place in the Deep South. She has been published in the *Xavier, Chautauqua, Arkansas* and *Sheepshead Reviews* among others. *The Meeting of Air and Water* is her first novel. It was inspired by the photographs of Fonville Winans which documented Cajun life in the 1920s and 30s. She lives in Lafayette, Louisiana.

Sharon can be reached at sharonannlacour@gmail.com.